Out of Darkness

Out of Darkness

Mary D. Brooks

Renaissance Alliance Publishing, Inc.
Nederland, Texas

ISBN 1-930928-15-7

First Printing 2001

9 8 7 6 5 4 3 2 1

Cover design by LJ Maas
Illustrations by Lúcia A. de Nóbrega

Published by:

Renaissance Alliance Publishing, Inc.
PMB 238, 8691 9th Avenue
Port Arthur, Texas 77642-8025

Find us on the World Wide Web at
http://www.rapbooks.com

Printed in the United States of America

This book is dedicated to my grandfather, Kiriakos Stathakis. He was an humble man who was in the Greek resistence in Larissa during World War Two. Pappou, you are a true Greek hero.

— Mary

In the Blood of the Greeks

INVICTUS

Out of the night that covers me,
Black as the Pit from pole to pole,
I thank whatever gods may be
For my unconquerable soul.

In the fell clutch of circumstance
I have not winced nor cried aloud.
Under the bludgeonings of chance
My head is bloody, but unbowed.

Beyond this place of wrath and tears
Looms but the Horror of the shade,
And yet the menace of the years
Finds and shall find me unafraid.

It matters not how strait the gate,
How charged with punishments the scroll
I am the master of my fate:
I am the captain of my soul.

William Ernest Henley
1849-1903

Chapter 1

Zoe Lambros leaned against the wall watching the army patrols begin their day. *Butchers!* she thought with disdain. She looked around the streets of her town—Larissa. It was a small farming town, the fertile countryside providing the community with cotton, olives and wheat. They sent their crops to Athens, or to Thessaloniki, which was only three hours away by train.

Following the progress of the hated German soldiers, her imagination peopled the street with friends and neighbors who were no longer among them. Larissa had seen its share of tragedy with the men of the town—actually more like young boys—going to war against Italy and dying for their country and their freedom. There was great jubilation in the town plaza with the news that the Italians were beaten back. It had resulted in a joyous celebration that stretched for days. Zoe sighed at the memory of better times. After the euphoria of the victory against the Italian invaders had faded, the realisation struck that the Axis powers had not been defeated, only stalled.

The Greek government stumbled from one crisis to another, trying to pull victory from the jaws of defeat. The inevitable happened in the spring of 1941, a day that many Greeks knew would come. Although they had hoped that their young men could beat back the advance of German might, it was not to be, and the Nazi war machine moved through the Greek countryside like locusts. And inescapably, one morning as the sun began its rise over Mount Ossa, in the tiny town of Larissa that nestled in the valley, the rumble of German tanks and the sounds of marching feet disturbed the silence. Larissa felt the full force of this advance. It was a trading town, and its location—350 kms from Athens and 150 km from Thessaloniki—made it important to the occupying German force.

The town lost a staggering number of its young men, and those who survived went underground. The resistance in the countryside had grown. The Germans had scoffed at the news of the Greek Resistance. Major Hans Muller, the commander of the German troops, was a much-despised man, a violent and irrational German, or so many Greeks believed. They had witnessed his callous treatment of them and the brutality that saw many of their families shot dead in retaliation for the increased Resistance activity. Zoe's own family had not escaped unscathed, and so she had a personal debt to settle with the invaders who occupied her beloved town.

The wind was blowing her long chestnut coloured hair into her eyes and she brushed away her bangs. She turned toward the sound of rushing feet and caught sight of Major Muller, a scowl on his face and a crumpled piece of paper in his hand. A little smile appeared on Zoe's face, as she knew where the major had been. The Resistance was going to give Major

Muller's new troops a welcoming parade. Zoe had wanted to go, but was prevented. She watched as Muller stormed up the steps of the house he had occupied and made into his own command and living quarters.

Zoe was about to turn to enter her own house when she saw another well-known figure coming up the cobblestone street. A sneer curled her lips. The tall figure of Eva Muller made its way slowly up the street. A hood covered her head, but it was unmistakably the German woman. Major Muller's daughter was walking towards the house, her two guards following behind. Zoe wondered if she went anywhere without her two shadows.

She watched the woman pass and, without thinking, she knelt and picked up a small stone. She fingered the stone in her hand and threw it, hitting Eva in the arm. Stung, she turned, and her gaze met Zoe's stormy emerald eyes. Eva turned to her guards, who were about to pounce on the young woman, and prevented them from going to arrest her.

Eva put her head down and walked away with the guards still shooting glares at the partisan. Zoe just smiled back at them, then turned to go inside the house. She had barely opened the door when she was pulled in and the door was forcibly shut behind her.

****

"What happened?" The German major stood waving a flyer in his hand. His face had turned the brightest shade of red and the veins in his neck stood out. The young man in front of him winced. The major crumpled the flyer in his hand and threw it out an open window.

Captain Jurgen Reinhardt stood in front of his commanding officer wishing he was somewhere else.

"Well, are you going to answer me or are you going to stand there mute?"

"They ambushed us, sir," Jurgen stammered

"How many did we lose?" the major yelled

"Twenty men and two trucks..."

The following minutes were filled with expletives and the sound of yelling that Jurgen was sure would cause his commanding office to suffer a major stroke. He followed the major out of the office and into another room where two guards stood to attention. The outer office was decorated with the swastika and a portrait of the Fuhrer himself.

"I want them rooted out—do you understand me, Captain? They are gloating. I want them rooted out."

"Yes, sir," stammered the young man

The major stopped talking as the door opened and a woman walked in. Jurgen let his eyes drift towards her. Eva Muller was a beautiful woman, that Jurgen knew quite well.

"Where have you been?" Muller demanded when she entered.

"I was in church," Eva said meeting the stormy blue eyes of her father.

"I don't know what you are doing there at this time of morning, but I have a much more pressing problem than protecting your whereabouts."

"I had my two guards with me, if that's what you are worried about," Eva said quietly.

"Two guards against a Resistance attack, Eva, will not save you." Muller noticed that she was carrying the twin to his flyer in her hand and snatched it from her in disgust. He sat down and slapped the annoying paper on his desktop. "Especially with this lot about."

The major had already read the flyer that the Greek Partisans had produced. It was indeed the same as the one he had flung through the window moments before in rage. It proudly accepted responsibility for the bombing of the column, and threatened to blow the Germans back to Germany in pieces. The major made a snorting noise and crumpled the flyer in his hand.

Muller sighed as he turned to his daughter. "Tell Despina I want breakfast."

"Yes, Father," Eva replied, then opened the door and left.

He turned to Reinhardt in a rage. "You! I want you to find out where these animals are and bring them to me," Muller yelled.

Eva stopped outside the door and shook her head and walked towards the kitchen where the housekeeper was preparing the morning meal.

****

Zoe was pushed against the wall and she was met with the angry face of her friend, Stavros. His black eyes bored into her green ones.

"What in the name of God are you trying to do?"

"What?"

"I saw you hit Muller's daughter. Are you mad?"

"No, I'm not mad, Stavros. I don't know why I did it. She walks around as if she's the queen of this village. She can go anywhere without anyone touching her."

Stavros let go of his friend and ran his hands through his hair. He had had this argument with her for what seemed like forever. "Killing her is not going to achieve anything," he said, knowing Zoe's response.

"Killing her may not get results, Stav, but I have to. I have to avenge the deaths. Are you going soft on them, Stav?"

"I'm not one to go soft on the krauts, little one, but all it will do is get us all killed. That demon is already demented, do you want him to kill us all?"

Zoe looked down at her scuffed shoe. "It would be easier than living like animals."

Stavros hugged the young girl in his embrace. "I'm sorry I got rough with you. I was terrified of what they might have done to you."

"What they might have done to me? You took a much bigger risk. How did it go?"

"Kaboom!" Stavros made the sound effects of bombs going off, which had Zoe grinning.

"Big kaboom?"

"Very big kaboom," Stavros grinned.

They had achieved their first goal of ambushing the German trucks and did quite a good job. The partisan movement was growing. He knew his countrymen would rally 'round, like they did with the Turks. They would overthrow this invader and Greece would once again be free. He watched the young woman go to a table where their maps were located. Zoe had a quick wit about her, and he enjoyed being with her. Zoe was new to the partisans, barely a year, just since both her parents were executed by the Germans.

Zoe sat at the table, her thoughts on the tall, dark-haired woman. She had been following her for a few weeks now.

"Does she go anywhere without a shadow?"

"Zoe, please drop the idea. It's only going to get you killed."

"I can't, Stav. I'm going to be seeing more of this she-demon anyway."

"How?

"You are talking to the newest maid for Miss Eva Muller! Once I get close to her, then I can execute my plan. Father Haralambos got me the job. Right out of the blue, you know. I was going past the church and he called me in. He asked if I wanted a job, and I said, "Sure I do." When he told me who it was for, I knew that it was perfect. I don't think he knew why I kissed him. It's a message from God, Stav."

Stravros groaned. "Zoe, you don't believe in God."

"I do now," Zoe said with a grin. "Stav, don't worry. You worry too much."

Chapter
2

Zoe leaned against the wall and looked out the window. The full moon shone through the window as the curfew on the town descended like a blanket. She looked out, scanning the street anxiously, hoping that Stavros had not been stopped by the hated patrols. The Germans were stopping any male in the street, but Stavros found that if he acted dumb, sometimes the soldiers wouldn't pick on him. She watched as the local priest, his shoulders hunched, his white beard blowing in the stiff breeze and his robes scraping on the ground, quickly walked towards the church. She saw him nod to the German soldiers who were barking orders to "Mach Schnell." She wondered if Father Haralambos still believed in a god.

When she had met the cleric only a few days before, she was rather surprised at his offer.

"Ah, there you are my child." The old cleric was stooped, as always. She always wondered how old he was since he had been around the village for as long

as she could remember.

"Father," she said and bowed and kissed his hand.

"We don't see you at the eklisia, is something wrong my child?" The cleric's blue eyes bored into the young girl who stood before him.

"War happened, Father."

"Indeed it did. Indeed it did. I have a job for you, if you are interested."

He then went on to explain that Major Muller wanted a personal maid for his daughter. He was quite surprised when she put her arms around him and kissed him. He didn't know why but his offer had made her very happy.

Zoe looked to the heavens and sighed. She wished she still believed in a god, any god. She could then pray that she wouldn't jeopardize their plans. Maybe she would pray and see if any deity did exist. She closed her eyes and fell to her knees, and made the sign of the cross.

"What are you doing, Zoe?" Stavros asked as he put down the meager food supplies. The food was getting scarce for everyone but the occupation forces as the war dragged on, leaving the Germans well fed and the Greeks starving.

"Praying. You're late. Did you get stopped?"

"I thought you didn't believe in God?"

"Just in case," Zoe said and opened her eyes and shrugged. "If He exists I want to ask Him to help me, and if He doesn't exist...then I'm talking to myself." Zoe got off the floor and went and closed the curtain. "Did you get stopped?"

"No. Apostolos met me and gave me a bottle of his new brew." He beckoned her over to the table to eat the bread and olives he had procured. Olives and *feta* cheese were the two items they could get their hands on easily. Zoe looked down at her breakfast and sighed. When the war ended, she was going to keep away from olives and *feta* cheese for the rest of her life.

"What is this supposed to be?" She indicated the bottle in front of her.

"Well, according to Apostolos, it's the next best thing to ouzo. He said it was his best brew yet."

They ate in silence and jumped when they heard the church bells sound. Zoe hated that sound, for it meant that another mother had lost her son in the war. It was the practice of the local *eklisia* to let the church bells ring out whenever a mother found out her son had died fighting for the motherland. Larissa had lost too many of her sons and daughters. Zoe remembered the first time she had heard the church bells ring out.

"Mama, why are the bells ringing?" Zoe looked around to where her mother had stop knitting. "It's not a Sunday."

"O Theos na tous prostatepsi," her mother whispered

"Why does God need to protect them? Who does he need to protect?"

Her mother looked at her, her eyes brimming with tears. "Ah mahtia mou, the war has come to our home," her mother said, and she held her child in her arms. "When those bells sound, it means a mother has lost her son."

Zoe looked around her and saw that the women had either stopped what they were doing or were crying.

"Our men will win this war, Mama. Greeks don't give up that easily! Remember we beat the Turks after

400 years of occupation!" the young girl said with the bravado and ignorance of youth.

Eleni Lambros smiled at her young daughter. A daughter growing up so fast. She was already in her 13th year. Already she was turning down offers of marriage. Many of the mothers who had sons were looking at her daughter as a prospective daughter-in-law. Not until this war is over, *she told her young daughter. Both of her sons had fought the Italians.*

"The Germans will be pushed back like the Italians have been. Remember Metaxas? He said 'Ohi!' to the Italians, and we beat them back," Zoe said, looking at the women, trying to get them to agree with her. "We can say 'ohi!' to the Germans...can't we?"

An elderly woman snorted. "Metaxas is dead, little one. We should all be so lucky."

"Soon the Germans will be at our doorstep. We will have to fight like our fathers did so many years ago...I remember the first war... Germani goorunia." An elderly woman spat on the ground and crossed herself. "Na pane sto thiabolo," she swore. Her voice broke as she wished them to go to hell.

"Yiayia! We will win!" Zoe exclaimed, not fully understanding her elders' pessimism or the elderly woman's curse.

"Believe in God, my child, Our Lord will keep you safe and also our beautiful country."

Zoe stared down at her plate as she ate absently. How those words were burned into her memory. God and country. She remembered the day so clearly. It was in May 1941. She saw her first German soldier and realized that God didn't listen to their prayers, nor would He. She stopped believing; and whenever Father Haralambos asked her, she echoed the words of

Metaxas and said "Ohi." She found that rather fitting. That was two years ago, and many things had changed in those years. She looked over to Stavros when he called her name.

"What are you thinking?" Stavros asked as he finished off his dinner.

"We didn't know the horror that would come to us. Metaxas may have been right not to let the English land. Koryzis made a very big mistake," Zoe said quietly.

"No, Metaxas was wrong, not Koryzis, Zo. We had to let the English come and then we relied on God to save us as well," Stavros whispered.

"You know something, Stav?"

"What?"

"There is no God."

"So says the fool..."

"What?" Zoe said, looking at him sharply.

Stavros held up his hand in surrender. "That's what Father Haralambos says. He said that's what the Bible says! Personally, I think there are a lot of fools in Greece."

"We are so bright and cheerful." Zoe smiled at him and gently hit him on the arm and they both laughed. "You know, Stav, we are way too depressed to be Greeks...I think we are Russians in disguise."

"Ah but we are Greek, and we do depressing well. We've had a lot of practice. Joy is for another time and another place."

Zoe stopped smiling and looked at her friend. "And you are too young to be without joy. It makes your black eyes even blacker."

"I don't think that's possible, Zo. As for the joy...we will find our joy after the war," Stavros mumbled. "Until then, we try and rid our country of the Germans." He picked up the glass and took a swallow and grimaced. "I swear Apostolos wants to kill us with this brew."

"Maybe we can give it to the Germans and the war will end," Zoe said as she took a sip herself and had to swallow or spit it out. "This tastes worse than his other brew. Did Apostolos have any news?"

Stavros looked down at the liquid and swirled his cup. "The Germans killed 20 men and women from Nea Smirnea in revenge for the truck bombing. We lost Andreas. He was..." Stavros threw the cup against the fireplace where it shattered. "Apostolos thinks we have a collaborator in our midst...maybe from the KKE." He ran his fingers through his hair.

He couldn't believe the stupidity of the KKE, and of course all the other Resistance groups, as well. They were fighting amongst themselves, each trying to outdo each other. All the while, the Germans were killing their people and raping their country.

Zoe went over and collected the broken pieces of the cup and put them in the rubbish container. She looked back at her friend who had his head down. "When is this madness going to end?"

Stavros had no answer to that, so he continued with his news. "He also told me that they are rounding up Greek Jews. He said they are being shipped somewhere."

"Why?" Zoe asked, drying her hands with a towel and then sitting down opposite her friend.

"I don't know. Apostolos told me that the three British and New Zealanders they helped escape last week told him some stories when they were in Trikala."

"What stories?"

"They say that they are shipping people like cattle, that they have seen men, women and children in boxcars, heading I-don't-know-where."

"Do you believe it?"

"Maybe. I don't know what to believe."

"Are you going ahead with the bombing?"

"Yes, of course. We have to. If we can get the supplies in, we can go and play blowups," Stavros said and banged on the table, startling Zoe.

"If we have a collaborator in our midst as Apostolos thinks, won't they know what you are going to do?"

"I don't know, Zo. I know I can trust you and that's the extent to which I trust anyone." He looked at Zoe and smiled. "I know you're not with the KKE."

Zoe gave Stavros a mock glare. "That's not funny, Stavros Mavropoulos! Those communists! Come on, Stav, do I look like a Stalinist?"

The two friends sat silently. Zoe looked up at him. "It's too bad you have to bomb Mrs. Vasos' house."

"Well, she will forgive us. It's not her house any more. It's a barracks. We will get to do some cockroach exterminating."

"You know, the Germans will kill you if they catch you."

"No, really? I thought I might go dancing with them IF they catch me. I'll teach them the *kalamatiano*," Stavros said and smiled.

"I don't think it's a good idea to bomb it. They killed all of those innocent people because of the truck bomb. What are they going to do when you blow up the barracks?"

"Yes, I know you don't agree, little one, but it's been decided," Stavros said gently, and tried to ease the young woman's fears. "What are they going to do? Kill us all? Who will be here to feed their bellies and who will make their wine? They need us. I will be here when you get back tomorrow."

"I have a bad feeling about this, Stavros."

"You forget, God is on our side," Stavros chided quietly.

"I'm a fool, remember? And we have a collaborator in our midst," Zoe said as she set out clearing the table. They both fell silent. Zoe took the dishes and began washing them as Stavros pored over the Greek underground newspaper.

"I'm going to bed." Zoe held the door open and looked back. "Maybe there is another way, Stavros..."

"This is the only answer I know, Zo. What do I know? I'm a sheep herder." He shrugged. "Go to bed, it's late."

Zoe gave him a half smile and closed the door behind her.

"May God protect you, little one," Stavros whispered as he watched the door close.

****

The curtain allowed a slight breeze into the room. It brought the smell of rain as Eva sat at her desk, her cup of tea by her side, writing to her beloved nanny. She would occasionally look up and watch her father reading. She missed her mother greatly.

"Did you hire a maid, Eva?" her father asked, not looking up from the papers he was studying.

"Yes, Father. A local girl. Father Haralambos recommended her to me, she's starting tomorrow."

"That's good," he said as he continued to read the reports. He stopped midway and took off his glasses. He got up and opened the door and gave some instructions to the guards outside. A few minutes later, Captain Jurgen Reinhardt entered and saluted.

"Did you read these reports?" he asked, indicating the pile of papers on his lap.

"Yes, sir."

"How reliable are they?" The major looked at him over the top of his glasses.

"Well, as reliable as the KKE can be, sir."

"That doesn't tell me anything, Captain."

"I think they are reliable."

The major continued to look down at the papers in front of him. "Let them."

"Sir?"

"Are you deaf, man?"

"No, sir."

"I said, let them. Get the troops out first, of course. Then have a reception waiting for them."

"Yes, sir."

"You can go." The captain turned to leave. "Jurgen, don't kill them. I have other plans."

"Yes, sir." Jurgen saluted and left.

Major Hans Muller sighed. He was tired of the war, tired of the Resistance movements. He picked up his wine and sipped it, contemplating life after the war.

Chapter 3

"Schnell! Schnell!"

"Anschlag oder ich schieße!"

The command was followed by gunfire and the sound of screams and abuse from the street woke Zoe from her sleep. She was disoriented at first as she struggled out of bed and pulled back the curtains. The tableau she saw before her made her blood run cold. A man lay on the road; already his blood stained the dirt, ebbing his life away. A German soldier stood above him and shot him again.

Zoe was shocked. Three men stood with their hands above their heads, defeated. One of the men looked up at the window.

"No," Zoe whispered.

Stavros was led away and there was nothing she could do about it. She could scream and holler until she was hoarse, but the image of the dead partisan, his blood staining the ground was too much for her to bear.

"You didn't hear my prayers again!" Zoe cried out, and aired her grievances against the God that didn't exist for her.

She hurriedly got dressed with the sole intention of sneaking past the patrols to see where the krauts had taken her compatriots. Even as she was collecting the necessary supplies, she was forming a plan to break them out. Zoe stopped and, with a thud, she let them drop to the floor.

"Who am I kidding?" She said as she sat on the floor and began to cry.

****

The morning found her still on the floor. She had sat there for hours and had finally fallen asleep. Getting up, she began to cry again. She dressed mechanically and walked out to the kitchen. Going to get a cup, she found a note. Her hands trembled as she picked it up.

> "*You know what I want for breakfast? Fresh eggs, lots of honey and good Greek coffee, and to sleep in but not in that order. Don't worry about me, little one. Everything will be alright. Apostolos brought along a friend tonight and we will be going earlier than planned. We should be back after things calmed down in a day or so. In the meantime do something about my order.*"
>
> *S*

She stared at the note for a long time. She didn't want to believe what she had seen in the night. She wanted to believe it was one huge nightmare; a nightmare within a nightmare. She went over to the small weapons cache they had and picked up a small handgun. She was going to kill that demon spawn, and she didn't care if she died trying!

She closed the door behind her and could hear her footsteps echoing in the quiet of the early morning, as light rain began to fall. She passed the area where the partisan had fallen, his blood soaking the ground. She pulled the shawl around her and put her head down and walked swiftly to her destination. She rounded the corner and slammed into Father Haralambos' ample figure, which caused her to drop her bag. The gun fell at the cleric's feet.

"I'm so sorry, Father," Zoe said as she knelt to collect her bag and the gun.

The cleric looked around, hoping the patrols had not spotted them. He helped her up. "Where are you going, my child?"

"An eye for an eye...isn't that what your precious Bible says?" Zoe spat, trying desperately not to scream at the priest.

"No, it doesn't say that, little one, well not exactly."

"Don't. Call. Me. That." Zoe looked into his eyes and ground out the words, regretting losing her temper at the old man.

"Alright, I won't call you that. Come with me."

"No."

"You want to stay out in the rain? You can if you wish, but I'm old and I don't think I'm going to get any younger or drier staying out here."

Zoe noticed that the drizzle had developed into light rain and she mutely followed the priest into the church. She halted for a moment and then crossed herself, more out of habit than belief, before going by the altar. Father Haralambos watched her in silence for a few moments.

"You still believe."

Zoe looked at the priest and shook her head. "No I don't. It's a bad habit."

"Are you trying to convince yourself that you hate our Lord and to deny Him in your heart?" the priest asked quietly, watching the young woman as he lit a candle.

"What do you care, Father? You are wasting your time. There are Greeks dying out there. Don't you hear them? You sit here and you preach about love and forgiveness. Who do I forgive, Father?"

"We all do our part."

"Bowing to our masters is what you are doing. Tell me Father why does the demon spawn visit a Greek Orthodox church?"

"What do you mean, my child?"

"Do you think we are all blind, Father? We have seen her come here and pray. Do you absolve her of her sins?"

"We all sin, Zoe, and we all need forgiveness."

"Do you know about loss, Father? You're not married. You can't know the loss of your wife, or children. You don't know what it's like to wake up and find out your loved one has been captured by the enemy. You don't know, do you?" She stared at him and then looked up at the image of the cross, shaking her head in disgust. "Will you be there for Samia tonight when Giorgos is six feet under? His blood has stained the ground, Father. Will you forgive the animal that killed him?

"Sometimes, my child, it is best if our left hand does not know what our right hand is doing."

"Are you going to join us, to free Greece?" She offered him the gun. "You can use both hands."

"I am doing my part. Now you have to do yours."

"I already am. Stavros told me you said that those who didn't believe there was a God were fools. You know, Father, I'm a fool; but a fool that is going to do her part to save our country."

"Is that why you crossed yourself when you came in?"

Zoe didn't answer the cleric for a moment. She fingered the gun in her hand. "I told you, that's a bad habit I picked up."

"You haven't killed anyone, have you?" He said it quietly as he watched her.

"No, but now is a good time to start—with that *strigla.*"

"Zoe, you are in a house of God, please don't swear."

Zoe mumbled her apology. "I haven't killed," she whispered.

"Don't start now. You are innocent of shed blood."

"I can't sit and watch, Father. Do you know what happened last night?"

The priest nodded his head. "Yes."

The church doors opened and a young man raced in. He stopped and knelt and crossed himself and went hurriedly to the priest.

"Father, Father!" The young man was breathless. He bent forward trying to catch his breath.

"Take it slowly, Kiriako."

"Father, they are rounding up everyone and sending them to the town square! They posted an announcement that our brothers that were caught last night would be hanged! I was told to come here and tell you! Hurry, Father."

Father Haralambos held Zoe as she collapsed in his arms. "No! Do something!" she yelled at the priest.

"I can't do anything, my child."

"Hurry up, Father, please! They want everyone to be there or else they will start shooting people."

The three of them hurried out into the busy street as the residents were herded towards the main town square. The German soldiers ringed the plaza and a scaffold stood in the center. The sound of grieving and babies' crying could be heard over the murmur of the townspeople. Zoe looked around and she froze as four soldiers passed them, flanking three shuffling men. Zoe would not have recognised them, their faces were disfigured so badly from bruises.

Father Haralambos held the distraught woman in his arms as Stavros shuffled away from her. He looked back and tried to smile at the young woman, but his attempt turned into a grimace. The soldier coming up from the rear pushed him along with the barrel of his weapon and he nearly fell into the mud. They slowly made it to the platform of the scaffold.

The crowd was silent; only the sounds of a dog barking and a child crying could be heard. Major Muller walked through the crowd, his guards pushing people aside, and stood next to the scaffold. A guard held a black umbrella over his commanding officer. Muller tapped his black boots in a small puddle, clasped his hands behind his back and looked out into the crowd.

"I see Father Haralambos is here. Father, would you give these men the last rites? I am a God fearing man, and I think that would be fair," the German said as he gazed at the falling rain.

His arm still around Zoe, the priest whispered in her ear. He looked around and spotted an elderly woman and beckoned her to be with Zoe. The old woman came up behind Zoe and embraced her as the cleric went up the steps to the scaffold. He began to administer the last rites. All three men bowed their heads; the youngest began to cry as the priest made the sign of the cross on their foreheads.

"Be brave, *palikaria,* we will continue the fight for you," he whispered to each man as he placed a kiss on his forehead.

"Hurry up, Father, I don't have all day," the major commanded, as he looked up at the priest.

Father Haralambos shuffled and deliberately slowed as his descended the stairs and went and stood by Zoe and the old woman. He held Zoe's hand.

"This is a warning to anyone who wishes to defy me." The major raised his voice and lifted his arm, then dropped it. The executioner saw the hand signal and the lever was pulled. The scaffold ropes creaked as the three men were hanged.

Zoe closed her eyes as she began to cry, the priest holding her as he up a silent prayer. A tiny voice was heard singing; it was soon joined by all those assembled.

We knew thee of old, Oh, divinely restored,
By the lights of thine eyes
And the light of thy Sword

Zoe looked up, her face tear stained, and realized the villagers were singing the *Ymnos eis tin Eleftherian,* The Hymn to Freedom—the soul inspiring national anthem of Greece, their only way to be defiant as the rain continued to pour. Zoe looked up at her dead friends and began to sing:

From the graves of our slain
Shall thy valour prevail
As we greet thee again—
Hail, Liberty! Hail!

Long time didst thou dwell
Mid the peoples that mourn,
Awaiting some voice
That should bid thee return.

Ah, slow broke that day
And no man dared call,
For the shadow of tyranny
Lay over all:

The voices swelled as one voice as the major looked on, his face set in a scowl. He turned to walk off, then stopped and turned to Captain Reinhardt. "Leave them up there."

"Yes, sir!" The captain saluted as the villagers continued to sing in open defiance.

And we saw thee sad-eyed,
The tears on thy cheeks
While thy raiment was dyed
In the blood of the Greeks.

Yet, behold now thy sons
With impetuous breath
Go forth to the fight
Seeking Freedom or Death.

From the graves of our slain
Shall thy valour prevail
As we greet thee again—
Hail, Liberty! Hail!

Chapter 4

The wind blew the curtain and swirled it around the figure at the window. The strains of the song washed over Eva as she leaned against the windowsill. She closed her eyes and prayed for the souls of the men that had been killed. Silent tears were shed as she listened.

In the blood of the Greeks. How appropriate that song was. She quickly wiped away her tears and turned from the window as the door opened and Major Hans Muller walked in, his uniform splattered with mud. Behind him came Captain Reinhardt.

"If I could, I would kill them all!" the major screamed.

"What happened to you?" Eva inquired calmly, as she sat down and picked up her cup of tea.

"Sir, it was a young child."

"I don't care! Those little monsters..." He went into another room to change, and Jurgen and Eva exchanged wry glances.

"A little child kicked him in the shins and then threw some mud at him as we were walking from the town square," Jurgen explained.

"He should have the child arrested." Eva laughed and then looked towards the window. "I heard them singing," Eva said as she glanced at the captain. "Very stirring song, don't you think?"

"They started after the three were hanged. Useless piece of defiance, if you ask me. Anthems don't win wars, Fraulein. Might wins wars.

"No, no they don't, but they stir a nation; and when a nation is stirred, passions are brought to the surface. Don't you think so, Captain?"

"Do you believe our beloved Third Reich will fall? We will stand for a thousand years, Fraulein. It is predestined."

"The Romans believed that their empire would remain for thousands of years, too. It's easy to believe, Captain, what your heart tells you."

The captain looked curiously at her and was about to ask her what she meant when the major came back inside wearing a clean uniform.

"Come, Captain, we have work to do!" He turned to his daughter. "And you, behave yourself." He gave her a smile and walked out the door.

The two walked out of the room as Eve pensively sat at her writing table. "I always do."

After a moment she walked to the door and signaled a guard. "I will go to church now," she instructed the guard, who had a very worried expression on his face. "Is something wrong?"

"Fraulein, I don't think it's a good time to go to church. I mean..."

"Why is that, Private?"

The young man looked distressed. He didn't want to tell the major's daughter what to do for fear she might report him to the major. Then it would surely be the front line tour of duty for him. But if he didn't warn her, and she were to get hurt... The private realized he couldn't win and, with a mental shrug, he proceeded. "There was a hanging and..."

"I know, Private, I heard about it. I don't think it was a secret. I'm sure I will be in good hands with you guarding me. Don't you think?" she asked with a mischievous smile and a raised eyebrow.

The other guard smirked as the private looked worried. "Y..Yes Fraulein."

"You're not sure if I will be safe?"

"N...No...I mean yes."

"Good, then we don't have a problem, do we?"

"N...No."

"Right, then let's go shall we?"

****

Father Haralambos knelt down and began praying. Seeing those men on the scaffold was hard enough for the cleric. He had seen much in his life. Young Zoe had been taken to lie down by Sister Evthokia; the child needed some love and attention. *Her temper will get that child killed one day*, the cleric thought.

A smile came to his face as he thought back to when little Dimitrios kicked the major in the shins. His mother was going to die from the sheer shock of it all. *I'm quite sure Zoe had something to do with that. Ah out of the mouths of babes, or in this case, the foot of babes.*

His thoughts were interrupted as a blast of cold air swept across his back. He turned to find a cloaked figure standing in the doorway, its face shrouded in shadows. But as the figure moved closer, a feeling of deja vu came over the priest. He had seen this person before, but where? As he bid the woman welcome and she knelt at the altar, he finally realized who she was.

He remembered the first time he saw her. It had shocked him, and he nearly blurted out what he wanted to say right in front of the major.

He was ushered into the major's office soon after Greece had lost the war. The major wanted to speak to the priest. He was a central figure in the village and thus a possible, if not, willing ally.

"Father Haralambos, I would like you to meet my daughter, Eva."

The beautiful woman in front of him extended her hand; he had frozen. He nearly blurted out the first thing that entered into his mind...Daphne. He recovered quickly, although Eva had looked at him rather strangely.

"I'm pleased to meet you, Father. I'm sure I will be seeing more of you in the coming months."

The cleric released her hand and smiled. "You are welcome to come and worship, my child. God welcomes all."

"Even Germans?" the major asked and laughed.

"Even Germans," the priest replied, and smiled.

That first meeting led to the young woman attending church to worship. Long after the villagers had left one morning, he found her kneeling at the altar.

"Is something bothering you, my child?"

Eva hesitated. She wasn't sure she could do this, but she needed to know. She began to ask and then stopped.

"You know you can say anything to me and I will not tell a soul. It's in the priest's guidebook," he joked.

Eva smiled and then her smile vanished as she

looked at the priest, twisting the ring on her finger. "Father, did you know my mother?"

"I know many people, my child. There are many who worship here."

"That's not answering the question, Father. I heard that the priest's guidebook says you must be honest."

"Ah, that little clause." He smiled. "What makes you think I knew your mother?"

"The fact you nearly passed out when you saw me, and also that my mother was born in this very village."

"Ah," the priest sighed.

"So you knew my mother?"

"Indeed. Daphne Mitsos. A very beautiful woman. You look very much like her. Yes, I knew your mother quite well."

"And you knew my father?"

"Your father is Major Muller..."

"Father, remember that clause?" Eva had said, and she had smiled at him, shaking her finger. "Father, I know Major Muller isn't my father. I may look like him, but he is not my father. I suspect you know who my father is, don't you? Is he in the village?"

The priest hesitated. "Yes, your father is in this village."

"Who is he? I want to find him. Can you please tell me?"

"Let me tell you a story. A very long time ago, a sheepherder fell in love with a young woman. As is customary, the woman's family had already picked out a husband for the young woman. The young woman, as things go, didn't want to listen to tradition. Her heart fell in love with the sheepherder, even though he was older and a very poor sheepherder, at that. Her

father was against this union, so they called a halt to it, much to the deep and aching sadness of this sheepherder and the young woman. There was a slight problem. The young woman was pregnant with his child."

"You are talking about my mother, aren't you?"

"Indeed." The priest hesitated. "Daphne was sent away before anyone learned she was with child. It was a miracle of sorts, because it's hard to keep a secret in such a small village as this. Her father had relatives in Austria, so he shipped her there—away from her friends, and away from the sheepherder. From there, I don't know what happened to her."

"That doesn't tell me who my father is?"

"Ah, but I haven't finished the story yet." He looked down into her eager blue eyes and softly said, "The sheepherder lost his one true love, or so he thought, and decided that no other would, or could, replace her in his heart. A little melodramatic perhaps, but he loved her so."

The priest cleared his throat and with all the courage he could muster said, "So the sheepherder decided to enter the priesthood..."

He watched as the realization surfaced on Eva's face. "You! You're my father?!" The shock was evident in her voice.

"I am your father," the cleric answered, and smiled. "And you are my daughter. You are more beautiful than I had imagined."

Through the tears and the trepidation, they managed to talk. One day Eva had passed on the news that the Germans were looking for two British airmen and if the priest knew where they were maybe he could warn them. Eva became the best source of information for the Resistance. No one knew where the priest was getting his information from, so they kept it secret, for if Eva's identity was known, it would get both of them killed.

Father Haralambos smiled at the young woman and wondered how God had maneuvered events. He did work in mysterious ways. *I just wish next time He wouldn't give me a near heart attack.*

"How are you, Eva? It is good to see you." He kissed her lightly on the cheek and motioned for her to sit down.

"I am so sorry, Father. I couldn't warn you in time," Eva said as she pulled back the hood of her cloak.

"I don't think there was anything you could have done. They are with our Lord; no one can touch them now, my child."

"I have some news." Eva reached into her cloak.

The inner door opened and a very tousled haired Zoe walked through. "Father, I...What in God's name are you doing here? *Hameni skila,*" Zoe spat out and pulled the gun she had concealed.

"Put the gun down, Zoe; and what have I told you about swearing in the house of God?"

"NO! Get away from her, Father, or else."

The cleric stood his ground. "Or else what? You will shoot me? Here? In the house of God?"

"If I have to," the young woman said defiantly.

"Haven't there been too many deaths already?" the priest tried to reason.

"This will be a justified death, Father. Now step away from her."

"Do you think I can't call on my guards at this very moment?" Eva asked, and sat down. She smiled at the woman. "It's not what you think it is."

"What do I think it is, *skila!*" Zoe snarled as she waved the gun at her. The priest sighed and reached out and grabbed the gun from her. "Father!" Zoe protested.

"I told you, no swearing in church. Now sit down and listen."

"Father, you can't expect me to be in the same room with this..." She was about to swear again, but stopped herself. "...with this woman!"

"Why not?"

Zoe looked at the priest as if he had grown another head. "Father, were you at the murder of our brothers today? Or did you forget giving the last rites to them?"

"I haven't forgotten, Zoe. It's not what you think. You remember when I said it is best if our left hand does not know what our right hand is doing."

"Yessss." Zoe let out a frustrated breath. "What does that have to do with...her?!"

"Zoe, Zoe, Zoe. You need to cultivate patience."

"Father, Father, Father, I need to get out of here before I kill someone in this church." Zoe got up, but was pushed down by Eva.

"You know, you are quite stubborn," Eva pointed out as she sat back down.

Zoe was outraged. "Father, if I didn't know better, I would say you were a collaborator."

"Aren't we all glad that you know that's not the case?" Father Haralambos said, and smiled at her.

Zoe looked between the cleric and Eva and shook her head.

"Zoe, this is Eva Muller."

"Father, I know who she is," Zoe spat out bitterly.

Frustrated to the brink of anger he retorted, "No, you don't, and stop interrupting me!"

"Zoe, what Father Haralambos is trying to say is that I'm not who you think I am."

"Oh, that's even better. I don't know who Father Haralambos is, you're not who I think you are, and you expect me to sit here and believe it? By the way, I'm not who you think I am either. In fact I'm a German spy sent here to live a miserable life as..."

"Zoe, do you remember when Stavros had to warn the British airmen that the Germans were trying to find them?" The priest sat down and clasped his hand over Zoe's and looked into her eyes.

"Yes. We got them out in time but what...?"

The priest pressed his fingers to her mouth to quiet her. "How do you think we got that information?"

Zoe shrugged. "I don't know. Maybe Fraulein Muller gave you the news. This is worse than that drama that Petrakis put on last summer, and that stank," she said sarcastically.

The priest looked at Eva, who nodded at him. Zoe looked between the two of them and sighed.

"A few months ago I approached Father Haralambos and gave him the news about the airmen's whereabouts being sought by the Germans."

"You are on *our* side?" Zoe asked incredulously.

"Yes," Eva said simply.

"Why?"

"I have my reasons," Eva said quietly as she looked into the stormy green eyes of the young woman in front of her.

"Oh, let me guess. You are really out to save Greek souls out of the kindness of your heart?"

Both Eva and Father Haralambos looked at each other.

"Because Eva is my daughter," Father Haralambos said.

Zoe felt a sudden chill in the church as her eyes widened in disbelief. She searched the faces of

Father and Eva, but there was no denying what she had just heard. Disbelief was all that was left to her. "Bloody hell!" she swore.

Chapter 5

Zoe stood at the window, her head resting on the glass as she watched the rain falling lightly against the pane, making a kaleidoscope trail down the window. She sighed as she traced a droplet with her finger, disappointment weighing heavily on her shoulders. She heard the door open and close, but she didn't bother to turn around.

"Do you want to talk?" Father Haralambos asked as he sat nearby. Father Haralambos' office overlooked the garden, and it helped when he wanted to think. He wasn't surprised that Zoe chose to hide in there.

"You've complicated matters."

"Oh, how so?"

"I was going to kill her," Zoe said quietly. "I had it all planned out. I was going to show Petrakis that I could be a useful member of the Resistance. Now you tell me she's your daughter."

"You are useful member, Zoe."

"Yeah, right," said Zoe as she continued to watch the rainfall. "Very useful."

Father Haralambos watched the young woman for a few moments. He got up and walked over to Zoe, gently placing his hands over hers. "You can be very useful, Zoe."

"If I was useful, Father, why didn't I help Stavros or Apostolos or Leftheri? How useful was I to Giorgos or to the others that have died?" She turned and looked at him, her green eyes glistened with unshed tears.

"You can't stop the war by yourself, my child. It's going to take the might of the Allied powers to deliver the deathblow to the Nazis. Just like a hand needs the rest of the body to accomplish its desired action, so do we. We need the Allies to help us to defeat them. You are useful."

"How? I haven't done anything, apart from a lot of crying and watching my friends die."

"You were very brave, Zoe. Brave enough to have witnessed the death of your friends so that they left this earth knowing their lives were not in vain. And you are here for moral support to your friends who still live. It takes a lot of courage to continue when death is all around you. Don't cry for the dead, Zoe, for they are with our Lord in heaven. Cry for the living who need your help. Remember the job you said you were going to accept?"

"Personal maid to Fraulein Muller? How can I forget?" retorted Zoe sarcastically.

"Why do you think I recommended you to Eva?"

"Because I can clean and cook?" Zoe suggested with a lopsided grin.

Father Haralambos laughed. "Indeed you can, but Eva is going to need someone to help her to get us any information she comes across that would be useful in our struggle. She has noticed that Captain Reinhardt has been watching her closely, so she would want you to deliver the information. So, what do you say?"

"Father, I won't kowtow to the krauts, I don't care if one of them is your daughter!"

"Zoe, it doesn't matter that she's my daughter; what matters is that we need you. You need to put aside your anger and understand that you will be doing your comrades a service and possibly saving lives as well. Can you see how you are needed here?"

"Yes."

"Killing Eva would only have caused more deaths to our *patriotis.*"

Zoe shivered as the darkest memory of her life once again made its way to the surface to torment her. A torment so painful that Zoe was not even aware of the tears silently rolling down her checks. Nor did she feel the embrace of Father Haralambos as he tried to comfort her. Zoe was completely absorbed in her torment and in her memories.

Once again the villagers were rounded up and forced to stand around without being told why. Finally through the crowds came the new commander, his grey and black uniform neatly creased and pristine. Zoe remembered thinking that it needed some mud on it to baptise it. A wry grin formed on her lips as she envisioned applying the mud herself, but she was abruptly brought out of her daydream when the sound of a gunshot pierced the air. She jumped at the noise of the bullet as it reached its target. In the blink of an eye, a feeble old man crumpled to the ground, the blood streaming, down his face. His eyes gazed up into the sky unseeing. The major was brandishing a gun, shooting people at will. There was no rhyme or reason to the executions. Fifty Greeks had died that day, a loss felt by every family in the village.

The villagers panicked but couldn't escape, as the village plaza was surrounded by German troops and those that tried to flee were shot. Zoe watched in horror as the young and the elderly fell. The major had stepped in front of Zoe and her mother. All Zoe could hear was the sound of the beating of her heart. Her mother whispered to her, but she didn't hear anything.

She only wanted to hide her face from this madness. She knew she would be safe in her mother's arms, but on this day, in a heartbeat, they were torn away from her. Scarred forever in her memory and her psyche, Zoe closed her eyes and held on tight. But her will could not stifle the sound of the gun popping so close that she felt the bullet when it exploded in its next victim. Mama.

Zoe felt her mother's arms release their grasp and timidly opened her eyes to see her beloved parent slump to the ground. The madness continued around her as she held her dying mother to her chest, the blood, mixing with the mud, caking her legs. Oh dear God, Mama!

Now, every time she closes her eyes she sees the blood. Every time she tries to sleep, the nightmares wake her up. She swore revenge for the death of her beloved mama and her belief in God died on that day along with her innocence.

"Zoe, Zoe are you all right?" the cleric asked as he held the crying young woman.

"Yes, I'm all right," Zoe whispered as the memories receded and she regained her composure.

"We have lost too many loved ones, I know, my child. We can grieve for them, but they are in a better place."

Zoe wiped away the tears and accepted the handkerchief that the cleric had handed to her. She nodded her thanks and sighed. "Father, remember when my mama died that day?"

The cleric nodded.

"My belief in God died with her," Zoe whispered.

"I know, my child, I know," the cleric whispered back.

He remembered the nights he had held the child in his arms as she cried and swore that God was responsible and he was a demon. The many nights she fought him.

Zoe sighed again loudly. "Father, what do I need to do?"

"Eva is expecting you, so I suggest you go and get cleaned up and report to *Kiria* Despina." Father Haralambos stood up and wiped a tear from her cheek. With a twinkle in his eye he chuckled. "And try to be meek and humble when you are talking to Major Muller."

Zoe glanced up at a drawing on the wall. It had a shaft of light descending from above, illuminating the figure of Daniel in the cave with lions around him. "Well I think I'm about to learn what Daniel felt like. At least those animals were tame compared to Major Muller."

"You have a guardian angel like Daniel did, Zoe."

"Well if I do, then I need to report him for not being on the job," Zoe replied as she continued to look at the painting.

"Zoe, would you like to pray with me? I know you don't believe in our Lord, but I do, and I would want you near me as I ask for His help," Father Haralambos said, taking her hand.

Zoe nodded. "All right Father, but I still don't trust your Nazi daughter." As they knelt, Father Haralambos put his arm around the young woman. They bowed their heads as he offered a prayer.

****

Zoe straightened her shirt one more time and then rounded the corner. Her palms were sweaty and she wiped them along her skirt as she spotted the major's residence. She looked heavenward.

"Now would be a good time to show up, guardian angel," she said to the heavens quietly.

She slowly made her way up the stone steps where two soldiers stood guard before the entrance. Above them the Nazi flag hung limply in the drizzling rain. One of the soldiers brandished his gun and pointed it at her. She stopped as she was about to take the final step to the landing.

Chapter 6

Eva sat at her desk, her long raven hair falling across her face as she looked at the photo she held in her hands. The smiling face of a young girl, her arms around an older woman, looked back at her. Eva remembered, so vividly, the day that photo was taken.

She had been excited to join the Bund Deutscher Madel, the League of German girls from 14 to 18 years of age. She raced home to tell her beloved *Mutti* how she and her friend Greta had signed up. They found out they were going to parade in front of their leader, and the following months saw them practicing how to march in formation. Greta had stayed over and neither of them had slept that night. The following morning, thousands of Hitler Youth paraded before the *Fuhrer*.

Eva closed her eyes and she could still see the stands at Nuremburg, the banners flying in the breeze. Adolf Hitler stood at the podium, waved at them and said, *"You, my youth, are our nation's most precious guarantee for a great future, and you are destined to be the leaders of a glorious new order under the supremacy of National Socialism. Never forget that one day you will rule the world!"*

The cheers reverberated from the stands as thousands of young voices were raised in enthusiastic response

And then *Kristallnacht* happened.

Eva shook her head at the memory and sighed.

"Oh *Mutti*, you would have been so ashamed of me," she whispered to the woman in the picture as she brushed away tears.

She looked up at the sound of knocking and quickly composed herself. "Enter."

The door opened and the rotund housekeeper, *Kiria* Despina, entered. Behind her came Zoe, clutching her bag. "Fraulein Muller..."

"Ah yes, Zoe, please come in. Thank you, Despina." The tall woman stood and came around the desk.

The housekeeper gave Zoe a wink as she left and closed the door behind her.

"So, this is how our masters live," Zoe stated flatly as she looked around the well-furnished room. A desk was positioned near the window, and a light breeze blew the curtain over the chair. A portrait of Adolf Hitler with a group of young people adorned the wall. Zoe looked up at the portrait. She recognised Eva quickly as the gangly teenager who was taller than the others, including Adolf Hitler, her dark hair in a ponytail. She stood next to Hitler as he held her hand in a handshake, both smiling broadly for the camera. *She has such radiant smile*, thought Zoe, as she studied the photo.

Eva went back to her desk and put away the photo, then walked over to where Zoe stood. She ignored Zoe's last remark. "How did the meeting with Captain Reinhardt go?"

"Nerve wracking. He wanted to know everything about me, why I wanted this job and if I could read and write Greek."

"You can read and write?"

"Of course! We're not all illiterates here, you know," Zoe said defensively. "I also understand some German, enough not to get me shot," she muttered.

"I'm sorry, I didn't mean it that way."

After a beat, Zoe looked up at Eva; their eyes met and Zoe smiled shyly. "Father Haralambos taught me to read and write," she explained. "You never know when it could be useful. Oh, like being a maid and personal assistant to Fraulein Muller," she said, and gave Eva a mischievous grin. "May I ask you a question?" Zoe requested as she sat down on the couch.

"Certainly. If I can answer it, I will."

"Why?" Zoe asked, watching the woman's face intently. She had wanted to ask this question since she found out that Eva was Father Haralambos' contact. "Why did you choose to betray your father?"

Eva looked down at her hands, twisting the ring on her finger. "I have my reasons."

"What? Did daddy not give you what you wanted?"

"Zoe, we are on the same side. I don't want to fight with you."

"We are on the same side, but I want to know your reasons. I'm doing it because this is where I live, and the Nazis have killed my family and friends," Zoe said belligerently as she stood again, walked over to the portrait of Hitler and pointed at the young Eva. "You are a Nazi and yet you want to help the Resistance. It doesn't add up."

"Have you ever done something that you were ashamed of? That you wished that you could go back and change?" Eva asked as she looked up from the couch at Zoe who had leaned against the wall.

"Yes. Many times."

"Do you know about the 'Night of Broken Glass'?"

"Germany's night of shame," Zoe whispered. She recalled hearing her brother read the article in the paper aloud to her family. She remembered being horrified by what the Nazis had done.

"Indeed, a night of shame," Eva said quietly. "Our group had assembled, and a few of the older girls and a few of the older boys heard about a plan to scare the Jews. Greta, she was my best friend, wanted to go." Eva stood and went to window and stared out. "Greta wanted to go and she wanted me along, so I went. Mutti thought I was at Greta's house." Eva tried to collect her thoughts. "I remember standing in the courtyard of a synagogue which was alight with flame. My friends were laughing and joking. For the first time I was ashamed to be in the Bund Deutscher Madel.

"Did you kill anyone?" Zoe asked, trying to reconcile the remorseful woman in front of her with what she had heard from the news reports and word of mouth about that ugly night.

"No, but I have blood on my hands."

"How, if you didn't kill anyone?"

"How, indeed," Eva said quietly. "I watched as the rabbi was beaten, Zoe. I watched and did nothing. I might as well have been the one who dealt the blows." After a moment, Eva continued. "I helped my friends destroy people's lives and I didn't stop them. I was a coward. I didn't try to help them," Eva said as tears fell down her cheeks. She wiped them away hurriedly, angry with herself for her loss of control. "I stood by and did nothing. I ran all the way home, and then I found out my mother had been killed."

"How?" Zoe asked quietly.

"Someone thought she was a Jewess and killed her," Eva said, trying to regain her composure before turning around to face Zoe.

"What happened to Greta?"

"I don't know. My father sent me to live with my aunt in Austria. I never saw her again. When the war started, my father was assigned here."

"Is that when you decided to work against the Nazis?"

"No. It was soon after we arrived and my father had been told of an attack by the Resistance." Eva closed her eyes and recalled, in total horror, her father's reaction. "There was an incident..."

"A massacre," Zoe corrected quietly.

"A massacre...in a nearby village...I don't know what happened, but all I remember is the sound of the guns and the screams. I felt helpless. I didn't want to be a part of the murdering again."

"I was there." Zoe lifted her eyes and met Eva's.

"You were?" Eva asked in surprise.

"Yes. My mama died that day."

"I'm sorry, Zoe," Eva whispered. "I would understand if you decided not to have anything to do with me."

Zoe sighed. "I wanted to kill you. I wanted it so bad," she whispered.

"Why didn't you?" Eva inquired quietly.

Zoe gave her a half smile. "The greater good." Eva looked at her expectantly. "Killing you would have condemned others to their deaths. I couldn't have had that on my conscience. I would have gotten revenge for my mama's death...Father Haralambos would have lost his child as well," she said quietly.

"The greater good," Eva repeated quietly.

They sat in silence for a while, each in their own world of pain trying to come to grips with their own demons.

For Eva, the gentle chimes of the antique clock were a decided relief, for they had broken what had been a puzzling train of thought. It was strange. Here she was, raised in a life of privilege, educated in the best schools, and yet in some strange way, she was awash in the feeling that she somehow did not quite measure up to this intense peasant girl with the hard green eyes whose face was as beautiful as her name.

But there was more to it than that, and Eva Muller knew it. Already she sensed that there was something about the lithe girl...something that was sparking emotions in her that she had not felt in a long time.

Yes, it was indeed strange. In fact, as she sat there in the thick silence, it finally occurred to her that what she was feeling at this very moment was almost exactly how she remembered feeling the first time she had laid eyes on that Reinhardt boy at a rally back in Germany. How handsome he had looked in his Hitler Youth uniform! She was sixteen at the time and she remembered how, with racing heart, she had pointed him out to her friend Greta.

Yes, it was so very strange. Because at this very moment, Eva Muller's heart was racing with excitement in precisely the same manner. Cupping her hand, Eve stared down at her perfectly manicured nails as if they encompassed in this moment all that made up the universe. For what seemed like an eternity after the clock's chime, Eva continued to sit there alongside the equally mute Zoe.

What was in this girl's mind? she wondered. *Could she possibly feel it too? Of course not, you fool!* she chided herself.

How could she, when you yourself don't know what it is you're feeling? No, the only thing in this one's heart was a burning desire for revenge, for swift and terrible retribution for what had been done to her homeland...to her mother. And who in God's name could blame her?

Finally, in a voice so low Zoe had to strain to hear, Eva said, "You realize, of course, the risk you are taking."

"Life is full of risks, both great and small," replied the girl. Zoe stared deeply into Eva's eyes and slowly added, "For all of us."

"Yes," said Eva, returning the girl's mesmerizing gaze. "I suppose that is true." *What is it about her that captivates me so?*

From down the hall the heavy tread of Despina reverberated as she labored up the stairs. Eva stood up and in a clear voice said, "You understand, then, what is expected of you?"

"Yes, Fraulein Muller," Zoe meekly replied, standing up as well. "I assure you, I am a quick learner."

As they heard the hesitant knock on the door Eva said, "Good. You will begin your duties immediately."

"Yes, Fraulein Muller."

"Come in, Despina."

In a voice that seemed perpetually out of breath, Despina said, "Your lunch is ready, Fraulein Muller."

"Very well," pronounced Eva. She turned to Zoe and said, "At the moment I wish to do some writing. You will please bring it up to me."

"As you wish." The tone of Zoe's voice was properly respectful, but as their eyes met, Eva thought she detected just a hint of grim amusement in the smaller girl's expression.

"This way," panted Despina.

Without looking back, Zoe followed her out the door and down the hall. Eva stood at the door and watched her as she patiently followed Despina, first as she waddled down the hall, and then as they disappeared down the steps.

They were gone now, but Eva's gaze lingered still for a moment or two before quietly closing the door once more.

Chapter 7

The sun began to peek through the clouds, and Eva looked heavenward. She walked slowly to the church, two of her guards behind her. The villagers were giving them outright hostile stares, but Eva held her head high and headed up the church steps. She motioned for the guards to remain outside.

She entered the church, covering her head as she passed the altar. She spied Father Haralambos talking to one of the elderly nuns. She patiently stood by until he had finished and then went over to speak to him. There were a few people milling around after the service.

"Ah, Fraulein Muller how nice to see you."

"Father, I hope you are well."

"Very well, my child."

A short elderly woman interrupted their conversation by raising her walking stick and striking Eva's arm.

"Mrs. Elimbos! Please, we can't have violence in the house of God!" Father Haralambos said as he removed the cane from her hand.

"Get this animal out of the house of God first!" the elderly woman replied, and spat in Eva's face.

Eva deliberately did not move, but let the old woman continue her tirade until she had exhausted herself, grabbed her cane from Father Haralambos and walk off quite satisfied with herself.

Father Haralambos hurriedly gave Eva a handkerchief so she could wipe away the spittle. "I'm so sorry, Fraulein."

"It's alright Father, it made her feel better." Eva smiled.

"Well I'll have a word with her next time I see her. Please come into my office."

They entered the office and the cleric ushered Eva into a seat. "I am sorry, Eva. I didn't know."

"Of course you didn't, Father. Mrs. Elimbos has probably wanted to do that for a long time. I have the new identity papers."

Father Haralambos looked perplexed. "I thought you were going to get Zoe to deliver these? Has Zoe decided not to help?"

"No, Zoe is fine." She handed the papers to the cleric and shrugged. "Captain Reinhardt was nearby and I didn't want to arouse his suspicions." She indicated the papers and said, "The Petrolakis family, I'm sure, will be happier."

The cleric looked at the identity papers and smiled. Pre-war Larissa had a small Jewish population and some had managed to flee before the Germans invaded, but others had been caught. Their neighbors sheltered the few that weren't immediately captured.

The penalty for hiding Jews was death, and Father Haralambos tried to get them out of the country as soon as he could. Eva had managed to get her father's signature on new identity papers. How she had done that was beyond him, and he wasn't going to ask. The cleric had met secretly with Monsignor Jean-Claude, from the French Resistance, who had given him some very inventive ways of getting people out of the country.

The two parted company and Eva rejoined the guards outside the church just as Captain Reinhardt rounded the corner.

"Ah, Fraulein Muller, out for Sunday worship I see."

"It gives me peace, Captain."

"I'm sure it does." They walked quietly along for a moment. "Your new maid is working out nicely?" inquired Reinhardt, breaking the silence between them

"Fine, thank you."

Captain Reinhardt stopped for a moment and indicated to the guards to continue on ahead.

"Eva..." He placed his hand on her arm gently.

"Captain, let go of my arm," Eva said frostily, trying not to flinch.

"Eva, why can't we talk?"

"Captain, I have nothing to say to you, and I'm quite sure that what has happened in the past, is in the past," Eva said and walked away, leaving the captain standing outside the church.

"Forever the Ice Queen," Reinhardt muttered, watching the woman walk away.

****

"Halt!"

Zoe sighed and turned to see the soldiers approaching. She had been stopped twice today already, and it was beginning to get on her nerves. She put the sack she was carrying down on the ground and pulled out her identity card. Without waiting for the soldier to ask her, she handed the card over.

"You are a smart one, aren't you?" the soldier sneered as he read the papers and then glanced back at the chestnut woman.

"No." Zoe attempted to be humble but she didn't think she could get away with it.

She realized she hadn't been successful when the soldier backhanded her, knocking her to the ground and spattering her clothes with mud. The other soldiers, along with the one who had struck her, snickered.

"That was for having a smart mouth. Get up!" the soldier ordered. "Where are you going with that?" he asked as he pointed to the sack.

Zoe glared at him, wiping the blood from her split lip with the back of her hand.

"What seems to be the problem here, Corporal?"

Zoe glanced behind her, relieved to see Captain Reinhardt had come over to see what the commotion was about.

"Well, I'm waiting, Corporal," Reinhardt said, since he hadn't gotten an immediate reply.

"I was checking her papers, sir."

"And giving her a fat lip in the process." He glanced at Zoe and then back to the corporal. "I'll take it from here." With that he dismissed them and watched as they walked off. "You seem to attract trouble, Fraulein Lambros," Jurgen said with a smirk.

"I don't mean to," Zoe mumbled.

"Where are you going?"

"Taking some vegetables back to *Kiria* Despina," Zoe said quietly as she felt around her lip with tentative fingers.

Reinhardt looked at her and lifted her chin with his finger, inspecting her bloody lip. Zoe met his grey eyes and then she dropped her gaze as she remembered Father Haralambos' instructions to appear meek and humble.

Reinhardt laughed. "You are a spitfire," he chuckled. "I don't think that look you have is quite humble enough. You need to work on it."

"I will," Zoe muttered as she looked down at her muddied clothes.

He turned away from her and looked at the fields where workers were stacking the wheat harvest. "A word of advice: be careful with Fraulein Muller. That one has ice in her veins and wouldn't think twice about killing you if she finds out you are in the Resistance."

Zoe's eyes registered shock that Reinhardt was aware of her involvement. It only produced more laughter from the captain.

"Come now, Fraulein, you didn't think I didn't know?" Reinhardt taunted as he continued to smirk.

"Is there a Greek that isn't in the Resistance?" Zoe countered.

The captain smiled. "Quite true, quite true." After a moment the captain said, "I like you, don't make me shoot you."

"That would be bad for me, huh?" Zoe commented dryly as she looked up and ran her hand through her unruly hair.

"Very bad. We understand each other, don't we?" the captain replied as he chuckled

Zoe nodded her response.

"Good. Now go on your way before the Ice Queen starts yelling. God knows I don't want to hear that," said Reinhardt as he watched Zoe pick up the sack and continue walking slowly down the dirt road.

He sighed. *Fraulein Muller. The Ice Queen.* He shook his head at the memory of the young woman he had met in their Hitler Youth days. She had changed. He tried to get close, but all he got was rejection. That girlfriend of hers, Greta, had always been in the way. Always around when he tried to court her. He took great delight in telling her father about her and her girlfriend. He recalled that Muller was controlling his temper with him, but he hadn't wanted to be in Eva's shoes when she returned.

"Ah well, no use crying over what might have been," he said as he pulled up the collar of his jacket up and walked away.

****

The rain clouds parted to allow slivers of sun to peak through. Zoe looked up at the sky and marveled for a moment at the patterns that were created. She paused outside the cemetery and made a decision. She walked towards the gate and entered. As she passed an elderly woman, she nodded and walked further in. She dropped the sack near a grave and knelt.

"Yassou, mama," she greeted her mother as she pulled the weeds from her grave. A simple cross adorned the grave of Eleni Lambros, 1900-1942.

"I know I haven't come to see you in a few weeks, but things have moved so quickly." She paused and watched an elderly man shuffle away from a nearby grave.

"Remember I told you how I was going to avenge your death?" Zoe sat on the damp grass. "It didn't go so well, and we lost Stavros; but I'm sure you know about it by now. They hung him, Mama." Zoe's voice caught. She wiped away the tears and, wiping at her eyes, she took a deep breath and continued.

"They caught him and Apostolos with Letheri, and they killed them. Giorgos too. They are all dying, Mama. All my friends are dying. Be sure to kiss them for me in heaven, especially Stavros. Tell him, he is a big dumb Turk for not listening to me."

The tears started to flow freely as she sat on the ground, her arms around her knees. "Mama, you won't believe what I'm doing now...even Papa would be laughing. I'm a personal maid to the beast's daughter. Can you believe it? Me, the one you kept yelling at to clean up after myself." Zoe chuckled through her tears at the memory.

"Mama, remember Father Haralambos? Well, he gave me quite a shock the other day. Did you know he used to have a girlfriend before he became a priest? I never thought of him as anything but a priest...funny that. Turns out that the beast's daughter isn't his daughter. She's Father Haralambos' daughter. It's worse than an ancient Greek drama. You would have loved that."

Zoe plucked some more weeds from the grave as she continued her one-sided conversation with her mother. "I was going to kill her, Mama, but now I can't because she is working with us. That's very strange. My head tells me to kill her but my heart...well, it has other ideas. She is pretty, Mama. She has the bluest eyes I've seen. They remind me of the time we spent on Lymnos and the Aegean was so blue."

She sighed. "And she's tall, nearly gave me a neck pain from looking up at her," Zoe laughed.

"I like her, Mama, she has a kind soul for a Nazi. I have to take the supplies to the housekeeper, but I'll visit you again soon. Kiss Papa for me. I hope God knows what a special person you are." She closed her eyes for a moment. "I miss you, Mama."

****

The housekeeper was bustling in the kitchen, heating pots of water for Fraulein Muller's bath, when Eva poked her head in, scaring Despina so she dropped the plate she was holding.

"Sweet Jesus, Son of God and the Holy Ghost!" the housekeeper said as the plate broke into pieces on the stone floor. She looked at the broken pieces and then backed away from Eva who had entered the kitchen. She stood with her hands on her hips.

Eva's eyebrows rose into her hairline at the expletive from the normally quiet housekeeper. "I'm sorry, Despina, I was looking for Zoe. Is she back yet?"

"No, Fraulein, she hasn't returned yet. She is late, I'm..."

The door burst open and Zoe bustled in, muddied and wet. "I'm sorry I'm late," Zoe said and stopped when she saw the housekeeper kneeling on the floor, picking up the broken plate and Eva standing there with her arms akimbo.

"Dear child, I thought something happened to you," Despina said as she rose slowly and then took the sack. She then noticed the mud and the split lip.

"What happened?" queried Eva, holding Zoe's face toward the light.

"A corporal took offence..."

"What did you do?" Eva asked as she was handed a piece of linen and began washing Zoe's face as soon as the younger woman was seated.

"I had gotten stopped by two patrols previously, and I just handed him my card. He wasn't impressed," Zoe said quietly. "It was my fault."

"It wasn't your fault," Eva said as she looked down into Zoe's emerald eyes. Her hand was about to continue cleaning Zoe's face, but she abruptly dropped her hand and averted her gaze. "Despina, can you please get my bath ready? I'll see you soon," Eva said quickly and walked out of the kitchen.

Zoe glanced at Despina who shrugged and went to put the water on to boil. Zoe looked again at the door through which Eva had departed and frowned.

Chapter 8

"Oh, that was bright!" Eva chastised herself as she closed the door to her bedroom. She felt an attraction to the younger woman, but Eva was determined not to put Zoe in danger. Not again.

"Not again." Eva closed her eyes tightly, trying to keep the foreboding memory of that last night with Greta and the Youth League from surfacing. But the vision of her father standing over her, his arm raised and ready to strike, sent chills down her spine. That dark night her mother was murdered. *Kristalnacht.*

She walked into the house, dropping her knapsack on the floor. The ambulance had just left with her mother's body. She felt empty inside. Her whole world had crumbled and the only person who understood her was gone. She slumped to the floor as tears flowed freely.

She heard her father and someone else leave the house, their voices subdued. She wasn't sure how long she had been sitting on the floor. The door opened and her father walked in. He was still wear-

ing his uniform, stained with blood, her beloved Mutti's blood.

"Eva, I am going to ask you a question, and I want you to answer me truthfully," her father said as he sat on a chair across from her.

Eva could see the fury in his eyes and knew that she had done something terrible, but for the life of her she could not fathom what. "Yes, Papa," Eva replied, her voice hoarse with emotion from crying.

"Where were you tonight?"

Eva brushed away tears as she looked up at her father, who she knew was barely controlling his temper. "I went with Greta and my friends and we...we burnt a synagogue," she replied quietly.

"Didn't I tell you to be here tonight? Didn't I tell you not to go out, to stay with your mother?"

"Yes, Papa. I told her I was going to be at Greta's house and then I was going to come back..."

"You lied to her and to me. You disobeyed me!"

Eva bit her lip, waiting on the answer.

"Do you know what your disobedience has produced?" Herr Muller started to raise his voice, his face turned a bright shade of red, the veins in his neck pulsed rapidly and the control he had held so tenuously on his temper evaporated. "YOU," he pointed at Eva who was cowering in a corner, "you killed your mother!"

"Oh Papa..." she cried.

He went over to the young woman, picked her up by the collar of her blouse and slammed her against the wall. Grabbing her by the hair, he screamed, "I will not tolerate your disobedience!" Then he slapped her so hard that it split her lip and she slumped in a heap. She dared not utter a sound and cowered against the wall trying to make herself a small target.

But his rage only served to urge him on as he beat her across the back and legs for several minutes, screaming incoherently. Finally his anger was satiated for a while and he sat down heavily, his head in his hands.. "You have disgraced me."

"I...I'm sorry, Papa," the young woman hiccupped, tears staining her battered and bloodied face.

His voiced rose as he neared the wide-eyed girl. "I will not tolerate a bastard child ruining my reputation!"

Eva looked at him, the confusion evident on her face.

Muller stood and removed his belt. "I had someone tell me of your perversion, Eva. Did this person tell me the truth about you and Greta?"

When Eva said nothing to deny her father's accusations, he exploded. "You disgust me!" he spat. "Do you know what that will do to my reputation? They will send me to the front for this. And you, do you know what they do to perverts in concentration camps?"

He folded the belt strap, popping it for effect and leaning over her, so close she could feel his breath, he hissed, "Is it true?" But Eva could not speak, her words frozen in fear. "Answer me, damn it!!" he demanded. Eva remained motionless, which only served to explode the rage once again boiling inside her father.

What followed was the worst, cruelest beating she had ever received. The leather belt, so mercilessly used against her back, left welts too painful to touch. But that pain was nothing compared to the mental anguish she now suffered. She had been beaten into the bottomless pit of guilt and shame and as she lay there sobbing, blood covering her back and legs, her father's words: "bastard child," tortured her until she wished she were dead.

"Fraulein Muller! Fraulein Muller!" Despina's worried voice penetrated Eva's consciousness from beyond the closed bedroom door. Eva shook her head to clear the memories and wiped away her tears.

"I'll be right there, Despina," she called out as she stood trying to compose herself.

****

Despina carried buckets of hot water from the kitchen into the bathing room. Zoe had been urged to clean up and soon began helping Despina with carrying the buckets of water and filling the tub.

Eva walked into the room and nodded to Despina who left some soap nearby. "Thank you, Despina." Eva stood at the window watching the sun set over the quiet village.

"Are you alright?" Zoe asked quietly, watching the tall woman still standing by the window. Eva remained quiet, willing herself to get better control of her emotions before facing Zoe. Turning toward Zoe, Eva observed her worried countenance. "I'm sorry I left so abruptly."

"You know, I've had a split lip before, I'll live," said Zoe, trying to lighten the mood. "Are you going to take a bath now, or should we get Despina to reheat it?" she asked with a smile. Her smile turned quickly to a frown when she saw the large bruise on Eva's arm. "What happened?"

Eva looked at her arm and shrugged. "Mrs. Elimbos objected to my presence at the church today and hit me with her cane." Eva removed her robe and settled in the bath as Zoe picked up the sea sponge to wash Eva's back. "I'm sure we will," Zoe's voice caught mid sentence at the sight of the faded welts on Eva's back. She gasped. "What happened?" Zoe whispered.

"It was my fault," Eva said quietly.

"How can this be your fault? You didn't hit yourself. Who did this, Eva?"

Eva remained silent for a while as she lathered her arms. "It was a long time ago, Zoe."

"Whoever hurt you should burn in hell," Zoe muttered as she gently sponged Eva's scarred back.

After Eva had finished her bath, she dried her hair and was about to comb through it when the brush was taken out of her hands and she was directed to sit in front of the mirror. Zoe began brushing her hair.

"Why are you so nice to me?"

"You pay me to be nice," Zoe replied with a smirk. She glanced at Eva's solemn face in the mirror. "You're not who I thought you were," Zoe observed as she brushed Eva's long hair. "No one deserves to be beaten, Eva."

"Not even if they were responsible for someone's death?" Eva softly asked

Zoe stopped brushing and turned Eva towards her. "Did you kill someone, Eva?"

"I might as well have."

"You're talking about Kristallnacht, aren't you?"

Eva nodded. "I told you that my mother was killed that night." Eva turned away, unable to face the young woman.

"My father...blamed me. He told me not to go out that night."

"How? How was it your fault?"

"He said if I hadn't disobeyed him when he told me to stay in...had I been there, I could have protected her."

After a few moments silence, Zoe put the brush down and took Eva's hands and looked into her eyes, blue depths that held unshed tears, and said, "About as much as I was able to protect mine."

Eva broke eye contact first and looked away. Zoe wrapped her arms around the woman and held her.

"He found out that Greta and I were...lovers," Eva whispered, her voice breaking. "He was terrified of what it would do...what it would do to his reputation."

"So he beat you?"

Eva nodded, unable to trust her voice, as tears rolled down her cheeks. Zoe's own tears fell as she held the woman in her arms.

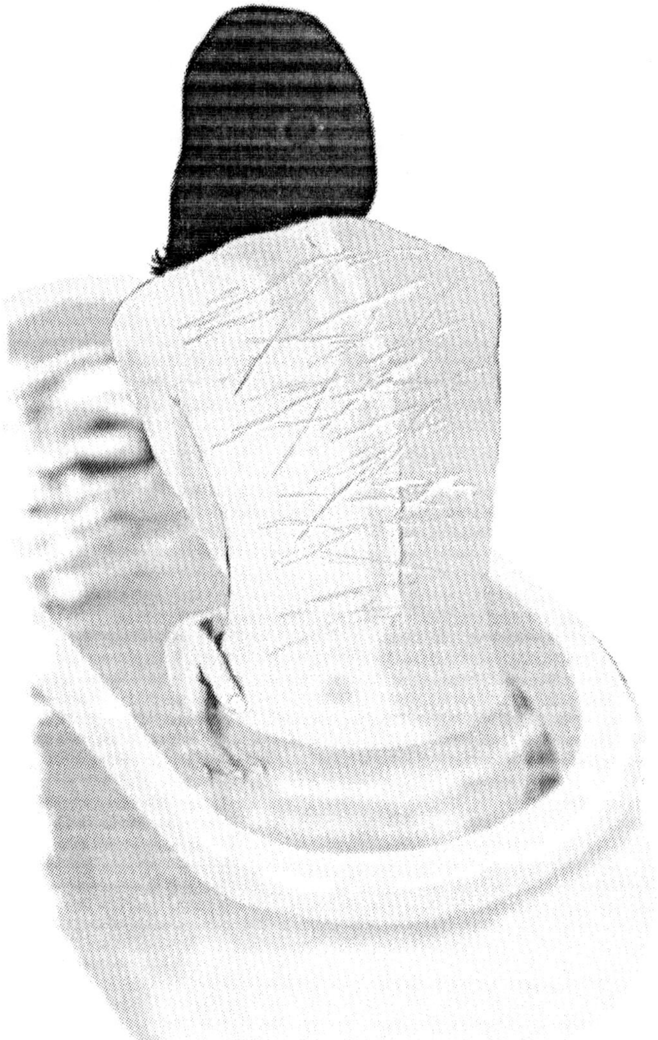

Chapter 9

Father Haralambos looked up into the bright early morning sun and squinted. He had a lot to do in church today and he was determined to get an early start. He rounded the corner to the small alleyway leading to the back entrance of the church, his mind on the matters of the day.

"Father."

Father Haralambos was startled at the sound of a voice coming from behind him. He turned and saw a man in his mid forties standing there, smiling at him. Father Haralambos embraced him and ruffled his dark hair. Athanasios Klaras' brown eyes shone with joy at seeing the old man.

"Athanasios, my boy, so good to see you! What are you doing here?" Father Haralambos inquired with a smile.

"I was homesick," Athanasios replied with a grin

"Have you eaten anything?"

Athanasios shook his head.

"Well then, we have to remedy that. Come,. we will go to my home and have some breakfast, and we can talk."

In deference to the cleric's age, the two men walked slowly through the back alleys, avoiding the early morning patrols. Athanasios smiled down at the man he loved as his father. When his own parents died when he was a young boy, the priest filled the void. He had spent many a summer's day talking to Father Haralambos and playing backgammon. In more recent times, when he found the war too hard to bear, he would close his eyes and remember those treasured moments: summer days at the river and water fights with the other orphaned boys. The priest had run the local orphanage and made it a point that the young boys learned to play, read the Bible and be honest and upstanding members of the school.

Athanasios was brought out of his musings as Father Haralambos led him to a small house. He opened the door and led him into a sparsely furnished room; two rickety old chairs stood again a wooden table. A large crucifix hung on the wall, the only decoration in the room.

"It's not much, but what is mine is yours," the cleric offered.

"Father, I have missed you so much," Athanasios said, and gave the old man another hug.

"I miss you too, Thanasi. I long for the days when I was just a priest and my only worry was how to break up water fights between you and Giorgos!" the cleric laughed.

"How is that old goat? I must go and see him and Samia."

The cleric frowned. "We lost Giorgos a week ago."

Athanasios sighed. He glanced up at the large crucifix. "A good man."

"We also lost Apostolos, Lefetheri and Stavros. They are at peace now. The village has been hit hard...God only knows what our future will be," the cleric said as he took out some cheese and bread and started to heat some water for tea. "So, how have you been?"

"Father, I've seen better days. We've had some successes and a lot of losses...too many losses. We also have another problem—the British don't want to help us. Churchill wants the King back, and I say: to hell with the King!"

"Communism isn't the answer, my son."

"What is, Father? If we have British support, we can unite everyone and form a strong Resistance. Like the French have done. We can do it, but no one wants to sit down. Everyone is thinking about the end of the war instead of thinking about the present. We can't form a government at the end of the war if we are all dead."

He took the cup of tea the priest had put in front of him and took a sip. "Our government can't organize a street parade, let alone this war, Father. The King is happy, and we are dying. Mark my words, Father, there will be a civil war in Greece after the krauts have been defeated. We stop one war and we begin another," he sighed.

"Let's hope it doesn't come to that."

"Father, there will be a civil war in Greece. Not if, but when."

"A civil war?" the cleric repeated. "More Greeks dying."

"Father, I don't know what the answer is—we get rid of the krauts and then what? We get the King back? That loser? He sits there waiting for us to do all the dirty work."

"And the answer is communism?"

"I don't know, but the monarchy hasn't worked. Maybe communism will work. But we have a more pressing problem. I was in Thessaloniki last week. A trainload of supplies and krauts are on a train that will be crossing the Gorgopotamos gorge, and it will also be carrying human cargo."

A railway line going from Thessaloniki to Athens spanned the Gorgopotamos Gorge. The Resistance had destroyed that line, making the Germans unable to move supplies to North Africa. It was a major blow to the Nazis until they had repaired it.

"Didn't the lads blow up that line?" The priest stopped in mid-sentence as he frowned at the man's last comment, "Human cargo?"

"Jews, Father. They are treated like cattle and sent to their deaths. Remember those boxcars we used to send sheep in?"

The priest nodded.

"They put those poor souls in boxcars and they go to their deaths...like sheep."

Father Haralambos stared at the man in shock. He was aware that the Jews were hunted by the Germans, but had not known how they were moving so many people. "That's inhuman," the cleric whispered. "Wasn't the line recently destroyed?"

"They blew it up and the krauts rebuilt it. We've been playing this game now quite a few times. We're going to blow up the line and the train."

"The train? You can't do that—all those people!" the cleric cried out.

"Father, we have to destroy that line and the train. Either way, lives are going to be lost. But if we destroy the rail, we send a clear message to those monsters that we will not submit! We have to fight them in any way we can, regardless of the risk. What is life under Hitler's regime anyway?"

"Thanasi, what about those poor souls?"

Athanasios looked up at the priest. "Father, those people are already dead. They live, but Hitler himself has ordered their deaths. What are you suggesting? That we don't act? We don't try and stop them? If we allow this train to pass, then they will be using this method to transport troops who will murder thousands. Didn't you tell me that it's a sin not to act when you can help a brother in need?"

"Thanasi, don't quote my own teachings back at me."

"Father, is it a sin not to act?"

"There must be another way. Can't we bomb just the line, or liberate the train?"

"I wish we could, Father. We don't have enough men to liberate the train. If we do that, the krauts will just start shooting and the prisoners will be killed. A few may get away but..."

"Isn't it better to let the few get away than to kill everyone?" the priest asked.

"Get away to where, Father? The whole country is overrun by Germans. Where do they go? They are destined to die. The Fates have already snipped their lives short."

"You are playing God."

"Father, if I could find a way to stop the train, I would do it in a heartbeat. We have to bomb that train. There is no other way. What do you suggest we do?"

"I don't know the solution to this particular problem. I don't have the Wisdom of Solomon, Thanasi. I don't have the answers and I don't know what to do. If we blow up the train, how many people will be punished and killed because of it? You know they will kill 50 Greeks for every German life lost...and those poor souls..."

"If we do nothing, Father, those on the train are destined to die," Thanasi said, looking at the distressed cleric. "As I said, I wish there was a way to liberate that train, but there isn't. We have to blow it up."

"We've been trying to get some of them out of the country," the cleric said quietly.

"How? How are you getting new identity papers?"

"We have help from the inside."

"Well, that works for one or two families at a time, not for hundreds of people." Thanasi looked across at the distressed cleric. "Do I know him, this person from the inside?"

The priest smiled. "Major Muller has been doing it for us. He just doesn't know it."

More questions were left unasked, as there was a knock on the door. Athanasios was quickly hidden in the adjoining room as the priest opened the door to a frazzled looking Zoe.

"Father, why aren't you in church?" Zoe asked as she entered and sat down.

"You were going to church, Zoe?"

"No. I was passing by and I saw the church closed. I came to see if you were alright." Zoe looked around and noticed the two plates and cups. "Father, did I interrupt anything?"

"You want a cup of tea?" Father Haralambos asked, trying to change the subject as he held up the teapot.

"You're not answering my question, Father."

"Sometime, Zoe, your inquisitive nature is going to get you in trouble."

"Story of my life," Zoe muttered. "So are you..."

The other door slowly opened and Athanasios stepped across the threshold with his gun in his hand. Zoe's eyes grew round with surprise. "Ares!"

Father Haralambos looked at the young girl with a frown. "The god of war? Zoe you're reading too much."

"No, Father, not that Ares, *that* Ares," and she pointed at Athanasios.

"What are you talking about, my dear child? This is my friend Athanasios."

Athanasios laughed. "Ah, Father, the Nazis know me as Ares Veloukhiotis."

"You chose to name yourself after the god of war?"

"Nice touch, don't you think?" Athanasios chuckled. "I knew those stories on mythology you used to read to me would come in handy one day!"

"I think it's great." Zoe piped in as she stared at the man she considered to be a true war hero. His exploits were legendary among the local Resistance groups and made him a man wanted by the Nazis.

Father Haralambos frowned at Zoe.

"Oh, Father, stop looking at me like that. We need heroes, and if he calls himself Ares, why not?"

"Ares was a blood thirsty god..."

"Father, I hate to break this to you, but Ares never existed remember?" Zoe said with a chuckle.

Father Haralambos ignored the young woman's last comment. He was extremely concerned now for the man's safety. He glanced at Thanasi who had a grin on his face and was enjoying the banter between the cleric and the young woman. "How did you recognise him?"

"I saw a poster of him in Captain Reinhardt's office when he interviewed me for the job," she said as she still looked up at the Resistance leader. "The poster doesn't come close." She realized what she had said and began to blush.

"Did you know about that?" the cleric asked Thanasi. He looked back at Zoe who was now looking down at the floor.

"They have a very old sketch of me, Father. I wouldn't worry. The Nazis love me...problem is, I don't love them," he said with a smile and a wink at Zoe.

"What if someone saw you come into the village?" The cleric began to panic.

"Don't worry, Father. No one knows I'm here."

"You are a real hero."

Athanasios sobered up and looked at Zoe. He knelt beside her chair. "What's your name?"

"Zoe."

He smiled. "You have a beautiful name, Zoe. I'm not a hero. I'm just doing what I have to do."

"You're still a hero...can I call you Athanasios?"

He nodded. "Or Ares," he smirked

"You are a hero to me," Zoe said softly. "My brother told me you saved his life on the front line with the Italians. He told me what you did."

"Who was your brother?"

"Mihali Lambros," Zoe answered.

"Ah that *manga*! How is he?" Thanasi smiled as he remembered a young man, his curly blond hair and hazel eyes that shone brightly when talking about his family and his home.

Zoe's smile faded. "He was killed when the Germans invaded."

"That's a real shame, I'm sorry Zoe. Mihali was a very brave man."

"Dimitri would love to meet you. You don't know how many people look up to you. You give people hope."

"Zoe, don't romanticize what I am. I'm a two-bit freedom fighter with more shrapnel in my body than brains. God gave me the opportunity to fight for the freedom of Greece. Who am I to refuse God's request?" he asked with a wink.

"You're still a hero to me," Zoe stated again. She stood and shook the man's hand. "I have to get back or Despina will wonder where I disappeared to." She smiled at Athanasios and opened the door.

As she left the house, she saw a squad of six soldiers coming toward her. "Oh shit."

Chapter 10

Zoe froze in mid step. Running towards her was a squadron of soldiers, screaming incoherently and brandishing their rifles. They reminded Zoe of a pack of wolves chasing its prey. For a fleeting moment Zoe imagined the worst, but instinct took over and she slowly backtracked her way inside Father's house. Timidly she closed the door, still not feeling secure, yet confident enough to peek outside to see what was happening. The soldiers, though, were not after her but some poor soul who could not escape their wild pack attack.

"What are you doing, Zoe?" Father Haralambos asked, watching the woman who had her head stuck outside the door.

"Soldiers."

"Yeah, I hear there are lots of them around nowadays," Thanasi said with a grin.

Zoe turned to the partisan and smirked. "Ha ha."

"I thought it was funny," Thanasi returned, and went back to eating as Zoe left the house.

****

She rounded the corner and stopped. She watched as two motorcycles, a car bearing the flag of a general, and a truck proceeded down the street. She hurriedly made her way back to the major's residence and watched from across the street as the general got out of his car. His aides fawned over him as they assisted him.

I wonder who that tight-assed kraut is, Zoe thought, as she went to the servant's entrance of Major Muller's quarters. She entered to find that Despina was in panic mode.

"Despina, what's going on?" she asked the harried housekeeper.

"Ah, there you are! Fraulein Eva was looking for you."

"What's going on?" Zoe persisted.

"Zoe, don't ask so many questions."

"I wouldn't have to ask if someone told me what was going on," Zoe muttered as she walked up the stairs and into Eva's study.

"Where have you been?" Eva asked as she heard the door open. She continued to write.

"Good morning to you, too, Fraulein Muller. I am fine, thank you, and you?" Zoe replied as she sat on the couch.

Eva looked up and grinned. "You know, Zoe, one of these days..."

"Don't tell me, I'll get into trouble. Trouble is my middle name, according to Father Haralambos."

"Where were you? You rose early today."

Zoe picked some nonexistent lint off the couch. "I went to the cemetery."

"Oh," Eva said quietly.

"Today was my mother's birthday. So I took her some new flowers and filled her in on what dastardly deeds we were up to." She grinned at the older woman. "Why is Despina in a tizz this morning?"

"General Rhimes has decided to pay us a visit," Eva replied and frowned. She didn't like the overbearing German general. He always found it amusing to pinch her in the rear and give her a slap for good measure. She had hoped she would be able to get out of greeting him, but her father had insisted.

"Who is General Rhimes?"

"He is in charge of Thessaloniki and the surrounding districts."

"That bastard!" Zoe spat out. She had heard stories of the infamous general but had never put a name to the face. His heavy-handed treatment of the Greek population had spread to Larissa. She also heard the stories about the brutality meted out to the Jews; a few things she had heard, she didn't want to believe. The reports were full of brutality and inhuman behaviour. "Do you know about the stories?"

Eva nodded. She didn't have to hear about them. She had seen for herself when Major Muller and she had visited Thessaloniki before arriving in Larissa.

They had stopped near the general's headquarters and admired the pier. She marveled at the deep blue of the water. The sun shone brightly and the smell of freshly made bread was in the air.

"Beautiful, isn't it?" Major Muller had said.

"It's too bad we are at war," Eva said and then noticed her father had gone on ahead, and was talking to an old man. She neared them.

"Where are you going, Jew?"

The old man trembled.

"Are you deaf?" The major raised his voice. Eva

cringed and took a step back.

"Home," the old man finally managed to reply.

"You swine don't deserve to have homes!" The major backhanded the old man and he stumbled. The meagre food he had fell on the road. Eva was rooted to the spot. "You are vermin!" the major spat out and hit the old man again.

"Ah, Major Muller, so nice to see you are cleaning the streets of my fair city!" The booming voice of General Erik Rhimes was heard as the general made his way across the street. His aide closely followed. "What seems to be the trouble?"

Major Muller turned and saw the general approaching. Immediately he clicked his heels and raised his arm in salute. "Hello old friend," the general said, returning the salute.

Muller grinned at his old school friend and the two embraced. "I thought you had rid the city of these pests," Muller said.

"I have, but you know how it is...cockroaches breed and they come back. So, you found a cockroach, I see?" He turned his attention to the old man who was lying on the ground bleeding. "Hans! You've dirtied my street. Do you know how difficult it is to get Jewish blood out of cobblestone?"

They laughed. Eva was sick to her stomach. She wanted desperately to help the old man, but more and more soldiers had gathered to see what the commotion was about and why their general was present.

"So dear friend, what are we going to do with this vermin?" Eric Rhimes asked, and raised an eyebrow at his friend.

"What do you normally do, Erik?" Major Muller, obviously proud of his handiwork, leaned against the lamppost and took out his cigarettes.

"Normally? I would get my fly squatter and kill

it." Rhimes acted out killing an insect and laughed.

"Okay," Muller said and, placing his cigarette between his teeth, he took out his gun and cocked it. The old man began to sob, "Please, Herr Major, have mercy!", but his pleas fell on deaf ears.

"Do we want to waste two bullets or one?" Muller tormented.

"Do you think you can do it with just one shot?" Rhimes goaded.

Muller looked around at his men, then back at Rhimes, "Perhaps if the animal would stop shaking..." he laughed.

Without thinking of the consequences, Eva screamed, "No, Papa!" but her voice was muffled by the cheering of the soldiers. She tried to reach her father and was stopped by a soldier who held her back.

"Don't want to get anything on that pretty dress," he told her. She could only watch as her father put the gun to the old man's head and pulled the trigger. Horrified at the sight, she rushed to the bank and violently threw up into the sea.

As she wiped the spittle from her mouth, her father demanded, "Are you all right?"

"Yes... yes, Father," she replied weakly.

"Ah, must be the sight of blood. My little one faints at the sight of blood."

Rhimes patted her on the back. "It's alright, Eva, we'll get this cleaned up and you won't have to see this mess when you go back to your hotel." He turned to Muller. "You set a good example for your child today, Muller. She will be a tribute to our glorious Fatherland."

The general's approval bolstered Muller's ego, and with a mock glare he said "Hans, you got more blood on the cobblestones."

They both laughed. He turned to his aide and waved his arms over the dead man. "Get this filth out of my sight and get someone to clean the cobblestones. One less Jew to search for. Find out where he lived."

Eva shivered at the memory. "They aren't just stories, Zoe."

"You mean they are real?"

"Yes, very real. The Jews are being hunted and exterminated."

"They can't do that! The Jews aren't animals." Zoe protested indignantly.

"They can, Zoe. A Jew is a nothing in the eyes of our Fuhrer." She looked up at the portrait of Adolf Hitler in disgust.

Zoe looked distressed. She was sickened by the war and by the stories of the cruelty of the Germans. She wondered if Eva felt *that* way about the Jews. "Can I ask you a question?"

"Always, Zoe. If I can, I will answer it."

Zoe hesitated. She wasn't sure how she was going to ask Eva if she felt the same way as Hitler did about the Jews.

"Do you...I mean," she stammered, "Do you hate the Jews?"

Eva looked up sharply, not anticipating that question. "No, I don't. Not all Germans are barbarians, Zoe." Eva looked down unable to meet Zoe's gaze.

"I didn't mean to hurt you," Zoe said, and went over to Eva and knelt beside her chair. "I just..."

"I know what you meant, Zoe. I'm sorry; I just wasn't expecting that question. I was in the Hitler Youth, but everyone in Germany was, before the war...I don't hate the Jews." Eva looked down at the young woman and their eyes met, Zoe allowing a tiny smile to emerge.

Zoe was glad that she had finally asked that question. She felt a growing affection for the woman. She had amazed herself when she first realized that she actually liked Eva. It had only been a few days, and yet she felt she had known her for a lifetime.

"I wish this war would end," Zoe sighed.

"What are you going to do when this war does end?" Eva asked with curiosity. She had been thinking about the end of the war and what she would be doing with her life. She didn't know what she wanted, but she knew she had found a friend in the blond-haired young woman. She wondered how her defences were breached so easily. She had built walls to protect herself but they had been breached. She found she could talk to Zoe so easily. She was tired of being lonely.

"What will I do when the war ends?" Zoe repeated. "Find myself the most comfortable bed, drink some real coffee and never eat feta cheese and olives again!" she grinned. "But not in that order!"

The two friends laughed.

"I want to go back to school, learn the things I missed out on and I want to travel," Zoe added wistfully. "I want to see the world...but it's only dreams."

"Zoe, never give up on your dreams," Eva encouraged, and smiled.

"I have to survive this war first, and then I can see to my dreams. What do you want to do? Find Greta?" Zoe asked. She found herself wishing that Eva would say no.

"Greta? No, I don't think so...I don't really know. I don't think I've allowed myself to dream."

They sat in silence, each with their own thoughts. Eva looked up at the clock. "I have to get ready to meet General Rhimes. Did you speak to Father Haralambos? He said he was going to give me some identity papers to alter."

"I went to find Father Haralambos, but he wasn't in church."

Eva stopped grinning. "He wasn't in church?"

"No, so I went to his house. I couldn't ask him because he had a visitor."

"Is he alright?" Eva asked, concerned for the old man she had come to love. They had spent time talking, getting to know each other. She found out he was a very gifted artist and quite a good singer. They had laughed when Father Haralambos insisted that he gave Eva his singing ability. He regaled her with his memories of a tone deaf Daphne. They had spent some time wiping the tears from their eyes as the priest shared memories of her mother. Memories she would treasure all her life.

"Oh yes, he was fine; he just had a visitor," Zoe said with a grin, remembering her encounter with the Resistance leader.

"Maybe you can go down and pick them up from him after I meet with General Rhimes."

****

"So what brings you to my backwater?" Muller asked has he handed the general some wine.

Erik Rhimes was a big rotund man; his uniform was stretched across his girth, and the buttons on his uniform appeared to want to break way. As he sat, he opened the collar of his uniform and exhaled. "Ah, that's better." He sipped his wine. "I came to warn you."

"You came all the way here to warn me? Don't tell me we have vermin?" Muller asked.

Rhimes' booming belly laugh erupted and Muller joined him. "No, no, no. You are going to get a visitor soon to your little backwater."

"Oh?"

"His name is Ares."

"The god of war is paying me a visit?" Muller chuckled. "These Greeks are so inventive. Lousy fighters, but inventive."

"Indeed. I must say that policy of one German for 50 Greeks does prove to be an excellent deterrent. I have to remember to thank General Kiefer for that idea. A stroke of genius. As I was saying, Ares Veloukhiotis is coming here."

"Why?"

"To blow up the line and..."

"Again? Damn it, Erik, that line has been blown up so many times I'm getting tired of telling my men to rebuild it!"

"They want to blow up the train as well."

"But they will be killing the Jews...I guess they will be saving us some work." They both laughed at Muller's joke. "I don't understand why he wants to blow up the train.

"Well, according to our informant...to teach us a lesson."

"If it's a lesson they want, then I'll be the one to teach it. Give me the men and I'll take care of every last one of them." Rhimes knew that Muller was deadly serious. He had witnessed many times the ruthlessness that Muller possessed. He admired the man.

"No. We're going to do something very different. I want you to put a prominent member of this little backwater on that train."

"Prominent member? How will that stop them from blowing it up?

The door opened and Eva walked in, with Zoe close behind. Eva had pulled her long dark hair into a pony tale and wore an elegant suit that matched her eyes. Zoe was rather pleased with how the outfit looked on Eva. She frowned when she spotted the general.

"Ah, Eva! How wonderful to see you." Rhimes got up and kissed Eva and then pinched her on the behind and gave her a good slap. Zoe's frown turned into a scowl.

"Hello, General," Eva said with a forced smile.

"Eva, my sweet, we have to find you a dashing young officer. I'm sure you must be lonely out here." He glanced at Zoe who had stood behind Eva trying to be inconspicuous. "And who is this?"

"This is Zoe Lambros, my personal maid and assistant."

"A Greek? Aren't you afraid she might take a knife to your throat?" the general laughed.

"No, I'm quite safe with Zoe around," Eva assured him.

He watched as Eva motioned for Zoe to leave the room as the door closed quietly. "Now, getting back to what we were discussing before the lovely Eva joined us." He motioned for her to join him on the couch. "I was just telling your father how the Resistance is going to blow up a train."

"Again?" Eva asked.

"Indeed. I think the Greeks believe in blowing something up until it doesn't exist!" The general smirked, quite amused at his own joke. He turned to Muller and repeated his previous order. "I want you to put a prominent member of this town on that train."

"So they won't blow up the train?" Eva asked.

"You've got it. They won't blow it up if some high and mighty local is on board. Isn't that just a brilliant idea?"

Muller grinned. "I take it you have someone in mind?"

"I do. I have found that the most prominent member of the community is the local priest. I want your priest on that train."

Eva gasped at the thought of that brave, innocent man being used as bait. She hoped that she could warn Father Haralambos and he could get away. Eva whispered a silent prayer that the Resistance wouldn't make the cleric another casualty of war.

"Ah, Father Haralambos. You know him well, don't you, Eva?"

Eva nodded. "He is a very good man. Isn't there another way?"

"I didn't know you cared so much about these Greeks, Eva," the General said, and frowned at the young woman.

"My Eva is deeply religious. I've told her to be careful when she goes down to that church. I heard what happened with that old woman hitting you," Major Muller said as he held his wine ready to drink and watched his daughter over the rim of the glass. "Getting close to that priest is not a good idea."

Eva nodded. She wasn't surprised to hear her father had kept an eye on her activities. Ever since *Kristallnacht* she had been aware that her father had someone spying on her.

"They can easily turn and kill you where you sleep. I wouldn't trust that servant of yours, either. Spending time with them is dangerous. They fill your young mind with ideas that are contrary to what we hold in our hearts," Rhimes said as he pulled out some papers from his briefcase. "I'm sure your Father

Haralambos is a God fearing man, but he is a Greek. He is prominent in the community, and he is perfect for what I had in mind."

"I will call him in tomorrow," Muller said, writing a note to himself.

"There was another matter I had to discuss with you." Rhimes handed the papers over to the Major..

"Identity papers?" Muller asked.

"Do you see anything strange about them?"

"Not really."

"Well we found these on two of the Resistance fighters. They appear to have originated from here."

"Did you ask them?"

"Unfortunately, we killed them before asking questions. They are good forgeries. Excellent in fact. Have you seen these before?" the general asked Muller who was studying them.

"Not that I would remember. Not unless Captain Reinhardt signed them on my behalf, but that's my signature. I don't understand it."

"Well then, you have a forger in your little backwater. A minor problem, but an annoying one. If we hadn't shot those two, you would never have known about the forgeries."

Eva paled as the blood drained from her face. The identity papers she and Father created were flawless, or so they thought. She had to get word to him, and quickly; and then get him to safety.

Chapter 11

Eva barely heard the two men talking. Her thoughts were on Father Haralambos and the dire predicament he was going to be in shortly. She was brought out of her thoughts when the two men began to discuss the state of the war. Eva had heard that the Allies had landed at Normandy, but from all accounts she was led to believe that the Reich was beating back the Allied advance. She had hoped at the time that it was the propaganda machine in action again.

"So we've lost Paris?" Muller exclaimed. He couldn't believe what his friend had told him. He believed the Allies were being pushed back across the channel. "When did this happen?"

"August," Rhimes said dejectedly.

"We're nearing October. You're telling me that we lost Paris in August? Damn it! Why didn't anyone tell us sooner?"

"I think they had a lot more concerns on their minds, old friend, than telling us about Paris. We lost Bucharest, the Russian bastards have overrun Estonia and the Americans...oh dear God, the Americans. We are fighting on too many fronts."

The two men sat smoking cigars. The smoke made Eva slightly ill but she wanted to remain to listen in on the conversation.

"We are going to lose the war, Hans," Rhimes said.

"Never! I don't believe that." Ever the good German, Hans was shocked that his friend would suggest such a thing. "We've had some losses but..."

"Hans, the war is going badly. Very badly. If we are lucky, we will salvage some sort of agreement. The Russians are mauling us. Barbaric people."

"What are we going to do here?"

General Rhimes pulled a piece of paper from his uniform pocket and gave it to the Major. Muller's eyebrows rose into his hairline as he read the orders from Central Command.

"That's why the train is important?" Muller queried.

"Yes. General Kiefer and I are organising a slow withdrawal of troops from Athens. We are leaving only a few there. Our Jewish problem will be eliminated. The Final Solution, Hans."

"Maybe we were given wrong information..."

"Hans, the Americans have crossed into the Fatherland."

Both Muller and Eva gasped, although not for the same reasons.

"When?" Muller whispered. He couldn't believe that the Allies had managed to cross into Germany. There must have been some mistake. It wasn't possible. "Are you sure?"

"I wish I could say I was wrong, Hans, but I can't. On the 13th, they marched into the Fatherland,"

Rhimes said quietly. He mentally shook himself, knowing that it was already too late.

Getting up from his chair, Muller swore and began pacing around the room.

"Excuse me, Father, General Rhimes," Eva said as she rose her from her chair. "I see that you have important matters to discuss, so I will leave you."

"Yes. Yes," her father replied absently, his thoughts on the Reich's impending defeat.

Eva walked out of her father's office, her thoughts jumbled as the good news was replaced with the more pressing problem of getting Father Haralambos out of Greece. She walked into the kitchen where Despina was busy preparing the noon meal.

"Despina, where is Zoe?"

"That child will be the death of me!" the housekeeper complained exasperatedly as she pushed back her hair from her eyes.

"Do you know where she is?" Eva asked again, becoming annoyed.

"No. She ran out of here like the devil was after her and with that child, he probably was."

Eva thanked the housekeeper, rushed to put on her coat, and hurriedly left the house. She would have to go and tell Father Haralambos herself. She couldn't delay any longer.

****

Light rain had begun to fall as Zoe headed out of the house. The housekeeper's words still echoed in her ears as Zoe tried to avoid any patrols. The good weather had changed so dramatically that Zoe wondered if the weather and the state of the war matched. She shook her head as she made her way to the priest's house. Avoiding the puddles that were beginning to form, Zoe walked up to the cleric's door and tapped lightly. Adjusting her collar to keep the rain out, she impatiently wondered why the priest was so slow in answering.

"Zoe, is everything alright?" Father Haralambos asked when he finally opened the door.

"Well, we have General Rhimes here," Zoe stated as she entered through the open doorway.

Athanasios entered the room again as the priest closed the door. "Big fat guy? *Gourouni* Rhimes"

Zoe giggled at the nickname. He did look like an overstuffed pig. "That's him. Big fat guy had a meeting with Muller. I don't know why, but Eva was with them."

"Who is Eva?" Thanasi asked as he leaned on the table.

Zoe glanced at the priest before answering. "Eva is Major Muller's daughter."

"And this Eva is important?" Thanasi continued, sensing that the two of them were keeping some secret from him.

"She is very important," Zoe exclaimed, and grinned at the surprised look on the cleric's face.

"The important question is why is Rhimes here?" Father Haralambos said to Thanasi.

"I wish we had a way of finding out."

"We do," Father Haralambos stated, "Eva."

"I'm now confused. How is the kraut's daughter going to help you?"

"She is our contact."

Athanasios stared incredulously at the priest. "She is your contact?" The priest nodded. "Dear God, man. Do you realize what you have done?" Thanasi threw up his hands in frustration. "And I suppose it was her idea to help you? Right?"

"She did volunteer."

"Great. This is just great! She has set you up, Father."

"You don't understand, Thanasi..."

"Father, what's there to understand?! You have been duped! I bet all those people you have helped are now dead. You don't honestly believe this woman came to help you?"

"Thanasi, you need to stop and listen. You're getting ahead of yourself. This is not like you. You don't panic. What's the matter?"

"Father, *you* don't understand," Thanasi sighed. "Does she know I'm here?" He addressed Zoe who was starting to get very angry with this man.

"No, I only told her that Father Haralambos had a visitor."

"Good," he said, running his hand through his hair and trying to figure out a way he could get the priest out of the area. "We can get you away."

"Do you always panic this way?" Zoe asked, frowning at the man as he paced.

"When you play with vipers, little girl, you get bitten. I'm not going to allow Father Haralambos to die because of this Eva," Thanasi spat out. He didn't understand why these people were so calm. Surely they had to realize that this German whelp was a spy.

"I am not a little girl." Zoe retorted. "I don't want him to die either, but Eva is as honest as the day is long. She is no more a spy than you are. She can't help it if her stepfather is a kraut." Zoe stopped when she realized what she had blurted out.

"What? Stepfather? What in God's name are you prattling about?!"

Father Haralambos gave Zoe an exasperated look. "Thanasi, you need to sit and calm down. Stop getting so excited. You're going to get a nosebleed."

"But Father..."

"Don't 'but Father' me, young man. I know what I'm doing."

"You don't! You don't know the first thing about the Resistance. You are a priest."

Zoe snorted at Thanasi's statement. "You sure don't get around much do you?"

Thanasi glared at her but Zoe ignored it.

"You two, behave."

"Father...you don't understand. I can't let those pigs get you. You are responsible for who I am. I'm not going to sit by and watch them kill you."

"Who said they will kill me, my son?" Father Haralambos asked.

"I am saying it, Father!" All three jerked their heads towards the door where Eva had just entered. Ares immediately cocked his gun, ready to protect the priest.

"Eva, what are you saying?" Father asked

"Eva, that's Eva? Stand aside, Father, she means to kill you," Thanasi demanded.

"Of course I don't! What gave you that idea?" Eva retorted, but that only caused Thanasi to become bolder, more determined.

"Oh, put that away," Father Haralambos said as the last reserves of his patience wore out. He grabbed the gun from a very startled Thanasi and secured it in the chapel's offering box that had been on the table. Zoe couldn't resist laughing at Ares as she looked at Eva who had a very confused look on her face. "You. SIT," he commanded, and Thanasi slumped into a chair. "And you," he leveled his gaze on Zoe, "stop smirking and behave yourself." Zoe slapped her hand over her mouth trying to comply. "And you, what are you talking about?" He directed his question at Eva.

"Did Zoe tell you that General Rhimes is here?"

The priest nodded.

"Well it seems they found some of the identity papers."

"Father, I can't believe you are trusting this kraut," Thanasi spat out.

"Who are you?" Eva asked the sulking Thanasi.

"That is Ares, the Resistance god!" Zoe said with a laugh. "More like the panic god."

"Athanasios Klaras?" Eva asked.

"You know me?" Thanasi said with some trepidation.

Eva nodded. "I know of you," she replied.

"Oh great. Just perfect," whined Thanasi.

"Oh, stop your whining. One would think you were 10 years old," Zoe said and shook her head.

"Listen, little girl..."

"Stop it!" Father Haralambos yelled. He had reached the end of his patience. "Eva, what's the problem with the identity papers?"

"I'm not a little girl," Zoe said as Father Haralambos glared at her. "Well I'm not," she insisted.

Eva looked at Zoe and then back at the priest. "Father, we have two problems actually. The first is that they shot two of our couriers. They had the papers with them."

"Those poor souls, may they rest in peace," Father Haralambos said, crossing himself. "But Eva, they can't link those back to us." He sat down across the table from Eva.

"Father, eventually they will find out who forged them."

"True," the priest said as he scratched his bearded chin. He sighed. "And what's our other problem?"

"There will be a train passing through here on its way from Athens to Thessaloniki, carrying troops. They are pulling out of Athens."

Three stunned faces looked back at Eva. "You mean they are actually pulling back?"

"Yes, I heard General Rhimes telling my father that they are slowly withdrawing troops."

"When?" Father Haralambos asked.

"In a few days, is how I understood it, and they said something about The Final Solution..."

"The Jews...they are moving out the remaining Jews from Athens and all the way back to Germany...that has to be it."

"They think the Resistance is going to blow up the train and the line."

"They know?" Thanasi asked.

"It seems so," the priest answered. "How is this a problem for us?"

"They want you to be on that train, Father. If you are on there, the Resistance will think twice about blowing it up."

Shock registered on Zoe's face, while the priest and Thanasi looked at each other. "You can't go on that train!" Zoe said angrily.

"If we don't blow up that train, many will die but..." Thanasi said quietly.

"What utter rot! Fifty Greeks will die if you do blow it up, smart man. And what about the Jews?" Zoe spat out. "Father Haralambos is not bait. He is a living, breathing kind man who you want to kill."

"Zoe, calm down," said Eva placing her hand on the younger woman's shoulder. "That's not going to happen." Eva looked at the priest. "She's right, Father."

"No, she's wrong," Father Haralambos said.

The three of them looked at the priest in shock. "Father, have you been drinking?" Zoe asked angrily.

"Zoe!" Eva swatted Zoe on the arm.

"Will you three please calm down? If I don't go on the train, then the Germans will know I'm in the Resistance, good people will die, and the line will be used to move the Germans out.

"Father, a good man will die that doesn't need to die," Eva said.

"We all have to go sometime, Eva."

"Not when I've just found you," Eva said quietly.

Thanasi frowned. "Father, we will find a way."

The priest exhaled loudly. "What part don't you understand, Thanasi? If I don't go on the train, Greeks die, Jews die and I die for Resistance activities. If I do go on the train, Greeks don't die, Eva is not implicated and..."

"And you still die, the Jews will die and I couldn't give a damn about the krauts! I hope they burn in hell!" Zoe's voice rose along with her anger at the frustration she was feeling at being unable to see a solution to this situation that did not include Father Haralambos' death.

"Zoe, either way I die," the priest replied

"I don't want you to die," Zoe said quietly.

"We all die sometime, my child," Father Haralambos reiterated, just as quietly.

"How can you be so final about this?" Eva asked, suppressing her tears.

The priest could not answer for fear of losing his resolve. Truth be told, he was shaking inside and said a silent prayer for strength. "Father," Eva whispered, "Oh, Father..." She was not addressing the priest, but her father that she'd only just met. They had spent such a short time together.

Father Haralambos rose and opened his arms and embraced Eva. "Don't worry, Eva, everything will be all right."

"I...I want to talk to you more about this, but I have to get back to the house. They will be wondering where I have gone," Eva said, burying her head in the priest's tunic. He could feel her tremble and held her closer until finally she broke away and walked to the door.

Eva stopped and looked back to see Zoe crying in the priest's arms. She stepped out into the drizzling rain and allowed her tears to flow. She was unaware of the cloaked figure that watched her leave the priest's house.

****

"So, you've made up your mind then?" Thanasi asked.

"I have to do what is best," the priest replied, still holding the sobbing young woman.

"I won't let you," Zoe said wiping away tears. "Even if I have to kill every last German myself, you are NOT going to die."

"Zoe, the needs of the many outweigh the needs of the one. It's for the greater good."

"Can't you see that the train will take you out of Greece? You may end up where the Jews are headed. You will die, Father and damn it, I'm not going to allow that!" Thanasi yelled.

"Thanasi, it is for the best, the Resistance will blow up the train, we can't allow any more people to be led to their deaths on that line."

"Father, please see reason. I wanted that train blown to kingdom come, but not with you on it. I wouldn't be able to live with myself knowing I caused your death. Don't you understand?" The young man pleaded with the cleric, hoping the old man would listen to him.

"Thanasi, sometimes the burden of leading is very difficult. We all make decisions that are too hard to bear. This is your torture stake, my son. I have to do what is right."

"Father, please listen to me!" Thanasi begged his mentor. "The Resistance will blow up that train, and I can't stop it."

"NO!" Zoe screamed at him and ran out of the house into the steady rain. Father Haralambos looked at the retreating figure and a tear made its way down his cheek. The priest wiped away his tears and left Thanasi. He went inside his bedroom and knelt, bowed his head and began to pray.

Chapter 12

Zoe ran. She ran until her heart pounded and her lungs ached for air. She didn't know for how long, and she didn't care; she just had to run until she could run no longer. Exhaustion finally slowed her down enough to bring her to a stop in front of the cemetery. Realizing where she was, she plodded through the mud to her mother's grave.

"Oh, Mama!" she cried, and collapsed to the ground, crying. "Mama, why is everyone leaving me?" she said as she tried to understand what was happening. Everyone she loved was gone, and now the man who was like a father to her would also die. She wiped away the tears. "This isn't fair. Eva just found her real papa, just when the Germans are leaving, and now this. It's not fair, Mama."

She looked to the heavens. "Dear God, I know I don't speak to you much, and I know you don't have to listen, but please, I beg you...please look after Father Haralambos. I know if you let him he will organise heaven for you." Zoe wiped her eyes again. "He is a good man and I love him so much." Her voice broke as she looked down at the sodden ground. "I don't have to tell you what he has done, how many people he has saved. Please make his death as painless as possible, don't let him suffer, I can't bear to think of him in pain and alone."

She rocked back and forth in the mud as the rain continued to fall on her forlorn figure. She wasn't sure exactly how long she had sat there in the mud, but she realized that the pelting rain had turned to drizzle and the sun had gone down.

She was slowly making her way back to the house when she heard a soldier commanding her to stop. Zoe sighed and turned. She grimaced when she found herself face to face with the corporal who had backhanded her several days before.

"So Fraulein, we meet again." The corporal grinned.

Zoe gave him a wry grin in return. "So it would seem."

"Where are you going?" he inquired.

"To Major Muller's residence," Zoe replied quietly. She was wet, cold and emotionally tired. She just didn't have any energy left.

"What are you doing out here at this time? Don't you know about the curfew?"

"Yes, sir, I do and I'm sorry," Zoe said quietly.

The soldier was taken by surprise. He expected a smart mouthed retort from this young girl. Taken aback, he just told her to get going and then stood for a few moments and watched her leave. Passing the church, Zoe looked up, and frowned when she saw that the door was open. She quickly ran up the steps.

****

The church was dark, the only light coming from the candles burning by the altar. Zoe stopped in the doorway when she noticed that Eva was kneeling in prayer. Not wanting to interrupt her, Zoe stood by a column and waited. But Eva was too emotionally overwrought to have noticed anyone as she looked up at the image of the crucified Christ.

"Lord, I can't believe that it is Your will to let Father Haralambos drink from this bitter cup." Her voice broke and she faltered. She wiped away the tears. "He's my father, Lord...I know I was brought here to find him and I know there is a reason for things to happen the way they do, but I can't see how this will benefit anyone. Please don't let him die. He has been my one saving grace in this nightmare." Eva choked on her words.

Tears welled up in Zoe's eyes as well, her heart going out to the older woman.

"I don't want to be alone again," Eva cried to the statue.

"You're not alone," Zoe said as she walked down the aisle and knelt beside her, taking her hand. "Not anymore." Zoe tenderly wiped a tear from Eva's cheek.

****

Father Haralambos hurriedly made his way to the church. He was going to make certain there was nothing left behind that could link Eva to the Resistance. He was sure he didn't have anything in his office that would incriminate her, but he wanted to double check. Thanasi had warned him about such things before he left, about the patrols that would stop him if he was out after dark, now that the curfew was in place. The cleric wondered where he had disappeared to, but knew there was no use in speculating; still, it didn't keep him from worrying about the lad. *Thanasi, God bless him, he means well but he is just too over protective*, Father thought to himself. Besides, he had to make sure things were in order before tomorrow came, and it was just a short distance from the house to the church, what could happen? The priest rounded the corner and stopped dead in his tracks.

The church doors were slightly ajar and he frowned. He was sure that he had told Sister Maria to close the door when she had finished preparing for Sunday's service. He shook his head and wearily climbed the steps. He made his way into the church and stopped. Before the altar two figures were kneeling, their heads covered, but he was quite certain he knew who the two people were. He smiled. "Thank you, Father," he said quietly and crossed himself. He then noticed the trail of mud from the entrance to the altar, shook his head and made his way out of the church.

****

Zoe and Eva rose and slowly made their way out. Eva stopped and saw the muddy trail. "Do you always like to play in the mud?" she teased, making an attempt to get a grin out of her friend.

"Only when it rains," Zoe replied. They grinned at each other and closed the church doors. They didn't encounter any patrols on the way back home. They stopped and watched as the car carrying General Rhimes sped off and they made their way around the house and into the kitchen.

"Oh my God!" Despina cried out as Zoe carried the mud from her boots onto the clean kitchen floor.

Her cleaned floor was now covered in water and mud. Zoe stood there with a sheepish grin and shrugged.

"Get out of here, NOW! You are..." the housekeeper yelled, but was stopped in mid sentence when she saw Eva follow Zoe inside. "Fraulein Muller, I'm sorry..."

"Sorry." She took off her muddy shoes and threw them out of the kitchen door and looked down to find her white socks were now a mucky brown colour.

"Get some hot water prepared for a bath, Despina," Eva requested, ignoring the glare Despina was giving Zoe as they both trudged up the stairs.

Despina watched the two as they disappeared from view and shook her head. "One of these days that child will be the death of me," she muttered as she placed a large pot of water on the fire.

****

Eva ushered Zoe into her bedroom, determined to get those wet and muddy clothes off of her before she developed pneumonia. Placing her on the bed as if she were a child, Eva removed her socks and tossed them aside. "What were you doing, Zoe? Did you jump in the river?" she asked as she unbuttoned Zoe's skirt and watched it fall around her bare feet. "I don't want you to get sick," she scolded; unaware of the effect the undressing was having on Zoe.

Zoe started to unbutton her blouse, but Eva pushed her hand away. "We can't have you catching a cold after..." she looked up for the first time then and saw the sheepish grin on Zoe's face, "...all, uh, can we?" Not sure how to interpret that expression, Eva stepped to the side and retrieved a blanket.

"This is very romantic, isn't it? Somehow I didn't think it would be quite like this...me being wet, cold and covered in mud, Despina yelling at me..." Zoe teased as she tossed her blouse to the floor, her shyness about revealing her own body forgotten. She looked up into blue eyes, losing herself in their depths.

Eva smiled. "You were thinking about it...about me?" she asked, placing the blanket around her friend's shoulders.

Zoe blushed. "Well...um...not all the time. I mean... oh hell, I don't know what I mean," she stammered, and let herself fall into Eva's embrace as Eva chuckled. Zoe looked back up into Eva's eyes, forgetting whatever it was she was going to say.

Eva just held Zoe. She had resisted her feelings for so long. Didn't want to get involved with anyone. She had cut herself off and maintained that icy exterior. She had built the walls around her heart to prevent anyone from hurting her again, and to protect herself from her father. She had managed to stay remote and aloof until she had met this young woman. Zoe had walked in and begun to disassemble the wall she had worked so hard at building.

They parted and held on to each other for a few moments. Zoe was quite content to stay where she was. She realized she wasn't cold anymore. *I wouldn't mind staying in her arms forever,* Zoe thought to herself as Eva snugged the blanket around her more tightly.

"I've never fallen in love with a woman before...I've never been *in* love before," Zoe said softly, finally admitting her feelings to Eva. She hoped Eva felt the same way.

"Well, that's...what did you say?" Eva asked as she realized what Zoe had just said. Eva thought she would never hear those words again. Not dared to hope.

"I've fallen in love with you," Zoe repeated softly but distinctly, looking into eyes that reminded her of the Aegean. "This is all new to me...I've never felt for anyone the way I feel about you."

"Maybe we..." Eva started, hesitantly. She wanted to believe what Zoe was telling her, wanted so much to feel that finally she could love again.

"When I said you weren't going to be alone, I meant it, Eva Muller. I just said I was new at this and, well, you are just going to have to show me."

"You surprise me, Zoe," Eva said quietly as she gazed at the blanket covered woman, her chestnut hair matted with mud but her eyes shining brightly. Those eyes looked up at Eva with emotions that she thought she would never again see directed at her.

"Oh? How so?" Zoe asked as she looked at her friend. She cocked her head sideways and watched the now fidgeting woman that held her.

"When I told you about Greta," Eva said, looking down at Zoe.

"I didn't freak out, is that it?"

Eva nodded. She wasn't sure what would happen when she revealed her love for another woman to Zoe. She couldn't believe it had only been a little over a week since she had confided in the younger woman. She remembered how Zoe held her as she told of her pain and the beatings. The regular beatings her father inflicted on her to get her "perversion" out of her. The beatings she endured at the hands of her uncle on orders from her father. The shame of being berated by her aunt. The rape by her uncle's friends as he tried to find her the "right man for the job." After her revelations, she and Zoe had spent the night talking. It felt good to be able to tell someone the whole truth.

She had revealed a little of what she went through to Father Haralambos, but not the full story. She didn't think she could voice her deeper pain. Until Zoe came into her life. Now, she had to make certain that Zoe knew where they were headed. She owed her that much.

"Why should I freak out...you were hurting and you needed a friend so badly," Zoe reminded her quietly, looking into Eva's eyes.

"You are special, very special, to me," Eva quietly said and, cupping Zoe's face in her hands, she slowly leaned over, pressing her lips to Zoe's. Gently at first, so as to explore the sweetness of this young woman, Eva slowly became more aggressive until she could feel the excited response from Zoe and sought to quench her desire.

"Oh boy!" Zoe whispered as they parted.

"Good or bad?" Eva asked with a bit of trepidation.

"Oh good! Better than good!" Zoe exclaimed as they shared another kiss. "Much better than when Tasos kissed me."

Eva looked down at her and her brows furrowed together, which caused Zoe to start laughing.

"Are you jealous, Fraulein Muller?" Zoe asked with a grin.

"No...I mean...yes...well...when did you kiss Tasos?"

"Let's see now." Zoe made as if she was trying to remember and then smiled up at her friend. "I was 12 years old, and it happened at the back of the chicken shed. Very sloppy kissing." She laughed. "My brother, Mihali, came out and stopped us. He told me that if I kissed a boy I would have a baby."

They both laughed as Zoe continued, "Which I believed, and so I never kissed anyone again!"

Eva looked down at her own tall frame. "Well I'm not a boy, so I can't get you pregnant."

Zoe looked Eva up and down. "You certainly are *not* a boy."

They looked at each other. Eva frowned. "You know this can be very dangerous for you." The thought of her father laying a hand on Zoe made her angry. She could withstand his beatings again if she had to, but could not bear for Zoe to suffer any punishment because of her.

"For me? What about you?" the young woman asked, wrapping the blanket around the older woman, as well.

"He will hurt you if he finds out. I don't want to see you going through what I've been through. You are a very gentle soul, Zoe, and if it means we can't take this further..."

"And you are a hard bitten Nazi, right? How do you feel about me, Eva?"

"I love you, Zoe, but because I love you, I don't want to put you in danger. I don't want to see you hurting."

Zoe sighed with frustration. She reached up and tenderly caressed Eva's cheek. "Eva, you may not have noticed this, but we are in a war. I'm in danger just walking down the street. I can get shot for nothing more than looking at a soldier the wrong way."

"My father..."

"Your father is an abusive man, who hurt you physically and mentally for loving someone. Father Haralambos told me that when we find love we accept it. We don't question it, we don't deny it."

"Father Haralambos said that?" Eva asked.

"Yes, he did. I don't think he was talking about us, but I do know how I feel about you. My brother described it once as Heavy Like." Zoe chuckled as she remembered her older brother describing his feelings for his newest girlfriend.

Zoe stopped and mimicked her older brother. "He said 'Zoe, there are three stages to a relationship: Like, Heavy Like and Deep Love. I'm in the second stage. Heavy Like. When I get to stage three you can shoot me, because I'll be useless.' So I'm in stage two and I think there isn't any cure to stop it from going to level three." She grinned up at Eva. "I wouldn't want to be cured."

Eva leaned down and softly kissed her again. They parted when Despina yelled through the door, "Fraulein, I have the water ready."

****

Despina looked up at the clock and sighed. She muttered to herself about Zoe being late. She had prepared Eva's breakfast and it stood waiting for Zoe to take it up. Making a decision, she picked up the breakfast tray and walked out of the kitchen and up the stairs. She waddled down the corridor to Eva's room, set the tray nearby on a low table, and knocked. She waited for a moment and then entered the room.

"I'm sor..." Despina stuttered to a halt.

Eva was lying in bed asleep; curled around the tall woman was Zoe, her dark head nestled in Eva's embrace.

"Mary, Mother of God and Baby Jesus!" Despina exclaimed and crossed herself twice. She stood for a moment and shook her head. She liked Fraulein Muller—she was much nicer than the rest of the Germans. She closed the door quietly behind her and went over to the sleeping pair. In the time she was their housekeeper, Despina had grown to love the tall woman.

"Zoe." She gently nudged the sleeping young woman. "Zoe!" she repeated, "Come on, child, wake up!"

Zoe stirred and opened her eyes to find Despina's worried face inches above her own. "Ahhhhh!" Zoe exclaimed and jumped, causing Eva to stir.

Blue eyes sleepily opened and turned to Zoe. "What?"

"What in God's name are you doing in that bed, child?!" Despina exclaimed.

"Ah..." Zoe looked around at Eva who had the beginnings of a smirk on her face.

"Ev...er...Fraulein...oh hell," Zoe said, as she tried to form some coherent thoughts and gave up.

"It's alright, child. I'm not going to tell anyone you were...asleep," Despina stated quietly and grinned at Eva.

"Thank you, Despina," Eva said as Despina nodded and set the tray nearby. "Zoe will be down shortly." Eva turned to Zoe who had tried to get out of bed, then realized she wasn't wearing anything and quickly decided to stay where she was. She smiled as she remembered how wonderful it had felt last night, kissing and making love to the woman in her arms. The timid kissing and caresses by the younger woman made her weep, and her soul cried out.

"Yes, ma'am," Despina said and waddled over to the door and closed it behind her.

Eva laughed as Zoe snuggled up against her, quite content to stay in bed.

"I sure hope this doesn't get around the village before I have a chance to get up," Zoe muttered.

"Don't worry, Despina won't tell a soul you slept in." Eva laughed at the look on Zoe's face and kissed her.

****

Zoe came down the stairs, grinning. This was the best morning she had ever spent in a long time. "This Heavy Like stuff is really good," she muttered as she reached the kitchen. If only they could get Father Haralambos away, it would be perfect. She quickly sobered up when she caught sight of Reinhardt leaving the kitchen, quite angry as he ran into her.

"Watch where you are going!" he yelled out and stomped off.

"I guess he didn't have a good morning," Zoe muttered as she entered the kitchen. She caught sight of Despina who was crying near the washbasin.

"Despina, what's the matter?"

The housekeeper dried her eyes with her apron. "Nothing, child. I'm alright," she stammered.

"Well you don't look like you are alright. What did that kraut do to you?" Zoe inquired, taking the heavyset woman by the shoulders and making her sit.

"Nothing. He just yelled. The war is going badly for them, I think. I hear things...things you don't know anything about."

"You'd be surprised," Zoe muttered.

"What?" the housekeeper asked.

"Nothing. So the war is going badly? And why did he yell at you?"

"I don't know, child. Men yell. These krauts yell louder than Greek men." She sighed and got up again to finish the cleaning.

Zoe stood watching the housekeeper as she busied herself around the kitchen. "Despina...um..."

"Yes, child?"

Zoe hated being called a child but she was willing to let it go since the woman was old enough to be her grandmother. "Please don't say anything about this morning to Major Muller."

Despina turned and looked at the younger woman and frowned. "Why would I do that?"

"Ah...well...um..." Zoe was at a loss for words. "He is a very violent man."

"Yes, I know that, Zoe," Despina said and stopped her activities and sat herself down. Zoe joined her at the table.

"I mean, he will hurt Eva."

"Yes, I know," Despina said. She had seen the young woman's scarred back when she helped with her baths. She was quite aware of how violent the major was. She was very surprised that Eva allowed this young slip of a girl to see her scars. "I don't intend to tell anyone that you slept in, or where you slept," she said, and smiled.

"Oh," Zoe said quietly, not quite certain how to perceive this newfound trust.

"Come on, child, we have work to do!" Despina got up and went over to the washbasin again.

Zoe followed her to the basin and quietly gave her a peck on the cheek, then quickly busied herself with the dishes. She didn't see the motherly smile on Despina's face as she put her hand to her cheek before joining her at the sink.

Chapter 13

Major Muller sat at his desk and stared up at the ceiling. He couldn't believe what he had heard from his old friend, General Rhimes. If it were anyone else who had told him about the Fatherland's losses...well he wouldn't have believed them.

"The Americans have crossed into the Fatherland."

"Mein Gott," Muller muttered. "My God, what a shambles," he said, and sighed.

His thoughts were interrupted by a knock on the door which he answered with a curt, "Come." Captain Reinhardt entered and saluted. Muller motioned for the young man to sit. "Has the train arrived?" he asked.

"Yes, sir, with three cattle cars."

"Good. You're probably wondering why there are soldiers on that train? Nicht?"

Reinhardt nodded. He had wondered that when he saw the train pull in first thing in the morning. He had asked a few of the soldiers, but they didn't know what was going on. All they had been told was they were being shipped to Thessaloniki and from there they didn't know what their orders were going to be.

"We have a problem," the major said. "We're pulling out of Greece."

Captain Reinhardt's eyes went wide and his mouth dropped open. If it weren't so serious Hans Muller would have laughed at the comical look on his second in command's face.

"Close your mouth, Jurgen, and listen."

"But..."

"I said listen. Did I say for you to ask me questions?" the major snapped at him. "The train that came in this morning is going to Thessaloniki. Men from here will join the soldiers from General Kiefer's command. The rest will be sent via truck convey. I've heard that there may be Resistance activity to blow up the train. Bring Father Haralambos here to me. He will be on that train."

"Yes, sir. May I make a suggestion?"

The major nodded.

"Why not get 100 villagers and put them on the train? One man won't matter much to the Resistance. Even if he is the priest. They will think twice about blowing up their countrymen."

Captain Reinhardt waited as his commanding officer turned his back on him and looked outside.

"Alright. Round up 100 villagers to go on the train," Muller said as he picked up a pen and began to sign papers. "Bring the priest here now."

"Sir, it's Sunday..."

Muller looked at the young man as if he had grown two heads. "So what? You don't bring priests in to me on a Sunday? Is there a problem?"

"No, sir."

"Well go and do it then." Major Muller yelled.

****

"And so when you do a kind deed, don't let everyone know of it, let God know." Father Haralambos finished his sermon on letting good deeds go unnoticed. His congregation was sparse today and he sighed. Only the old women and a scattering of old men were present. The young didn't have time for God with the war raging. Even Eva was missing today, and he was worried. She was always there unless she was ill. He was sure that she had been fine when he had seen her here last night.

He was startled when the doors to the church were opened and Captain Reinhardt and six solders entered the church.

"You're a bit late for the sermon, Captain," the priest quipped, knowing full well the reason the captain was there.

Reinhardt grimaced. "I'm not here for that. You are to come with me."

"May I ask where to?" he asked, hoping to prolong the inevitable.

"Major Muller wants to speak to you," he answered the priest, and then turned to the corporal on his left. "Gather everyone here and take them down to the train."

He led the priest out of the church as the soldiers rounded up the priest's congregation. The priest looked back and frowned. "I said I was coming with you, what have these people done?" The priest tried to plead with the Captain, but he could see he was not going to appeal to the man's kindness.

"Don't ask so many questions, Father. You may not like the answers," Reinhardt answered as he walked quickly back to Major Muller's residence. The old man shuffled along, quite unconcerned at the hurried pace of the younger man and he deliberately slowed down. "Come on, Father. Move!"

"Captain, I am old enough to be your grandfather, would you talk to him in that manner? And please slow down," the priest asked.

Reinhardt stopped. An incredulous look crossed his face. He couldn't believe how the priest had spoken to him, as if he wasn't afraid of him. He laughed. "Come on, Father, Major Muller is waiting.

Reinhardt liked the old man. He had spirit and quite a good sense of humour for a priest. A priest who was quite sullen and all fire and brimstone had educated him. This man was very human. He ushered him into Major Muller's office where the major had sat watching the priest enter.

"Ah, Father Haralambos."

"Good day to you, Major." The priest greeted the German as he sat down, uninvited. The major frowned.

"You're going on a trip," Major Muller stated and signed some forms without looking up at the cleric.

"I am? How lovely. To where?" Father Haralambos answered and smiled.

Reinhardt suppressed a grin. He really liked this old man. He turned to his commanding officer and watched as a scowl formed on the older man's face.

"That doesn't concern you at the moment."

"I'm going on a trip and you won't tell me where? Ah, must be a German thing," the priest said as he folded his hands and rested them on his lap.

"Father Haralambos, your lack of concern interests me...why is that?" the German asked. He tapped the pen on the desk and looked at the priest quizzically.

"Why am I not scared, or why am I looking forward to a trip when I don't know where I'm going to?" the priest quipped.

Reinhardt coughed to suppress the chuckle that had bubbled forth. Muller frowned at the captain and then turned his attention to the priest. "You are not amusing, Father."

"I'm not trying to be, Major. I'm an old man; I've lived a long life and I've seen a lot. I know you can kill this old body, but you cannot kill my soul," the cleric said, and he smiled at the Nazi.

Major Muller was stunned. He wasn't used to people being so honest with him. He was used to fear and hatred, but not open honesty. He turned to Reinhardt, "Leave us."

The door closed behind the captain and Major Muller turned his attention to the priest. Muller leaned back on his chair and looked at the priest.

"What secrets do you hold, Father?" Major Muller wanted to know why his daughter thought so much of this man. Reinhardt had told him of his meetings with her, the hours they had spent together. He was suspicious.

"I am the keeper of many secrets, Major, most of them spiritual. I'm a simple priest," the cleric replied.

"You're not the simple priest you want me to believe you are."

"You mean I'm not a priest? The Archbishop will be most surprised." His eyes were still smiling, but the major could sense a steely resolve. "It's a lovely dance we are dancing, Major, but I'm getting older so why don't we say what we want to say," the priest suggested.

"Tell me, Father, why does my daughter Eva come to church so much?"

"Why do people come to church?" the priest asked back as he looked back at the major. "Eva is a spiritual child, Major."

"She is a perverted child," Muller mumbled. "I know what she has been doing, Father."

Father Haralambos realized he was being baited and he inwardly smiled. Muller was just a pup when it came to these tiresome mind games. "She has been cleansing her soul, Major. The death of her mother caused her so much grief. I'm sure, as her father, you are aware of that. She has been in pain and she needs the solace of the Lord."

Major Muller watched the old man for a few moments. "Tell me, Father, what has my daughter told you about her mother's death?"

"A child is scarred from such an experience, Major." The priest lost his good humour and his blue eyes turned cold as he looked at the man responsible for his daughter's pain. *No child should ever be treated like an animal*, he thought.

Major Muller was startled. The good humoured priest's eyes showed hatred for a moment, and then the priest smiled. "Major, any child that loses a parent is lost. Eva is no different. As I said, she has found solace in the Lord."

The major decided to let that issue drop as he was rather unsettled by what had transpired. He fussed with some papers on his desk. "You will report to Captain Reinhardt for your train trip," he ordered, not looking at the priest.

"Ah yes, my little trip. Will I have time to let the good Sisters know I will be gone for a time?"

The major nodded. "Tomorrow you will board the train," he said, refusing to meet the priest's eyes. "Leave," he directed, turning his chair around away from the priest. He was unaware of the smile that crossed the priest's face.

"Have a good day, Major."

Muller didn't answer as the door closed quietly when the cleric left. Muller felt that the old priest had challenged him, and somehow he had lost. He shook his head.

****

Father Haralambos was deep in thought as he made his way through the forest, the autumn chill creeping into his robes. He reached the end of the trail and settled down as he gazed out across the northern horizon.

The forest that surrounded the area appeared to be succumbing to the weather—their leaves falling, leaving the shriveled, bare branches to face the coming winter. He found a secluded area overlooking the northern mountains, the clouds skimmed across the mountain peaks, the mountains themselves looking grey and depleted. The river, a vital resource for the war ravaged community, was a center of activity for the many local farmers, its crystal clear water and powerful currents bringing a sense of intensity and vigour to the atmosphere. The rich, opulent fields of wheat flourishing as the time for harvest neared gave an almost golden hue to the skyline.

There was an eerie silence that forced the Father's thoughts to focus on his imminent future. He sat on the boulder and contemplated his life. He was fortunate, he thought, that he could take a moment to reflect on his life. Others were not so lucky as their life was cut short. He could find some time to organise his affairs and say goodbye to those his loved.

Maybe that's a curse and not a blessing, he thought to himself.

He had found his only child and now to see her being taken away from him again hurt him a great deal. She was a spirited and deeply religious woman who he was proud of. He didn't think he could ask for more in a child. He smiled. When he looked at her, it was like he could see the love of his life, Daphne.

He heard a rustling and he turned and saw Zoe coming towards him. He smiled and she promptly sat beside him.

"I thought I would find you here," Zoe said, looking out over the valley. She had seen the priest leave Muller's residence. She had hoped to stop him before he left, but Despina held her back with some chores that needed doing which took her some time.

"It's quiet here," Father Haralambos said, fingering the well-read Bible in his hands.

They sat in silence for some time, Zoe playing with a stick as she watched the clouds slowly pass.

"I'm going to miss you," she said quietly.

"I'm going to miss you too, Zoe."

"Don't give God a hard time okay? I know you want to organise everything," she said and gave the priest a grin.

Father Haralambos laughed. "I promise not to give God a hard time. I'll tell Him you told me to behave."

"I've already told Him," Zoe said shyly and looked away.

"Are you speaking to Him now?" the priest asked.

Zoe nodded and prodded some dead leaves with the stick. "I asked Him to take care of you and told Him that you are a bossy boots." She grinned at the priest who was laughing. She hadn't seen him laugh so much in years. His whole face changed and it made him look younger.

"Can I ask you to do something for me?" the priest asked

"Anything," Zoe replied.

"Behave when I'm gone," the priest said as he hugged the young woman. He looked down to see tears running down her face. He kissed the top of her head and rubbed her back with is hand. They sat like that for some time, each with their own thoughts, gazing out to the mountains. A memory surfaced as Father Haralambos smiled at the memory of a very young girl putting her hand up eagerly to answer the question he had put to the class.

"Alright, children, which is the highest mountain in Larissa? Who can tell me," Father Haralambos said as he looked out at the sea of faces before him. The young children scrunched up their faces trying to think. The priest smiled as he watched them.

A little hand shot up. The child's honey coloured pigtails bobbed up and down as she tried to get his attention.

"Yes, Zoe?"

"Father, the highest mountain in Larissa is Mount Olympus!" she said with conviction and sat back down.

The priest smiled. The children looked at Zoe and laughed. The child was crestfallen and began to pout.

"Now, now children. Zoe is nearly right. Mount Olympus is the highest mountain in Greece and you can see the mountain from here if you look hard enough. The highest mountain in Larissa is Mount Ossa."

"What's so funny?" Zoe asked of the grinning priest.

"Ah, I was just remembering a very young girl and Mount Ossa," he said cryptically.

Zoe looked at the mountains and smiled. "Mount Olympus is the highest mountain in Greece."

Zoe looked shyly at the priest who was looking out at the mountain ranges. She tried rehearsing what she wanted to say to him on the way out there but it sounded so silly to her. She wasn't sure how to tell the cleric about her love for Eva or how much Eva meant to her. She wiped her palms against her skirt, quite surprised to find she was worried. She mustered her courage and said, "Father, I have something to tell you."

"You do?" Father Haralambos asked. He was wondering when the subject of Eva and Zoe being together would come up. *I am an old man but I am not blind*, he thought to himself as he watched the young woman.

"Um...You know about Eva and what happened in Germany with her...I mean Major Muller..."

"He beat her, I know that," the priest replied. When Eva had told him he was so angry he wanted to confront the major, but he quickly realized that it wasn't the best laid plan and it would only hurt his daughter more if he had done so.

"Hmm...did she tell you why?" Zoe asked. She wasn't certain how much Eva had confided in the priest. The priest nodded. "Um...well..." Zoe stuttered and looked away.

"You love Eva," the priest said quietly and smiled.

Zoe looked up at him. "You know?"

"Yes I know. How does Eva feel about you?" he asked, knowing the answer to that question already.

He had seen how Eva looked at the young woman when they were together.

"Um...she feels the same way," Zoe said self-consciously. "Uh...we..." She couldn't bring herself to tell the priest they had made love the previous night. "We...uh..."

The priest smiled at her and took her hands and held them. "Zoe, never be ashamed of loving someone. You don't get many chances in life and when they come, treasure them. Bottle them up and treasure them, my child. Eva is a precious human being. She has gone through the fires of hell, and she needs someone to love her and help her. You are a special person, Zoe. You have lost much, but I see a fire that burns so brightly. You have a gentle heart and a loving soul. Give her that love, my child, and she will love you with equal measure. You have my blessing."

Zoe looked up into his eyes and she could see glistening unshed tears. She nodded mutely. They sat in silence for a moment. The cleric picked up his Bible and turned to the young woman.

"Zoe, I want to read something to you." He opened his Bible and found the passage that he wanted to read to her. "When the time comes I want you to remember this."

Zoe nodded. She didn't trust her voice to speak.

The priest began to read. "And He will wipe out every tear from their eyes, and death will be no more, neither will mourning nor outcry nor pain be anymore. The former things have passed way." The priest's voice broke. "I am going to a better place, my child. I will not be alone. Whenever you are afraid I want you to remember what the Psalmist wrote: 'The Lord is my shepherd, I shall lack nothing. In grassy pastures he makes me lie down. By well watered resting places he leads me. My soul he refreshes. He leads me in the tracks of righteousness for his name's sake. Even though I walk in the valley of death, I fear nothing bad for you are with me. Your rod and your staff are the things that comfort me.'"

The priest stopped as Zoe sobbed beside him. He held her for a moment and then continued, "Surely goodness and loving kindness themselves will pursue me all the days of my life; And I will dwell in the house of God forever." He finished and closed the Bible.

"I want you to have my Bible, my child. Keep it with you and read it. I'm going to be keeping an eye on you." He handed the black book, the corners upturned and well used, to Zoe who took it and held it close to her chest.

She held the Bible in her hands. His Bible. A small possession that she would treasure for the rest of her life. "I love you, Father," Zoe said and leaned against the priest as he held her.

"I love you too, Zoe," the priest replied, holding the young woman in his arms. He was certain his prayers were answered and that Zoe had come to realize that God was not to blame for the war or the terrible fate that had befallen the country. He was satisfied that his work was done.

Chapter 14

Father Haralambos left Zoe at Athena's Bluff and made his way back to the church to let the Sisters know he would be gone for a while. There was no reason to get them upset. He was sure they would be able to carry on in his absence. He needed to write a letter to the Archbishop asking for a replacement. *I have so much to do,* he thought as he climbed the stone steps.

He entered to find Eva talking to one of the sisters. "Ah, Eva. Are you alright?" the priest asked as he took her hand.

"Yes, Father..." The priest ushering her into his office interrupted her.

"Sit, sit," the priest urged the young woman. "Now where were you this morning? I was worried you might be ill."

Eva smiled. She wasn't sure how to tell her father that she was in bed with Zoe, or why they had been in bed, though she didn't think she could lie to him, either. "Uh...we...I mean I was in bed," Eva stammered.

The priest turned to get a pitcher of lemonade and grinned. He did so enjoy trying to tease the girls. "You were in bed?" he repeated, and offered her the drink.

"Yes, Father," Eva said quietly, thinking that she might as well dig a hole and bury herself in it. She hadn't thought it was going to be so hard to tell him.

"I hope you didn't tire Zoe too much. Despina would be most unhappy," the priest said with a gleam in his eye. Eva stared at him in shock; her eyes went round and her mouth dropped. "Are you alright, child?" the priest asked, grinning. He sat back and folded his hands on his lap.

"Uh..." Eva was stunned. She wasn't sure what to expect, but she hadn't expected that reaction.

Father Haralambos continued to smile. "You have something to ask me? By the way, did you hurt yourself?" the priest asked as he leaned over to have a closer look at the tiny bruise at Eva's neck.

Eva tried to get her thoughts to form a coherent sentence, but all she could get out was, "Oh hell." Realizing that she had just blasphemed in church, Eva turned a crimson shade of red and covered her eyes with both hands, shaking her head.

Father Haralambos laughed. "Don't swear in church, I don't think God likes it."

She looked at him and grinned. "You are wicked."

The priest came over and sat with his daughter, wishing he had more time to get to know her better. She had a personality he so enjoyed and he was comfortable in joking with her, even if she was mortified at the time. "Tell Zoe not to bite so hard next time," the priest whispered to her.

"Father!" Eva was shocked even more.

"Ah, Eva. I missed out on watching you grow, humour me in my old age," the priest said and grinned

The priest watched Eva grin back. He was so proud of her, and happy to see his daughter find someone who could love her for who she was. They sat together drinking the lemonade in silence. Father Haralambos knew they had to discuss what would happen the next day; it would be difficult to say goodbye. "I'm leaving tomorrow," Father Haralambos said quietly.

"Father, maybe Ares can take you away," Eva said, as she tried once again to convince him to leave Larissa, to escape.

"This is my cup, my child. I can't give it to someone else," the priest replied, knowing that no matter what he said Eva would try and change his mind, just as Zoe had tried.

"Ares said they will blow up the train. I don't want to lose you," Eva said as she looked at the priest, trying desperately to get him to change his mind, knowing it was a lost cause; but if she had learnt anything during this nightmare of a war, it was not to give up.

"I don't want to lose you either, but my time has come. You have to be strong. You have to help Zoe as she will help you. You're not alone anymore," he said, trying to ease the young woman's fears.

"Because I have Zoe, does that mean I have to let you go?" Eva asked, her voice breaking. "Can't I have you and Zoe in my life?"

"Eva, I can't let Major Muller know that I know what will happen to the train. He is not a stupid man, he is an evil man, but not stupid. He will make the connection. I don't want you to suffer again at his hands. Do you understand?"

"Father, maybe I can escape with you and then he won't be able to get his hands on either of us." Eva was desperately clutching at straws.

Father Haralambos sighed. "What of Zoe? Will you leave her behind?"

"No. But she..."

Father Haralambos stopped her with a finger against her lips. "My child, if I could do that, I would, but we can't all escape. That would risk many lives. I have lived a long life, a very good life. I don't have a death wish but Eva, my darling daughter, there is no other way. I won't sacrifice your life. You have lost too much already."

Eva sighed and sagged against the cleric. Father Haralambos kissed her tenderly. "I think you need to go to Zoe. She needs you now. You both need each other. She came to see me at Athena's Bluff. She's still there."

Eva nodded, brushing away the tears. She wanted to get her father away from this nightmare. She had spoken to Ares and it was set, but she realized he wasn't going to listen.

"She told me how she felt about you. Do you love her Eva?" Father Haralambos asked as he tenderly wiped away her tears with his handkerchief.

Eva nodded. She found a lump in her throat and she drank some lemonade. "She is everything to me, Father."

"Love her with all your heart, child. She is a rose among weeds. As I said to Zoe, you don't get many chances in life and when they come, treasure them. Bottle them up and treasure them. Love one another and treat each day as if it is the last day you will be alive. Believe in God and He will never fail you. Will you do that for me?" he asked her.

"Yes, Father," Eva said quietly as she held the old man's hands.

"I want you to do something else for me," the priest continued "I want you to get out of Greece when the war ends. I want you and Zoe to leave. Thanasi tells me there is more bloodshed coming. He said Greece will be plunged into civil war and I don't want you two to be here. Just remember that I'll be with you in spirit. Zoe's asked me not to try and reorganise heaven, so I will need something to occupy my time," Father Haralambos joked. "Take care of Zoe," he added.

Eva nodded, not trusting her voice.

"Remember my child, I will always love you, and I thank God every day that He brought you to me," he said as he brushed back the dark bangs from her eyes. "Don't forget now, remember to pray," he admonished, and kissed her tenderly on the cheek.

****

Eva had an idea as she left the church. She wasn't going to give up trying to find a way to rescue her father. She owed him that much. If she had learnt anything from living in Larissa over the course of two years, it was the unyielding spirit of the Greeks against the occupation. They never gave up hope; they found ways to survive and to thwart the Germans. She slowed as she came to the train station.

It was tightly guarded on all sides. The soldiers were milling around and she wondered if they were from General Kiefer in Athens. The piteous cries coming from the boxcars broke her heart. She watched as the soldiers poured water onto boxcars to quiet the yells and screams that were coming from inside of them. The weather had turned cold, and it sickened her to think of the poor souls in the boxcars being drenched with the cold water. She shook her head and said a silent prayer. Turning away in disgust, she stumbled into Captain Reinhardt, who held her to keep her from falling.

"Ah Fraulein Muller. Don't fall now...we wouldn't want that cold mud on you," Reinhardt said and grinned. He had been watching as she had looked over at the boxcars.

"Captain. Thank you for your concern," she said as she tried to extricate herself from the captain's embrace.

"My pleasure, Eva," he said as he let her go. "What are you doing here?"

"I was curious," Eva replied. She hadn't anticipated being stopped. There were some advantages to being the major's daughter. The soldiers knew her and didn't attempt to ask her questions. Except for Captain Reinhardt, who had made it his personal mission to make her life uncomfortable since her arrival.

"Curious?" Reinhardt repeated. "Would you like to see some of the scum that we took off the train?" he asked as he scrutinised Eva's face. He smiled at her discomfort.

"No, that's fine. I'd better be going," Eva said, trying to get away from the smug looking German.

"By all means, have a good evening," Reinhardt responded, as he watched the woman walking away. He frowned when she headed in the opposite direction from the major's residence. "Now where are you going little Eva? Hmm?" He decided to follow her.

Eva walked down the cobbled streets towards Athena's Bluff. Distracted by her thoughts of the poor Jews, Father and Zoe, she was unaware of her surroundings; unaware of the children playing in the street or the dog that barked at her passing. She was too distracted to see Captain Reinhardt follow close behind.

Finally reaching the bluff that Father was so fond of, she saw Zoe sitting on the cliff reading. Smiling, she took a moment to drink in the sight of this lovely young woman who filled her heart with hope and joy. Just the sight of her could lift Eva's heart, and the power of that was not lost on her either.

Zoe turned around when she heard the scrunching of the dead leaves. She smiled when she saw Eva. "Hi. You look exhausted." Zoe said and made room for Eva on the ledge. Eva sat down and put her arm around the younger woman. She caressed Eva's cheek. "You spoke with Father Haralambos?"

Eva nodded. "He is such a stubborn old goat."

"What if we can sabotage the train before it leaves?" Zoe asked.

"It will only postpone the inevitable," Eva responded dejectedly.

"What if Ares can get Father out of the train?" Zoe tried again. She had been thinking of ways to get the priest off that train since Father Haralambos had left her at the bluff.

"I've seen the train, Zoe. It's guarded by so many soldiers no one can get close without being stopped. There are four boxcars," Eva replied, unable to dispel the image of the soldier pouring the water into the boxcar and the screams that she had heard.

"What's in the boxcars?" Zoe asked, gazing up at Eva. She frowned when a tear rolled down Eva's face. "What's the matter, Eva?" she asked, and brushed away the tear with her fingers.

"They," she paused, "they hold Jews. I could hear their screams, Zo. The soldiers were pouring water into the cars to quiet them down," Eva said as she rubbed at her eyes.

Zoe stared away. She closed her eyes and sighed. The barbarism of the invaders was widely known. Larissa had lost so much. Every family suffered, but it was the Jews that suffered the most. Being unable to help these poor souls when they were forced out of their homes made her more determined to help the Resistance with trying to overthrow the occupation.

Eva held Zoe closer as they sat in silence watching the sun set. The mountains had turned a golden hue as the last rays of the sun saw them for the final time that day.

"Eva, after the war ends, will you come with me?" Zoe asked quietly. "Share my dream?"

Eva remembered when Zoe had told her about her dreams of the future, after the war. At the time she thought the younger woman had given her a glimpse into the real Zoe. She was so taken by the younger woman's hope for the future. Despite all that had happened, she held on to a dream.

Eva asked Zoe what her plans were going to be after the war. Eva herself had no plans. She would remain a prisoner within her own home as long as her father was alive.

"What will I do when the war ends?" Zoe had repeated. "Find myself the most comfortable bed, drink some real coffee and never eat feta cheese and olives again!" She grinned. "But not in that order!"

The new friends laughed.

"I want to go back to school, learn the things I missed out on, and I want to travel," Zoe said wistfully. "I want to see the world...but it's only dreams."

"I want to share your dream, Zo. I would follow you anywhere," Eva replied and leaned down and kissed the younger woman.

The two lovers were unaware of Captain Reinhardt hidden in the brushes watching them. The captain grimaced as he watched the two women kissing. He was disgusted by their behavior. "Little Eva, you are still a pervert," Reinhardt whispered to himself. Major Muller had been right to order him to watch Eva.

Captain Reinhardt stood stiffly to attention. He was proud of his new commission and his new assignment with Major Muller. He had known the major before the war when he was trying to court his daughter. He and Eva Muller had been in the Hitler Youth together. He never understood why he couldn't even get her to go with him to the park, until the day he saw her with another young woman. They were holding hands and kissing. He was disgusted. He knew then it was his duty to report this perversion to the authorities, but he held back.

On Kristalnacht, when they went to the synagogue, he watched again as Greta held Eva and tried to stop the tears that flowed because she had seen the old Jew being killed. When Greta kissed her that had been the final straw for the young man. He had to tell her father; it would be a betrayal of the Fatherland to let the perversion take root. He remembered his instructor saying that homosexuals were deviants and needed to be reformed. There was hope for them if they were not too far gone into the perversion.

He remembered what happened when he told her father, who was then still a captain. Captain Muller's eyes went an ice cold blue, and Jurgen was afraid he would feel the brunt of the man's anger. But he thanked him for coming to him and asked him not to report what he had told him to the authorities. He said he would see that Eva got the proper treatment for her sickness. Only later did he find out that the captain had beaten the woman severely. He couldn't find out any other information and wondered if the treatment her father had talked about worked.

Major Muller had looked the young man up and down and grinned. "So, Jurgen, you're all grown up and a captain."

"Yes, sir." The young man grinned and stood a little bit straighter.

"Sit down, boy, before you break your spine standing so straight," Major Muller said as he sat down.

They had gone on to discuss his current assignment. He hated Greek food, but that's where the Fuhrer wanted him, so that's where he would go. At least it wasn't the Russian front.

"Now, Captain. I have another assignment for you. I'm sure you remember my daughter Eva?"

Reinhardt nodded.

"I want you to keep an eye on her. If you see..." the Major had stopped and exhaled loudly, "if you see any kind of perversion, you are to let me know. She has been treated for this sickness."

"Yes, sir," he said.

"She hasn't had a relapse, so I don't think it will be a problem," the major said, and went on to give him his other assigned duties.

"I wonder how you seduced that child," Reinhardt muttered as he watched the two holding each other and kissing. He admired the fire in the young Greek which remained unquenched, despite the hardships she had endured. He hoped he would be able to save Zoe, *if* she could be saved. He would see to it. He continued to watch as the two rose from the bluff and, hand in hand, walked back to the house. Reinhardt spat on the ground and allowed them to leave before he set out himself.

Chapter 15

Father Haralambos sat on his bed, the early morning sun shining through the threadbare curtains. His suitcase stood in the corner, and the priest frowned. Sister Maria brought him a woolen scarf she had made, saying that he would need it since she had heard that the weather in Thessaloniki had turned cold. He had tried to decline, but the good Sister was quite stubborn—even more than him—so he relented. He was surprised even more when Sister Gregoria gave him a woolen jacket. He had spent the rest of the day writing letters to the Archbishop and getting the church ready for the Sunday sermon, which was to be delivered by the organist since he wasn't going to be back in time.

He was brought back from the goings on of the previous day by a knock on the door. The cleric frowned and took out his pocket watch. It was only 7:00 a.m.—too early for his call to go to the train. He opened the door. Thanasi stood there thumping his feet on the ground because of the cold. The priest ushered him inside. "What are you doing here, Thanasi?" the priest asked as he watched the younger man remove his scarf and coat.

"Father, I know I said goodbye last night, but I had to see you one more time," Thanasi said. He was going to try and convince the priest that he could escape; there was still time.

"I thought we already had this discussion yesterday?" the cleric said as he went to the teapot to brew some tea.

"Father, please, I beg you, please reconsider," Thanasi pleaded. If it meant groveling he would do so. He was prepared to die for this man.

The priest sighed and turned to Thanasi. "Don't you know how much I would dearly love to stay? To watch my daughter find happiness, to watch you find peace. Do you think I haven't thought about escaping? Don't make it more difficult for me, Thanasi. Today I know maybe one tenth of what Jesus must have felt like in the Garden of Gethsemane. Don't you know that I would dearly love to hand this bitter cup to someone else?" he said as he turned away from the younger man. He hurriedly brushed away the tears.

Thanasi sat there not knowing what to say to him. He watched as the priest poured him a cup of tea and then sat down. "I'm sorry, Father," Thanasi apologized quietly.

"I know, my son, I know. I want you to promise me something."

"Anything," Thanasi said, and knelt near the priest.

"I want you to promise me you will keep an eye on Zoe and Eva. Watch over them. They are going to need your help. When the war ends, I want you to take them out of the country. I don't want them to be here when the civil war starts. Can you do that for me?" the priest asked as he looked at Thanasi.

"I promise, Father."

"Good boy. Remember what I've taught you, love God and your country," the priest said as Thanasi put his head on the priest's lap and began to cry. He held the young man and patted his head. "Now, now...come on, have courage." He lifted the man's face and brushed away the tears with his hand.

"I love you, Father."

"I love you, too, my boy. Now go and make me proud." he said, and kissed Athanasi on the top of his head. He watched as he put his jacket back on and then his scarf. Thanasi brushed away the tears and went to the door.

"Father, you are my hero," Thanasi said, and walked out the door and down the alleyway.

Father Haralambos watched the door close and smiled. "His hero," the priest repeated, and shook his head. He finished his tea and cleaned the kitchen. He looked at his timepiece again. "Well, it's time I made way to the train station," he said aloud. He stopped in front of the crucifix and crossed himself. "Dear Lord, you know what is to come. Use me as you see fit in the remaining time I have left." He kissed the icon and picked up his suitcase. "I hope Saint Peter doesn't keep me waiting at the Pearly Gate, I hate waiting," he said aloud as he left the house and walked out.

He glanced up at the sky, which was cloud free, and shook his head. He shuffled along and rounded the corner to the church, stopping for a moment to watch the routine activity around him. Dimitri the baker was starting his day; he saw him and bade him a good morning. The priest raised his hand and waved back. He had watched this town's residents grow up and get married, had baptized their young and watched their young repeat the cycle. He wondered if life ever truly stopped. *Probably not,* he thought and started walking again.

"Ah, Father Haralambos. Beautiful day isn't it?" Father Haralambos turned around and saw Captain Reinhardt.

"Good day to you, Captain. Yes, it's a beautiful day," the priest replied and began walking.

"Are you looking forward to your trip?" the captain inquired, easily keeping pace with the older man

"Quite. I hear Thessaloniki is quite cold at the moment. Beautiful city. I'm looking forward to seeing Father Makarios when I get there," the priest said and continued to walk towards the station.

"Can I ask you a question?" Captain Reinhardt asked. He didn't usually request permission to speak to the villagers. He just went ahead and asked them the questions he wanted answered. Somehow this man's occupation and position in the community made him respectful.

The priest stopped and looked up at the golden-haired young man. "Certainly. What would you like to know?" He smiled.

"Would you consider sitting up front with the troops?" the captain asked.

The priest frowned. "Where are the rest of the villagers going to be located?"

"In the boxcars. There isn't much room..."

The priest smiled at him. "I would rather be with them as we make our journey to Thessaloniki. I'm sure we can find something to amuse ourselves," the priest replied as he watched Reinhardt nod.

"I have to go ensure that it leaves on time. You don't need to hurry, Father," he stated as he walked away.

The priest shook his head. He picked up his suitcase and shuffled along. He glanced up at the major's residence and spotted Eva at the window. Beside her was Zoe, who looked like she had slept in her clothes. He shook his head. He smiled up at them and waved. Eva blew him a kiss and mouthed, "I love you."

The priest nodded and walked away. He didn't want to turn back and have another look. He would lose his composure if he did. He finally arrived at the train station where soldiers milled about.

"Halt. This area is restricted," a young German soldier said in broken Greek.

"I am to board the train," the priest informed him, and handed his papers to the soldier.

The soldier looked at the papers. He wondered why he wasn't with the rest of the villagers who had been in the train since the day before. He shrugged. *None of my business,* he thought and waved the priest through.

The priest stood on the platform as the chaos swirled around him. He sniffed the air and grimaced. The smell of decay was all around the train. Before he could discover the source, the door opened on one of the boxcars and a body was thrown out. The soldiers held their noses as their comrades dragged the man from the platform and threw him into the ditch near the tracks, causing the body to roll down the embankment and land with a thud at the bottom.

Father Haralambos bowed his head and said a silent prayer. He looked up and met the eyes of the soldier that had pushed the man into the ditch. "Forgive them, Father," the priest prayed quietly.

"You!" the soldier pointed at him, "There is a space here." He pointed to the boxcar.

The priest picked up his suitcase and walked to the car.

"Maybe you can convert these animals before they meet Jesus," the soldier said and sneered, and his comrades laughed.

"I'm sure Jesus will be most happy to meet them, I'm not so sure what he will say about you," the priest said as he walked into the car leaving the soldier slack jawed.

The stench hit him as he stepped into the crowded car. The priest inhaled sharply. The occupants looked at him wearily and bowed their heads again. Their pain was too overpowering to be worrying why a Greek Orthodox priest was in the car with them. He found a small spot near the rear of the car and put his suitcase down and sat on it. He mentally kicked himself for not bringing food with him.

He bowed his head and prayed. When he looked up, he saw a young child looking at him. The little girl smiled at him. Her big brown eyes were red from crying and tears stained her grubby cheeks; her dark hair was matted and her clothes were dirty. He tried to see if her parents were with her, but no one was paying any attention to the young girl. He smiled at her and waved her over. "What is your name?" he asked gently.

"Rebecca Stavrithis. What's yours?" Rebecca asked, looking at the man with the long white beard and the black robe. His gold crucifix stood starkly against the black of his robe.

"Panayiotis Haralambos. Are you here alone?"

"My daddy was here but they..." the young girl stopped, and starting crying. The priest hugged the young child as he realized that the body of the man that was dragged out was indeed the child's father. He held the child as she sobbed.

"Do you want me to tell you a story?" the priest offered as he wiped away the tears.

Rebecca hiccupped and nodded and rubbed her eyes.

"Okay, do you know the story of the donkey that talked?" the priest asked. Rebecca shook her head, and the priest began his tale as the train started to move.

Chapter 16

"WHAT?" Major Muller lowered the telephone handset and just stared at it, unbelieving. *Propaganda, it had to be. Propaganda made up by the Resistance. Athens couldn't fall that quickly.* While it was true that the majority of the troops had left with the train bound for Thessalonki, the troops that remained were hardened soldiers.

The major moved his attention back to the phone as he raised the handset to his ear. "What about General Kiefer?" he asked, running his other hand through his hair and holding the back of his head. "Are you sure? Yes...yes, fine...I'll see what I can do here." He hung up the phone and fell into his chair, pinching the bridge of his nose between a thumb and forefinger as he loudly blew out a breath.

There was a knock on the door, and after a pause Captain Reinhardt walked in, moving to the front of the major's desk and patiently standing at attention for several moments.

"Athens has fallen," the major stated, not looking up.

Reinhardt's eyes grew as big as saucers and his jaw dropped as the news registered. "What about General Kiefer?" he asked.

"He is being held as a prisoner of war by the Americans."

The phone's shrill tone startled them both. Muller picked it up. "Yes?"

Reinhardt watched his commander's face turn a pasty white as he slumped further into his chair. He was sure that if the major hadn't been sitting, he would have fallen down.

"When?" the major asked as he glanced at Reinhardt. "Yes, General. Heil Hitler." He replaced the phone on the hook. "What else could go wrong today?!"

"What happened, sir?"

"The troop train going to Thessaloniki was bombed an hour ago by the Resistance. The train fell down the gorge."

"Father Haralambos," Reinhardt whispered, feeling a pang of remorse at the thought that the old man had died.

"What?"

"Nothing, sir. What are you going to do?"

"We are pulling out. General Rhimes has ordered us to withdraw to Thessaloniki. Well, we can't catch another train on those tracks. The bridge and line have been totally destroyed. The only way out is by truck. See to it," he said dismissively, and turned to start collecting paperwork.

Captain Reinhardt still remained, a look of total indecision on his face. Muller frowned as he noted Reinhardt hadn't left to start carrying out his orders. "Is there anything else, Captain?"

"Uh..." Reinhardt was of two minds, and wasn't sure how to broach the subject of Eva's latest indiscretion.

Muller looked up sharply at the sound. "Out with it man, I don't have all day!"

"It's about Eva, sir."

"What about Eva? Did she spurn your advances again? Is it so important that you have to tell me now?"

"Yes, sir. We have a problem."

"One of many, Captain," Muller growled, now annoyed with him. "Out with it, man! What problem do you have with Eva?"

Reinhardt swallowed. "Her perversion has come to the surface...again."

Muller's blue eyes turned to ice. Reinhardt was glad he wasn't on the receiving end of Muller's fury. The man's face had turned a bright shade of red as he sat at his desk, his fists balling up in fierce anger. A problem with Eva, especially this problem, was the last thing Muller had wanted to hear in the middle of this crisis. "I thought you told me differently in your last report?" he asked dangerously.

"Yes, sir, but..."

"Captain, you will tell me what you know. I will not play a question and answer game with you!"

"I observed Eva at the train station yesterday, and we accidentally bumped into each other," the captain said quickly as Muller's face reflected his irritation. "We talked, then she told me that she was going back home. She didn't. She went north. So I followed her. She went to Athena's Bluff and she met Fraulein Lambros there, sir."

"Who?"

"Zoe, sir, her maid. They sat for a while and then they kissed. It wasn't...uh..." Reinhard was unsure of how much he should tell Major Muller. His commanding officer already looked ready to have a stroke. "There is no doubt in my mind, sir, that she has corrupted the young woman."

"Mein Gott," Muller whispered, sitting back in his chair. With all that was happening, he wasn't ready to deal with Eva's betrayal again. But he knew he had to deal with it now, decisively and with no remorse.

Major Muller sat back up and trained dangerous eyes on Reinhardt. "How long has this been going on? Under my very nose? In my house?" The Major's voice rose as he thumped his desk. Reinhardt jumped.

"I—I don't believe, it's been..."

"I don't care what you believe!!" Muller screamed. "I gave you an assignment to watch her, and what do you do? You bring that whore into my house!"

"I..."

Muller looked daggers at him. "I have no daughter from this moment on." His calm voice belied his rage. "I will get someone else to start the redeployment. Your assignment now is Eva. Take care of it," Muller said, staring at his second in command. He had warned Eva, had told her in no uncertain terms that if she relapsed, he would kill her. Her betrayal of him now, when he was in such a vulnerable position, was inexcusable, and Reinhardt's ineptitude compounded the problem.

The man still standing at attention in front of his desk was looking nervous and uncomfortable. *As well he should,* Muller thought. His anger flared again and he narrowed his eyes at the captain. "I will deal with you after you have dealt with this problem. Your incompetence astounds me, Reinhardt. Now get out of my sight!"

"How...I mean the problem, how should I handle it, sir?"

Muller cursed. "Do I have to tell you everything? How did you become a captain? Did your father buy you this commission? Eradicate this perversion from my house. Get the hell out of my office and go and deal with it! Now *get out*!!"

****

"Athens is free!" Thanasi declared, and raised his arm in salute at the other grinning Resistance members. They cheered loudly and began to sing "Ymnos eis tin Eleftherian," The Hymn to Freedom. Their voices harmonised even as they laughed. Finally, their dreams of a free Greece were going to be realized and the war would soon end. Thanasi saw Zoe standing out near the edge of the group. He frowned for a moment and left the circle of celebrating men. Walking over to Zoe, he gently took her arm and silently guided her over to one side.

"Zoe...we got word that the line was destroyed about an hour ago."

Zoe lowered her head and Thanasi held her for a few moments. "Did anyone...?" she asked softly against Thanasi's shoulder.

"No. No survivors. The train went down the gorge..."

They stood there, amidst the celebrations, each feeling their own grief at losing a beloved friend.

"Alright, we've been told the Americans are on the move. I'm not sure when they will get here, but I think it's our duty to help our kraut friends out the door." Dimitri, the Thessalian Resistance leader, yelled, trying to be heard above the din of the celebrations.

Dimitri came over to where Thanasi and Zoe were now standing apart. He clasped the older man on the shoulder and grinned. His smile turned to a frown when he saw their faces. "What's the matter?"

"The train was blown," Zoe said quietly.

"Oh." Dimitri looked down and sighed. He had forgotten about the train amidst the good news from Athens. They had lost another 101 people from the village. *We will mourn when the war ends*, he thought to himself. They still needed to focus on killing as many Germans as they could. He turned to Thanasi. "Leftheri has gone to Muller's place. As soon as the bomb is detonated we can begin..."

"What bomb?" Zoe interrupted the man, her eyes wide with alarm.

"The one that will blow Muller straight to hell," Dimitri replied.

"No, wait!" Zoe cried out, "Eva is in the house!"

"So?" Dimitri asked and shrugged.

"But you can't kill her!"

"She's a kraut, Zoe. Or are you going soft on krauts?"

"Shut up, you idiot!" she yelled right in Dimitri's face. "You don't understand, Eva and Father Haralambos were working together!" Grabbing his arm, she pleaded with him, "When was Leftheri going to detonate the bomb?"

Dimitri checked his watch. "In ten minutes...you'd better run. You don't have much time to get her out."

"I have to stop him!" Zoe cried, running out of the house and down the alleyway. Her heart was beating so hard it felt like it would explode from her chest as she ran, her thoughts only on Eva and reaching the house in time. Her attention blinked back just in time to see the slow moving horse and cart ahead of her. It stopped, blocking the exit from the alley. Running up to the cart, she saw that its load had shifted and fallen to one side, the contents of the wheat-filled bags spilling on the ground all around the cart. There wasn't enough space to squeeze around the sides, and the spilled bags blocked the route underneath. She was trapped in this godforsaken alley while precious seconds ticked away against Eva's life. Meanwhile, the old man driving the cart still hadn't moved from his seat. He was sitting halfway turned, forlornly gazing at his spilled cargo.

"Come on!" she yelled at the old man, "Move!"

"What's your hurry, little Zoe? Is the devil after you? You young people have no patience," the old man grumbled, as he slowly climbed down to the cobble-stoned surface, limping around to take hold of the horse's lead and trying to coax it to move.

"Damn it, pappou!" Zoe cursed and scrambled up the piles of wheat, slipping several times before she made it to the cart and climbed over it. Jumping off the seat to the ground, she tripped as she landed awkwardly on her ankle. She got to her feet and began to run, despite the pains shooting up her leg with every step. She had to get to Eva in time, before Leftheri blew up the house.

****

Reinhardt was shaken. He closed the door to Muller's office and stood there for a moment trying to get his control back. The guards looked at him but didn't say a word. They had heard the yelling coming from Muller's office.

He straightened his uniform and checked his gun. With a scowl, he turned and stomped up the timber steps to Eva's office and, without knocking, he threw the door open and walked in.

Eva looked up as she heard the loud footsteps head for her door. Instead of the usual knock, the door flew open and she saw Reinhardt heading straight for her.

"What the hell?" Eva started, rising from her chair as Reinhardt reached her.

"Shut up," Reinhardt commanded and backhanded the woman. Eva fell to the floor, looking up in surprise and shock with a hand to her cheek where she'd been hit.

"Get up! You're going to write a note to your whore. You will tell her you need to meet her at Athena's Bluff, at the cabin." He was yelling the orders at her as he grabbed her arm painfully and yanked her to her feet.

She stood unsteadily, still reeling with confusion and shock, before being jerked toward her desk by the hand still tightly gripping her arm. She was shoved into her chair, and a gun was being waved in her face.

"I said *do it*!" Reinhardt snarled at the woman.

Her hands shaking, she picked up her pen and began to write the note. When she finished, Reinhardt grabbed it and folded it in half, setting it before her again. "Write 'Zoe' on it in big letters!" he demanded and then he set it on the front of her desk, prominently displaying the "ZOE" to get the woman's attention.

"Get up. You give me any trouble now and I swear. I will have that whore of yours begging me to kill her. Now move!" Reinhardt growled, as he took Eva by the arm again and halfway dragged her downstairs. He poked his head in the kitchen to where Despina was cooking.

"Despina! Fraulein Muller and I will be at Athena's Bluff. Make sure Zoe knows where we are, and tell her to meet us there," he instructed her and then left without waiting for a response.

Despina frowned at the now empty doorway. "That man has the manners of a pig," she spat out.

A few minutes later, the kitchen door opened and a curly topped young man entered. "Leftheri, what are you doing here?" the housekeeper asked.

"Kiria Despina, I have to get you out of here!" the young man said and took the older woman by the arm, turning to drag her out of the house. Despina stood her ground, and the young man fell backwards to land with a thump on the kitchen floor.

"What is going on here?" she demanded.

Leftheri sighed and got up from the floor. "Look, the house is going to get bombed! Now please, can we get the hell out of here?"

"Well, why didn't you just say so?" the older woman groused. She took off her apron and followed Leftheri out the door.

The two Greeks walked outside, calmly crossing the street and heading down the sidewalk toward the alleyway. It appeared they were just out for a stroll, the younger man politely assisting the old woman. The guards watched them, and one of them recognised Despina. He shrugged and shifted his attention elsewhere, unconcerned. After a moment longer, the other guard did the same.

Despina and Leftheri had just managed to turn the corner into the alley when the building exploded, sending debris flying everywhere and starting fires. Leftheri peeked around the side of the wall and grinned. "Boom Boom!" he said to himself. They watched, staying hidden in the shadows, as the remaining solders ran to the remains of the building to try and put the fire out and look for survivors. They never got the chance.

As the soldiers reached the front of the burning building and waited for orders, the remaining Resistance fighters began their assault from hidden positions. A gun battle quickly ensued, but the German soldiers were rapidly finding themselves on the losing end, many of them having foolishly left their weapons behind in the panic that ensued immediately following the explosion.

Leftheri, watching the battle, felt his shirt being tugged and Despina urgently calling his name. He looked at her to see her pointing the other direction and crying, "Look! Isn't that Zoe?"

Looking down the street in the direction she was indicating, he saw a figure running awkwardly toward them. After a second, he did recognise the figure as Zoe, a pained and panicked expression on her face.

"Zoe!" he yelled to her, with no effect. Before the stumbling woman reached the alley, Leftheri jumped out in front of her to get her attention. He couldn't let her run right into a raging gun battle. When she still appeared to ignore him and tried to hobble past, he quickly grabbed her around the waist and carried the struggling woman into the alley.

"EVA!" Zoe screamed, having seem the remains of the building, realizing she had been too late to save her lover.

Zoe fought against Leftheri's hold, and he gripped her even tighter, enduring her hits and kicks. As she tried to twist and squirm away, he finally lost his balance, collapsing against the alley wall, still desperately hanging on to the screaming and sobbing Zoe. They slid down into a heap, Leftheri finally able to wrap his legs around hers, and grabbing her wrists to hold her still.

Zoe was reduced to sobbing, the long run and then the struggles to get free having sapped her remaining strength. "Eva...oh, Eva..." She was half sobbing, half wailing the name.

Despina watched as Leftheri finally got the distraught woman under control, and was instantly at Zoe's side, holding her and stroking her hair, trying to help Leftheri calm her feeble hysterics. "Shhhh...there there, little one." She gently tilted Zoe's face, wet with tears, so she could look at her. "You could have gotten hurt if Leftheri hadn't stopped you! Didn't you see the soldiers and hear the guns?" she asked, concerned.

"B—But the building...Eva...oh God...I had to get to her!" Zoe stumbled over the words in between sobs.

"Eva wasn't there, sweet child," Despina said with a soft smile as she started drying Zoe's face with a small kerchief. "She wasn't in the building, Zoe. She left earlier with Captain Reinhardt." She gave Zoe a small kiss on her forehead, seeing the young woman calming at her words.

Leftheri finally released Zoe and helped her to her feet, seeing her favor one leg a bit. He helped brush her off, then brushed off his own clothes as Zoe and Despina hugged each other.

"But," Zoe was saying, "she really wasn't there? You saw her leave?" She saw the older woman nod her head.

"Eva has gone to Athena's Bluff. She and Captain Reinhardt said you were to meet them there."

Zoe looked at the housekeeper and frowned. "Why would Eva go with Reinhardt? Unless..." The blood drained from her face as Zoe realized that

Muller must have found out about her and Eva. "Oh dear God!" She turned to Leftheri and grabbed his arms, "Leftheri, can you run and get Thanasi? Tell him Eva is in danger and Reinhardt has her. We have to save her. Tell him to meet me at Athena's Bluff."

Leftheri looked at her, confused.

Zoe shook him gently, her eyes pleading with him. "Leftheri, please? Please don't let her die! You must find Thanasi, quickly!" She released him when he nodded at her, then started painfully running towards the bluff as Leftheri went to find the Resistance leader.

****

"So, little Eva, we're here. Now, where is your slut?" Reinhardt finally said as he sat across from the bound woman. They had tied her arms and legs to the chair and placed the chair in the center of the room.

"You're a pig, Jurgen," Eva said and her eyes shot daggers at her former friend. She hoped Zoe wouldn't see the note they left on the desk.

"You know, Eva, I did so enjoy watching Greta being pushed onto the train with those Jewish swine. I wish you would have been there to see it," Reinhardt said with a grin. "She didn't look all too healthy to me."

"You bastard," Eva spat out and tugged at her bonds to get free. The chair creaked as she struggled to no avail, the ropes keeping her immobile.

"You know, your father wanted me to kill you. Did you know that? He said that you weren't his daughter anymore," Reinhardt said, wanting the denunciation to hurt the woman.

"Doesn't surprise me," Eva sighed. Her father would have killed her back in Germany if he had thought he could get away with it. But in the Fuhrer's regime, he would have appeared weak and useless if it got out. A man who cannot even control his own daughter wouldn't be worth much to the Fatherland.

Reinhardt laughed. "Ah, yes, I suppose it doesn't surprise you. You know, I would have enjoyed watching the beating you took; it would have made up for all the times you refused my advances. You had the opportunity to become an officer's wife! You could have been somebody. Instead, you are a nobody. Nothing. You're worthless, and so ugly that no man would touch you now." He motioned to one of the guards to keep his gun trained on her as he moved behind her. Roughly pushing her forward, he grabbed the fabric of her shirt and ripped it open to reveal the scars that crossed her back.

"See that, boys? That's what you get when you're a pervert. Very nice work. I should congratulate Major Muller and tell him how much I admire his skill." He laughed as he traced several of the scars across her back. Eva struggled in vain to move away from his touch, and two of the soldiers grabbed her shoulders to keep her still. Reinhardt walked back to sit in front of the woman.

"Do you think your opinion matters to me?" Eva spat at him as he resumed his chair.

Reinhardt shrugged. "I don't care. You're already going to die. But before that happens, you'll see that Greek slut of yours get some action." He chuckled, and the guards joined him. "Was she a virgin when you perverted her, Eva? Maybe little Zoe didn't have a good man around to show her how it's done," he grinned.

Eva was sickened by the thought of what they had in mind for Zoe when she arrived. She prayed for the younger woman to be delayed, or that Despina would have sent her on an errand—just something, anything to keep her from seeing that note on her desk.

"So why don't you just kill me and get it over with?" Eva taunted him. She was certain of her fate, but the thought of her friend and lover being killed sent a stabbing pain through her heart. She knew Zoe would follow her after seeing the note. If she could provoke Reinhardt enough, he might kill her now, the gunshots alerting Zoe or someone else and keeping them away from the door.

Reinhardt smiled coldly. "Not yet, we're still waiting for someone. It would be quite rude to start without the guest of honor. You know, I really liked that kid, smart mouth and all. It's too bad she's been corrupted and I have to kill her." He leaned forward to rest his elbows on his knees. "Tell me Eva, how did you seduce the poor girl? Such a sweet innocent child. Has she seen your ugliness?"

Eva looked away and remained mute.

"You see, it is our duty to root out perversion and destroy it," Reinhardt continued. "And you, you are a freak, a perversion."

"Who will root out your perversion?" Eva snapped at him, unable to control her temper.

The blow came quickly as Reinhardt backhanded her. It threw her head back, splitting her lower lip badly. She looked up at Reinhardt, standing over her, and grimaced. The blood ran down her chin and dripped onto the white shirt she wore.

Reinhart was furious, his face had turned red and the veins in his neck were visible. He backhanded her again with the hand that held his gun, the butt of the pistol striking her in the side of the head, laying the skin open above her eyebrow. The chair fell sideways and she lay on the floor, blood starting to pool beneath her head.

"You dare call me perverted? The Reich is my father and my mother. That is no perversion." He bent down to yell at her as she lay bleeding on the floor. "You were with me in the Hitler Youth, Eva. You were touched by the Fuhrer. He stood right there in front of us and shook our hands. Didn't you feel like you were in the presence of Christ himself?"

"And I didn't wash my hand afterward for a month," Eva retorted weakly, knowing that would infuriate Reinhardt further.

"You filthy whore! How dare you speak of our great leader like that. Oh, now I'm going to take great pleasure in killing you." He kicked her several times in the ribs and then sent a kick to her head. "You bitch." Reinhardt spat out, and prepared to kick her again when his corporal distracted him.

"Sir?" the man timidly said.

"What?"

"Sir, perhaps we should wait for the other girl," the young soldier said.

Reinhardt paused, then nodded. The soldier was right. She was trying to goad him, make him mad enough to kill her. He straightened his jacket, which was splattered with droplets of her blood, and went over to sit back down. "It's not going to work, bitch. You'll still see her die before your eyes."

Eva struggled to breathe. Her world was rapidly spinning out of control, and she was close to blacking out. She was sure he had broken her ribs, and there was a lot of blood running down the side of her face from the laceration above her eye, her torn lip, and another cut on her head from his kick. She lay on the floor trying to get her bearings. Reinhardt signaled to the guards to haul her back up. She stifled a groan as she and the chair were roughly handled and set upright.

"Was that as good for you as it was for me?" Eva hoarsely whispered, though truth be told she could barely focus, let alone breathe.

Reinhardt glared at her. "No, sweet Eva. I've got something much better planned. Something I will enjoy a lot more," Reinhardt said as he controlled his temper.

The door to the cabin opened, and all eyes went to the door. Eva sighed in relief as she saw a soldier walk in. Reinhardt sighed in frustration. That girl was taking too long. He was sure the note would be seen. He even made sure the old housekeeper knew where they were headed, in case Zoe didn't see the note.

The young solder that had just entered saluted his commanding officer. "Sir..."

"What now?" Reinhardt asked, glaring at Eva.

"The Resistance has bombed Major Muller's residence." the solder blurted out looking at the captain and then his fellow solders.

"What?"

"Resistance forces have also attacked the soldiers at the building after the explosion. Also, we got word that the American tanks are hours away from her"

Finally, my own command, thought Reinhardt. *The Americans weren't important.* Major Muller was surely dead and he was in charge. His priorities had shifted. He needed to start thinking of the welfare of his troops. Well, his first order would be to move his forces to Thessaloniki as the major had told him earlier.

"Have the men prepare to move out. Commandeer every available truck. We will fall back to Thessaloniki. Go!" Reinhardt ordered. He watched as the guards that were with him ran out of the cabin. He turned to Eva, his eyes filling with hate.

"I didn't want us to part this quickly, Eva, but I have other pressing matters. May you burn in hell with the rest of the perverted. Oh, and send my regards to Greta." He pointed the pistol at her, "Die, bitch!" and pulled the trigger.

Eva didn't hear the gunfire, her eyes going wide as the bullet hit her in the chest. Her body reacted to the noise, however, causing the chair to fall over backwards. She hit the floor, still tightly bound in the chair, her previously white shirt stained red from her blood. "Oh, Zoe!" she cried out before blackness overtook her.

****

"Where is he?" Zoe muttered as Thanasi knelt beside her. The members of the Resistance cell hid behind the rocks and brushes, watching the cabin. They had been waiting for their scout to come back and report on the number of soldiers inside the cabin

"Patience, Zoe," Thanasi counseled.

"Yeah? Well, I'm telling you, Thanasi, if she dies while I'm being patient..."

"They won't kill her. Not right now," the Resistance leader said as he watched the scout running carefully back, dodging behind cover to hide his movement.

"They have her, and there are six soldiers plus Reinhardt," the scout panted, then looked at Zoe. "She doesn't look good, they've beaten her quite badly. They're not doing anything now, just standing around like they're waiting for something."

"What?" Thanasi asked.

Zoe looked back at the cabin, her anger coming to the surface. "Not what. Who. He's waiting for me," she said as she looked at the Resistance leader, making a decision. "They want me? Well, why don't we give them what they want?"

"No way am I going to let you go in there! I promised Father Haralambos!" Thanasi said, shaking his head.

Zoe glared at him. "I don't give a pig's arse what you promised. Eva is in there! I'm not going to stand out here arguing with you and let that woman die. Got me?" Zoe seethed, trying to keep her volume down. "Thanasi, if she dies, I'll die. Then we can both tell Father Haralambos how we stuffed it up. I'm going in there and if you want, you..." Zoe stopped talking as the cabin door opened and the six soldiers ran out, heading for the vehicles parked along the road, not too far from their positions.

Zoe looked out at the cabin once again and then towards the men. She'd had enough of talking. "Alright, can you stop this chin wagging and let's get moving." She was interrupted by a single gunshot from the cabin, and was out of the bushes and heading for it before Thanasi could grab hold of her.

The entire Resistance cell started running behind Zoe. Thanasi shook his head and followed. They started firing at the soldiers, who were too startled to put up much of a fight.

Zoe picked up a dead soldier's gun and rushed through the door of the cabin. She stood at the threshold, stunned. Reinhardt was standing over the prone body of her lover, who was still tied to the chair. Blood covered Eva and had pooled around her body. He was just standing there, laughing.

"Get away from her!" Zoe yelled.

Reinhardt turned and grinned, raising his pistol in Zoe's direction. "Well. You took your time coming here. I had wanted..." Reinhardt didn't finish his sentence as Zoe raised her gun and fired. Reinhardt looked down at his chest in surprise and then crumpled to the floor. Zoe approached him, still firing at his body, emptying the clip.

"Go to hell you bastard!" she screamed, and spat on him. Dropping the gun, she fell to her knees, untying Eva's arms and legs from the chair. She gathered the woman into her arms, ignoring all the blood. "Don't you die on me!" Zoe yelled at the unconscious woman.

Chapter ·17

The rain had started to fall again. Zoe looked out of the window and shook her head. All around her were American medical personnel treating soldiers and civilians. The large tent was filled with bodies. She couldn't understand a word they were saying, but she was happy to see them.

It was a moment in her life she would remember forever. Reinhardt standing over Eva's body made her furious. She shot the captain so many times she didn't think anyone would recognise the kraut if they tried. Now she knew what it meant to kill and even though it made her ill at the thought, she knew she had done it to save Eva's life. Thanasi had come into the cabin and taken over.

He had organised everything, and for that she would love the man for an eternity. He had come through for them when she thought everything was lost. Seeing Eve on the floor in a pool of blood broke her heart. She wasn't even aware of how long she sat there while Thanasi tried to stop the bleeding. It was all a blur for Zoe.

The good news had been that the bullet entered her shoulder, broke her collarbone, and exited out the back. This, added to her other injuries, was going to keep Eva out of action for some time.

She looked down at the woman on the cot and smiled. She brushed away the dark bangs. Blue eyes opened, and Eva turned her head and gave a weak smile to the disheveled chestnut colour-haired woman. "Water?" Eva requested hoarsely.

Zoe went and poured some water in a cup and gently put the cup to Eva's lips, helping her to drink. She laid the woman back, fussing over her. "What happened?"

"The force of nature that is Zoe happened," Athanasios Klaras said as he dropped down on his haunches and greeted Eva.

"Morning, Thanasi," Zoe greeted the Resistance leader and glanced at the young American by his side. His orange hair stuck up at awkward angles and a smattering of freckles on his face made Zoe grin. "Funny. Now you're a comedian."

"I try, little one, I try," Thanasi retorted and grinned. He turned to Eva. "Well, what happened...While Reinhardt was taking you for his date in the cabin, the Resistance blew up some buildings, we made a lot of noise and the Americans came."

"I missed out on all the fun," Eva complained and grimaced with the effort.

"Oh yeah. So when Hurricane Zoe found out that Reinhardt had taken you, she called in the cavalry. We went on a search and destroy mission, and here we are. Anyway this is Captain Anthony Jenkins. He is a medic. He looks like he is only 14, but he isn't. They breed them to look young." He turned to the young man and repeated what he had said in English.

Anthony laughed and went to Eva's side. "*Thelo na se...*" Anthony said and frowned. He turned to Thanasi. "What's the Greek word for examine?" Thanasi told him and he turned back to Eva. "*Thelo na se eksetaso.*" He grinned when he realized his patient understood that he wanted to examine her and see how she was. He completed his examination and pulled the blanket back up around Eva, then quietly gave some instructions to Thanasi before getting up to attend to his other patients.

"*Kalimera kiria Zoe, eise... askemi*" Anthony said as he stood looking down at Zoe. He was rather taken with the young woman.

Zoe's grin turned to a frown. She wasn't a married woman and he had just called her ugly. Thanasi laughed at his new friend's use of the language. He explained to the young man what he had said, and his face turned the brightest shade of red that Zoe had ever seen.

"Oh no! Tell her I think she's beautiful." the American stammered.

"Come on, let's get you away before you get Hurricane Zoe on to you," Thanasi replied, as he steered the man way from the two women.

Zoe took Eva's hand and smiled. "We're moving. Thanasi is going to America and he said we can come, too."

"Why?"

"He promised Father Haralambos that he would take us out of Greece."

"But you have your family and friends here."

"Eva, you are my family and my friend. I don't want to stay here anymore. I don't have anyone but you. So that means I go where you go. You don't want to stay in Greece, do you?"

"No," Eva admitted quietly.

"Germany is in ruins, we can't go there. That orange-haired kid said we can leave when you are able to travel."

"Zoe, what happened to Reinhardt?"

"I killed him. He was taking something that didn't belong to him. You belong to me. I'm not sorry I did it, Eva. He hurt you," Zoe said as she saw glistening tears in Eva's eyes. "Don't cry." She brushed away the tear that had fallen. "I would do it again if I had to. I love you, Eva." She bent down and gently kissed Eva, oblivious to the people around them.

"I love you, too," Eva replied

They sat looking at each other, Zoe fussing over the injured woman. She straightened the blankets around Eva and tried to make her comfortable.

"What happened to Major Muller?" Eva asked. She didn't want to acknowledge any relationship to that beast that she grew up with as her father. Father Haralambos was more a father to her in the short time she had spent with him.

"Leftheri bombed the house..."

"What about Despina?" Eva asked in alarm. She loved the old woman.

"Don't worry, Despina was taken out of the house before that. We found out that Athens had fallen and then all hell broke loose. Even little Andreas, he climbed the flagpole and tore down the swastika and put the blue and white up. I didn't see it, but Dimitri told me it brought tears to his eyes. Then the Americans rumbled into town and here we are. Now, I think we've talked too much. Just shut up and rest," Zoe ordered with a grin.

It hurt half her face to smile, but Eva gave a lopsided grin at Zoe's command. She closed her eyes and Zoe sat there watching the older woman sleep until her stomach grumbled, then she got up and stretched. She left the tent and walked outside.

They had managed to live through the war. She never thought this day would come. She would go to church later and thank God for helping her through. She never thought she would go back to church, but Eva had helped her see that God was not to blame for the death and the misery. She would thank God for helping Eva. If only Father Haralambos was here to share in her joy. "I hope you're behaving yourself, Father H," she muttered and looked to the heavens.

She looked over at the flagpoles and saw the blue and white cross of Greece and the American flag. Her new country. She wondered how it was going to be, what new customs, and the language. No matter. They would manage. They had survived the war; they would survive America.

Now, to find someone who could teach me some English before we got there. She spied Captain Jenkins and Thanasi at the mess tent, and she walked purposefully over to them.

Land of Milk and Honey

Chapter 1

The sun was setting behind Sydney Harbour Bridge, casting its golden glow over the turquoise sea. It rode the waves up to the large grey bridge where the sailboats bobbed in the quiet calm. Another day set over the Emerald City.

Zoe Lambros was sprawled on the grass on a hill-top overlooking the harbour. She was thinking how much she liked this new land, and of the events that had led she and her lover here instead of to America as they had originally planned. She remembered how Thanasi had gotten them out of Greece to Egypt and the Australian soldiers she met there who told her of the land of milk and honey—Australia. Her musings were interrupted by yet another fly buzzing around her head. She swatted it away and sighed. Flies. She hated flies, and she discovered Australia had lots of them, especially in summer. The flies didn't bother her companion, Eva Muller, who sat in her chair—face to the sun—with her eyes closed. Her long legs were spread out in front of her, and she had her head tilted back to catch the final rays of the setting sun. Zoe grinned as she noticed Eva's skin had acquired a bronzed appearance. Zoe had more difficulty in getting a tan, her fair complexion resulted in the lobster look, a look she didn't particularly like. Zoe sighed and looked up at the sky as the clouds drifted lazily by.

She loved this vantage point—it gave them an unrestricted view of the beautiful harbour. They had found the site when they were strolling one day and promptly fell in love with the spot. Zoe considered it their place; although Eva did point out the council signs all over the place, it didn't stop Zoe from claiming it. They regularly had picnics at the lookout as they were doing now. The long summer days gave them time to wander down to the spot and relax.

Zoe went back to the letter on the grass. Eva, her dark hair neatly combed back, got out of her chair and sat cross-legged beside Zoe on the cool grass.

"Did you read this?" Zoe asked as she turned her head to see Eva.

"No, not yet," Eva replied. "I was waiting for you to come back so we could read it together."

"Oh that's sweet. No wonder I love you," Zoe replied and scrambled up to kiss the older woman before returning to her place on the grass.

"I knew there had to be a reason," Eva said and grinned. "Are you going to read it or stare at it?"

"Okay, hang on." Zoe opened the letter, laid it flat on the grass in front of her and began to read it aloud.

"My dear sisters," Zoe read, "I hope this letter finds you well and happy. I want to thank you for the food package you sent over to me. Some of it was quite tasty. I do have a

question about one thing you sent. This jar of Vegemite—am I supposed to eat it, or use it to grease my truck? I tried it, but I think you left out the instructions to use it on my truck. I did and the truck goes really well now! Ha ha ha."

Both Eva and Zoe burst out laughing. They could just imagine the look on their friend's face when he tried the Vegemite. Zoe had learned to love the yeast extract while in Egypt with the Australians, but Eva couldn't stomach the taste, and was horrified every time Zoe spread the black substance on her toast. When they both had stopped chuckling over Thanasi's new found truck grease, Zoe went back to the letter.

"Despina sends her love and tells me to let you know she misses both of you and wishes you all the happiness in the world. Dimitri wanted to know if you ride kangaroos. Well, do you? Everyone wishes you the best in the land of milk and honey. The news from here is not that good. Greece has descended into anarchy. We've had the Turks, the Italians and the krauts, and now we are our own worst enemy. Brother is fighting brother. My dear sisters, I don't know what this country will become, but at the moment Greek blood is being spilt by our own brothers. I am so glad I listened to Father Haralambos and got you out of here. I'm quite sure Zoe would have found even more trouble to get into, Eva. I am well. I was wounded in the leg the other day but I'm still going strong although hobbling a bit. Little Andreas was killed in the fighting. He was a very brave boy. I still remember

Dimitri telling me how he bravely climbed the flagpole and ripped the swastika from it. The monarchists killed the little man. When is this madness going to end? Petracles was captured but we got him back, a little worse than when we lost him but he is a strong boy and he will come through. I will leave you now, and again I want to thank you for the parcel, but please, next time no more Vegemite. If I have trouble with the truck, I may use it again. May God bless you, my sisters, and know I am thinking of you every day. One day I will emigrate to the land of milk and honey and be with you, but my place for now is here—fighting for my homeland. Love, Thanasi."

They sat in silence, their thoughts and prayers going out to the man they considered a brother. Athanasios Klaras had been the Resistance leader of the communist cell. His friendship with them was born from their mutual love for the village priest, Father Haralambos. The cleric's death bound them together and allowed their friendship to grow.

"We'll go to church tomorrow and light a candle for Andreas," Eva said quietly as she held Zoe's hand. "Oh, I almost forgot. The letter from the Immigration Department came today." She held out another letter.

Eva had decided to change her surname from Muller to Haralambos. She had been using Haralambos ever since Egypt, but she wanted to make it official. She smiled at the thought that Father Panayiotis Haralambos, her father, would be very proud. She despised her previous surname of Muller and everything it stood for. Her supervisor at her work in the biscuit factory had started calling her Harry because he couldn't pronounce Haralambos without making it sound like he was strangling a cat. She didn't mind, as long as she wasn't called a wog. That particular insult had grated on her, her hackles going up automatically whenever she heard the word. She found that most new arrivals to this land were called wogs. She could never figure out what that word meant, but it was definitely intended as an insult since it was hurled at them whenever they found it difficult to communicate. The Australians had no patience with people from non-English speaking countries, especially Italians and Greeks. It was far better than "Nazi" or "kraut," that some other German immigrants were subjected to.

"What did they say?" Zoe interrupted Eva's musing, turning to her lover.

"They didn't see it as a problem," Eva replied, grinning.

Zoe flashed a wide smile as she got up from her place on the grass and tackled the older woman to the ground. She rolled onto her side and held Eva as they laughed together at the good news.

"Father H would have loved that," Zoe said and proceeded to tickle the older woman. Eva squealed and fought with Zoe's hands as she also tried to tickle Zoe back at the same time.

"Excuse me," a young man cleared his throat. He had watched the two women playing.

They paused in their tickle fight at the sound of the intruding voice, both still breathing hard, and turned with red faces to see a man standing near the bushes that blocked the road from the outlook. Eva disentangled herself from Zoe and stood up, her six-foot frame easily towering over the man. "Yes?"

He was a short man wearing a cheap grey suit that was slightly rumpled from sleeping in his car. His brown eyes were behind round spectacles, and his black hair was combed back. Friedrich Jacobs stood there for a moment trying to decide which woman to talk to. He had been told to contact them and had followed them for a few days. The tall one intimidated him and he looked at the other woman who had a matching scowl on her face. He took out a handkerchief and dabbed it on his sweaty face. He wasn't used to the summer heat and the woolen suit wasn't making life any easier.

"My name is Friedrich Jacobs," he said and stuck out his hand. Realizing he was speaking in Greek, Eva examined him a moment longer before she took his hand and shook it.

"Don't tell you're a salesman." Zoe said from where she still sat cross-legged on the grass.

"No, I'm not. Can we go somewhere private to talk?"

"Who's going to hear you where we are now? The birds?" Zoe challenged.

"Zoe!" Eva turned to her love and wagged a finger at her, but had a twinkle in her eye. She turned back to the man in the frumpy grey suit. "What is it that you want, Mr. Jacobs?"

"Well it's a bit difficult to talk out here."

"We know you can do it, it's not that hard," Zoe muttered. Eva glared at her while trying not to grin.

The man didn't appear to notice. "As I said, my name is Friedrich Jacobs. I work for a group of investigators."

"You're a spy?" Zoe interrupted him again.

Friedrich laughed. He couldn't imagine himself as a spy. He would make a very bad spy, and would surely be dead before nightfall if he were. "No, Miss Lambros..."

"How do you know her name?" Eva asked him. She was understandably suspicious, having been raised surrounded by Nazi paranoia.

"I know a lot about you."

"Oh, you do? Are we going to play question and answer games now?" Zoe retorted, as she got up from her spot and began to collect the picnic basket. "Come on, Eva. I don't want to listen to this man any longer."

"No, please wait! There is a good reason why I'm here."

Eva stopped Zoe and held her arm as she was reaching for their blanket. "Let's at least hear what he has to say, Zoe. Okay?" Zoe paused, then nodded and straightened up.

"Look, why don't I come by your flat later and we can talk?" Friedrich asked, looking at the two women.

"That would be suitable. You can come at 7:00 p.m. tonight after we've had our dinner. I assume you already know where we live?" Eva saw the man nod in confirmation.

"Very well, I'll see you tonight at seven." Friedrich smiled at them and tipped his hat before he turned and left.

"I wonder what he wants?" Zoe asked, watching the man walk away.

"I don't know, but I'm sure we'll find out tonight," Eva replied pragmatically.

Chapter 2

Eva stood on the tiny balcony of their flat, holding a cold glass of lemonade in her hand and watching the heavy rain clouds gather. The lightning flashed across the skyline of the city. It was so typical of summer in Sydney, where the heat of the day was cooled by a southerly change. It made life bearable when the heat inside the biscuit factory where she worked topped the 100-degree mark, and all Eva could do was wish for relief. She hated the job, but she needed it. They needed it. She was determined to give Zoe the chances she didn't have back in Greece. Here she could study and learn and try to make the dream a reality.

"Hey you, what are you thinking?" Zoe asked as she walked out with a bowl of cut watermelon.

"If I tell you, will you kiss me?" Eva bargained and winked.

Zoe grinned. "Decisions, decisions. Maybe." Zoe looked up at the ceiling as if weighing her options. "Okay." She reached up and pulled down the tall woman and kissed her. "Okay, now what were you thinking?"

"How much I love you," Eva grinned.

"So a stormy night makes you think of how much you love me? That's deep, Evy."

They both laughed as they settled on the wicker chairs. Raindrops fell just in front of them, and Zoe stuck her legs out catching the cool droplets.

"So what are we going to do about that little man?" Zoe asked as she handed Eva a bowl.

"I don't know. Let's hear what he has to say."

"I don't like him," Zoe commented, munching on the watermelon. She spit the seed out and watched it fall down from the balcony.

"I sure hope Mr. Jenkins wasn't down there," Eva said as she looked down, relieved not to find their cranky landlord. "He is a strange man."

"Well I don't like him, either. He is a racist pig. Did you hear what he called Elena yesterday?" Zoe queried, as she took another stab at the watermelon slice. Elena Manheim was their neighbour and a dear friend. She wasn't much older than Zoe, and she was just as outgoing. She was the only one in her family to survive the concentration camps, and though she didn't like to talk about the horrifying experience, one could still see the fear in her eyes. They had become fast friends with the young girl as they traveled here on the same refugee ship. Elena and their landlord, a cantankerous old man, were always at loggerheads about some issue.

"No, what did he do now?" Eva asked.

"He called her a Jew," Zoe replied.

"Honey, she is a Jew. That isn't racist."

"I know that. It's what he said after that made me angry. He told her that Hitler had the right idea. That little *boofhead,*" Zoe said and spat another seed over the rail of the balcony.

Eva scowled. Their landlord needed to be taught how to be a human being with common courtesy. She had discussed it with Mrs. Jenkins who said her husband was scarred by the war and what the Japanese had done to him. "Everyone was scarred," she told the older woman, but she had let the matter drop. "We can't do anything, Zoe. He is like that."

"He's still a boofhead," Zoe replied, interspersing the Australian slang she had picked up with her Greek.

Eva grinned at how easily their conversations were now being peppered with slang words from their adopted country. Boofhead was the new word Zoe liked to use to describe the various people she thought of as idiotic. It was colourful.

"Mrs. Jenkins asked me whether you wanted to go out with her nephew, Danny."

"How many nephews does this woman have? What did you say?" Eva asked. The landlord's wife was always trying to get the two of them to go out with any number of her nephews. She liked the old woman, but she was running out of excuses for declining the landlady's attempts at matchmaking.

"I said Danny's not your type," Zoe replied in between munching on watermelon. "He isn't Greek," she added with a smirk.

Eva laughed and shook her head. When they rented the flat they told Mr. Jenkins they were sisters. He mumbled something about them not looking the same, but his wife interrupted and said that her sister didn't look anything like her either, which settled the matter. Her thoughts were interrupted as a knock on the door was heard, and she went in to answer it.

She opened the door and found Friedrich Jacobs standing outside. His grey suit was wet and his hair was plastered to his face.

"Mr. Jacobs, please come in," Eva said and opened the door wider. "Zoe, Mr. Jacobs is here."

"Oh goody," Zoe muttered and walked into the flat holding the bowls. She deposited them on the kitchen counter and wiped her hands on a kitchen towel.

"Be nice," Eva whispered as they both sat down opposite Friedrich. "So Mr. Jacobs, what is it you wish to discuss with us?"

Friedrich coughed. "Please call me Friedrich."

"Okay, Friedrich. It's been a long day, so can you just tell us what's so important?" Zoe asked and looked at the bespectacled figure.

"You're not one to beat around the bush, huh?" Friedrich observed, and chuckled. "I work for a group of investigators and I'm here to ask for your help."

Zoe and Eva looked at the man, both wearing matching frowns. "I'm sorry, Friedrich, but I think you lost me. How can we help you?" Eva asked.

Friedrich fidgeted. He had rehearsed what he was going to say all the way to the block of flats. "I'm not sure if you are aware that the Allies are going to be holding a war crimes trial at Nuremberg next year." It was a statement, but the tone was inquiring.

Eva nodded. She had heard about the war crimes trial. It was ironic that it would be held in the very place that Hitler had held huge rallies, the place she first met the evil, charismatic leader. "I'm aware of it. What does that have to do with us?"

"Part of my job is to find Nazi war criminals..."

"Are you accusing Eva of being a war criminal?" Zoe exclaimed, gritting her teeth. "You have no idea what this woman went through. How dare you come into our home..."

Eva's eyes filled with pride for the fireball sitting beside her. She loved the protective side of Zoe and truth be told, was excited by her fighting spirit. "Zoe, love, come on, calm down. Let's hear what Friedrich has to say," Eva whispered to the angry woman.

"I'm going to toss him off the balcony if he accuses you of being a war criminal," Zoe whispered back.

"Look, Miss Lambros," Friedrich looked between the two women and opened his briefcase. He looked inside and produced a folder. "I'm not accusing Miss Mu..."

He didn't see how quickly Zoe left Eva's side and stuck a finger in his chest. "She is not Muller, you got me, little man? Her father was Panayiotis Haralambos, a Greek. Eva is as Greek as I am. Now take your bag and get the hell out of our home. Muller sent his dogs to kill her. Do you understand? The only thing that saved her was me and the Resistance; we got there in time." Zoe shuddered at the image of the bound and defenseless woman in the cabin.

Eva slowly got up and held Zoe away from Friedrich. "Zoe, calm down, love." She tried to soothe the angry young woman.

Zoe looked up at Eva. "I'm not going to let them hurt you again, Evy. I'm not. These bastards will never go away, but I'm not a little Greek girl in Larissa anymore. I was helpless then..."

"You're not helpless now, love." Eva said kissing Zoe on the cheek. "Let's hear the rest of what Friedrich has to say. It's okay."

Friedrich watched the two women in silence. "I'm sorry I used your former family name. I know you changed it and why you changed it."

"It's alright, Mr. Jacobs," Eva said "Go on."

"I'm not accusing you of being a war criminal. We are well aware of what Miss Haralambos has done and was doing for the Resistance. Our job is to track down and bring to justice escaped war criminals. We believe that quite a few Nazis have fled to America, South America, England and Australia. The war crimes trials at Nuremberg are important to us."

"Who is we?" Eva asked.

"The Allies. We need to convict these people..."

"They aren't *people*, Mr. Jacobs. They are animals. Were you in Europe when the Nazis rampaged through?" Zoe asked.

"No, I wasn't, but I lost my family in Germany. They were Jews; I'm a Jew. I realise both of you lived through the horror," Friedrich said. He was angry with himself. He knew the wounds were still raw, and he was told to be mindful of that, but he hadn't been prepared to be verbally assaulted by the younger woman. If anything, he was expecting Eva to be the one to lead the angry barrage against him.

They sat there trying to calm down from the verbal exchange. Friedrich knew if he was going to get their assistance he would need to have a clear head. "Miss Harala..."

"Call me Eva," Eva said. She felt sorry for the man.

"Eva, our work is very important. We need to bring these people to justice, to answer for their crimes against humanity. We've tracked two former Nazis here to Sydney. There are many more, but these two are extra special cases."

"How does this involve us?" Zoe asked.

"Do you recognise this man?" he asked Eva as he passed her several photographs.

Eva curiously took the photos from Friedrich and looked closely at them. Instantly her face paled and her throat dried as she recognised her stepfather, Hans Muller. His face was scarred and his posture sagged, but it was him. She let out a gasp and dropped the pictures. "I...I thought he was dead," she muttered. Zoe looked worriedly at Eva and then picked up the photos. She too recognised the monster and her heart instantly went out to her lover. Holding a shaking Eva, she asked, "What do you want, Mr. Jacobs?"

Friedrich sat there trying to come up with an answer. He wasn't expecting that kind of reaction from the older woman who was now shaking. He was told that her stepfather ordered her death, but he wasn't privy to the details. He wondered which of the two was the stronger one, but he realised both were strong or they wouldn't have survived the horrors of the war. Zoe was trying to calm Eva with soothing words, whispering to her. She turned to look at Friedrich, and he was sure he would be dead if those daggers she was shooting at him were real.

"Mr. Jacobs, I don't know what your game is, and frankly I don't care. That animal is dead," Zoe spat out

"He didn't die, Miss Lambros. When the building was bombed, everyone assumed he was dead. We were told that he was severely hurt and he somehow managed to escape. Everyone's focus was on the fighting and no one paid any attention. He got away."

"Again, what does that have to do with us?" Zoe questioned, and frowned.

"We believe that if he knew you were here, it would flush him out of hiding and..." Before he could finish, Zoe had bolted from her companion's side and pushed him to the floor.

"Get the hell out of our home!" she yelled. "You are not going to use Eva as bait. Hasn't she suffered enough?"

"Zo, please, it's all right." Eva reached her lover before she lost all control. Rubbing Zoe's arm in an attempt to calm her, she pulled her away from the shocked man on the floor. Friedrich got up tentatively and resumed his seat, watching as the two women whispered to each other.

"Look, Mr. Jacobs, I think we need to talk about this. Maybe you can come back tomorrow and we can discuss it further," Eva said, holding back the angry woman in her arms.

Friedrich looked at both women and nodded. It was getting heated. "Same time tomorrow?" he asked, and Eva nodded. Eva walked him to the door and then went back to the living room.

"I'm not going to let them hurt you, Evy. I'm not going to let that bastard have another go," Zoe said and wrapped herself protectively around the taller woman.

"He can't hurt me now, love. I was just shocked to see his face again. It's all right."

A knock was heard and Eva went to the door and opened it. Their friend Elena was standing there with a mop. Eva smiled.

"I've come to help...where's the fire?" Elena asked, grinning.

Elena stood in the doorway wearing her ratty old housecoat with her dark hair pulled back in a bun. She would have been almost comical standing there with a mop in her hands, if not for the concern she had for her two friends. She had rushed over when she heard the yelling, knowing that the two of them didn't fight and that all the shouting in Greek was quite unusual. When she saw the little man scurrying down the corridor, she knew she had to go and see if everything was all right.

"Come in, Elena."

Elena walked in, put the mop down near the door, and went into the living room. Zoe was on the couch sulking.

"What's up, little matey?" Elena asked, mimicking a well-known comedian that all three friends loved to listen to on the wireless.

"Did you see that guy leave?" Zoe asked her friend.

"The one that looked like he was scared witless?" Elena replied and grinned.

"That's the one," Eva said, sitting beside Zoe. "He met Cyclone Zoe and you should have seen him run!" Eva ruffled Zoe's hair as she got up to go back into the kitchen.

"So everything is okay?"

"Yeah, just fine, Elena, nothing to worry about," Zoe replied. She didn't want to involve the young woman in their troubles; she had enough nightmares to deal with. "Why are you looking so frumpy?"

All three friends laughed as Eva went back into the kitchen. She could hear the two women discuss Elena's run in with their landlord. Eva put the pot of water on for tea and stared outside into the darkness. Her stepfather was here. She wondered if she would ever have peace from that man. If it wasn't for Zoe, she doubted she would be alive. The teakettle began to whistle, which brought her out of her reverie. She looked over her shoulder and watched as Zoe came over; she smiled at her lover. Zoe reached over, took the kettle from Eva, and then gently kissed her. She winked and walked into the living room. Eva shook her head and followed her back into the living room.

Chapter 3

The strains of a piano concerto greeted the man as he entered the small flat. The curtains were drawn, and the air in the dark room was thick with the smell of cheap whiskey. He sighed as he put down the bags of groceries he had in his arms and walked over to the bedroom door. Standing at the doorway, he watched his long time friend guzzle yet another bottle in several swallows. The man was sitting on his bed, surrounded by other empty whiskey bottles. The music complemented the melancholy feel to the place.

"Hans, you can't sit here all day," Erik Rhimes said as he walked into the bedroom. "Drinking is bad for you. You know what the doctor said."

Hans Muller was once a tall, handsome man in his late fifties. His wife had died several years before, and though he did love her in his own way, he had pretty much gotten over her death. A major in the German army during the war, he had everything he wanted—a good command, prestige, and power. The war was the best thing that could have happened to him. He had the respect he always craved. He was somebody. He had the world at his feet until that September morning when his world suddenly collapsed around him. Earlier that same morning he had received the news from his second in command that his daughter had reverted to her deviancy. Then, the Resistance bombed his command center. After the explosion, he couldn't remember how he escaped. All he could remember was his friend Erik hovering above him yelling orders.

Hans sighed as the last of the music faded and turned to Erik, who was standing there watching him holding the empty bottle. "What else is there to do, my friend?" he retorted with a drunken slur. "I can't go out...There is a reason I can't go out, isn't there?" He was so drunk he was forgetting what he was talking about.

"Hans, the doctor told you not to drink. It won't help." Erik tried to get the bottle that was still in the man's hand.

"I drink to forget," Muller muttered.

"It's not over, my friend," Erik tried reasoning with him. "There is a doctor in Argentina..."

"Why do we have to leave again?" Muller asked, trying to take another mouthful from the bottle of whisky, forgetting it was empty.

"Hans, we need to leave Sydney."

"Why would I want to do that? Wait... didn't I just ask that question?"

"I was told by our friends that we are going to be arrested!"

"Arrested for doing our jobs? That's a joke, Erik."

"They write the rules, my friend." Rhimes sat down next to Muller, and finally pried the empty whiskey bottle out of his hand. "I heard that they will be setting up court at Nuremburg."

"Bastards."

"Ja, well they are bastards, we are bastards and the Jews thrive," Rhimes replied. He looked at the bottle in his hand and threw it out the open door. It hit the couch and bounced off. Erik Rhimes had commanded the Northern Greece German forces. He was proud of it. He did his job and followed orders; then the war turned against them. Athens fell, Larissa fell, and then Thessaloniki. He was lucky to still be alive. They had barely managed to escape, and it was a cat and mouse game to try and outrun the Americans.

"Hans, I haven't asked you this before, but what happened to Eva?"

"Eva?"

"Your daughter, Hans."

"She was killed by Reinhardt. What happened to Reinhardt?" Muller slurred and then frowned. He had forgotten about his second in command. Reinhardt was an inept fool.

"What? Why?"

"Why what?"

"Why did Reinhardt kill Eva?"

"Oh. She wasn't my daughter, you know." Hans turned to his shocked friend. "Ja, that's true. Daphne...oh, my Daphne...well Daphne...you remember my wife?"

"Yes, I remember Daphne," Rhimes replied. The young, dark-haired woman captured his heart when they first met, but his friend married her first. He mentally shrugged.

"Well, Daphne was a bad girl. She went off with some Greek peasant that her father didn't like, and he shipped her off to Austria. She had the baby...Eva...and I married her."

"Why?"

"Why did I marry her? Ah, my friend, that is a very good question...a very good question," Muller replied. He tried to smile, but with half his face scarred, he could only manage a deformed grimace. "I needed a wife. A good German officer needed a wife...with a baby. A family, every good German officer needs a family..." he trailed off and then turned to his friend. "I can't have children, Erik."

Rhimes sat there in shock. This was the first time his friend had opened up to him like this. He had known Hans Muller for fifteen years and now realised he really didn't know him at all.

"Ja, so here is this Greek peasant, with a daughter, and here I am, I need a wife and a child... Too bad she wasn't a boy. Ah...yes, then it would have been perfect. Well, she sure got it on like a boy!" Muller chuckled at his own crude joke. "She was strange, that one..."

"She was a beautiful young woman, Hans."

"Ja, I suppose... but she was a lesbian, Erik."

Rhimes looked at his friend in stunned silence. The man was drunk. Surely he wasn't aware of what he was saying. His son, Heinrich even went out with the young woman.

"You don't believe me, huh?"

"It's not that I don't believe you, my friend, it's just that..."

"That's why Reinhardt killed her...why she had to die. Do you remember Franz's daughter, Greta?"

"Ja, but what..."

"Greta and Eva were lovers...Ja! Can you believe that?"

"Greta? A lesbian?"

"Ja, she was. A big, honking les...lesbian." Muller threw another bottle out of the room and it also crashed next to the couch.

"What happened to Greta?"

Muller shrugged. "I don't know, Franz never told me. What ever happened to Franz?"

"He died at the Russian Front," Rhimes replied.

"Ah ja, that's where I would have ended up. The Russian Front...Reinhardt killed her, you know."

"Why? Because she was a lesbian?"

"Of course. That fool Reinhardt brought the whore to her, and they had sex in my house. My house, Erik! Can you believe it?" Muller opened another bottle and took several long drinks. "My house," he muttered. "Did you see Reinhardt?"

"I don't know. We were slightly in a hurry to get out of Thessaloniki."

"Thessaloniki. They had nice ouzo. Wish I had some..."

"Come on, my friend, I think you need to sleep this off."

"My face hurts, Erik," Muller moaned as he sank back on the bed and promptly fell asleep.

Rhimes watched him sleep and shook his head. He needed to get them out of Sydney, and quickly, or else they would be arrested.

****

Friedrich Jacobs was tired. He sat at his desk in clothes that still hadn't finished drying, and yawned. His wet jacket hung near the heater. Zoe Lambros had made an impression on him, and he was surprised he didn't have a bruise on his chest from where she had prodded and pushed him. He shook his head. He'd handled the whole thing the wrong way, and he had underestimated the younger woman. He wouldn't make the same mistake the next time. He yawned again. He had been working long hours, and he really needed to get a decent night's sleep. He removed the photos of Hans Muller and Erik Rhimes from his briefcase and looked at them again for a moment before placing them on his desk.

He looked up when the door opened to see his colleague, David, walk through.

"Hey, Freddy. You slacker. Where were you this afternoon? I thought you had gone home for a change. You do remember where your house is, don't you?" David kidded as he placed more files on Friedrich's desk.

"Ha ha, funny. I know where I live. Sort of," Friedrich quipped back, ignoring the shortening of his name, which he really detested. "I was out working."

"Did you go to Muller's flat?"

"Haralambos," Friedrich replied. David looked at him quizzically. "She goes by the name of Haralambos now."

"Why?"

"Muller was only her stepfather. Panayiotis Haralambos is the natural father," Friedrich replied and yawned again.

"So where's the father?"

"Dead. He was killed in a train crash, from what I could find out. The Resistance blew up the train he was on."

"Did he know she was his daughter?" David asked, taking the seat opposite Friedrich's desk.

Friedrich shrugged. "I don't know."

"So did you tell them?" David persisted as he picked up the photo of Muller from Friedrich's desk. "He is an ugly bastard, huh?"

"I told them...and nearly got shoved back into last week," Friedrich replied.

"What? Did Miss H hit you?"

"No, her flatmate did." Friedrich grinned sheepishly as David laughed.

"So that woman that she lives with, is that her sister?"

"Do they look like sisters?" Friedrich questioned with a mischievous look.

"Hardly! Eva looks like a Greek goddess. The other one is cute, but I think she'd tear out my eyes if she didn't like me. I wonder if Eva would go out with me if I asked."

"Not your type," Friedrich shot back.

"I can try, Friedrich my boy, I can try."

"You can try till you're old and grey, but she still won't go out with you."

"Why? I'm good looking!" David boasted, preening a little bit. David considered himself a good-looking bloke with his blond hair and green eyes. He had what women considered to be the good ol' bronzed Aussie look.

Friedrich rolled his eyes. "Maybe. You're just not the right gender."

"Huh?"

Friedrich sighed. "She's a lesbian." David was surprised and Friedrich had to laugh at the look on his face. "She and Zoe are partners."

David whistled. "Huh. I had no clue. Oh well," he shrugged.

"Any news from Daniel?" Friedrich shifted the conversation back to work.

"Daniel came back an hour ago. He's tracked Rhimes to this address." David handed a piece of paper to his friend.

Friedrich read the paper in his hand. "Do they both live here?"

"Don't know. It might be where one of them lives. He didn't see Muller, only Rhimes entering with some groceries. So, will Miss H help us?"

"I don't know. I'm going back there tomorrow." Friedrich placed the paper on top of the photos and leaned back in his chair.

"Why?"

"I showed her the photo, and she was shocked to realise the bastard is still alive. Then Miss Lambros got rather upset with me, and we ended up not getting much accomplished. Miss Haralambos said they needed to talk about it and asked me to come back tomorrow evening."

"Do you want a bodyguard tomorrow?" David joked.

Friedrich gave him a dirty look. "I think I can handle myself."

"Oh yeah, like you did tonight." David was laughing as he picked up his coat and went to the door. "Well I have a hot date tonight, Freddy, so I'm going off to meet and greet this young woman. Go home and get some rest," David told him as he left the office.

"David, you heathen." Friedrich muttered as he went back to studying the pictures.

Chapter 4

"ARGH!" Zoe screamed in frustration that verged on panic. "Damn it to hell!" She had to find that ring. She just couldn't lose it.

"What's the matter, you silly goat?" Elena asked as she walked in through the open door of Zoe's flat. Her brown eyes widened when she saw the state of the lounge room. It looked like a cyclone had hit it. Cushions and papers were all over the floor.

"I lost it!" Zoe yelled from behind the sofa.

"Old news, Zoe. You lost it a long time ago."

"Oh, you *are* a funny woman."

"I think so," Elena replied, and watched as Zoe searched the sofa trying to find whatever she had lost. "What are you looking for?"

"My ring." Zoe stood and scowled at Elena. "Are you going to stand there and yap, or help me?"

"You are such a grouch." Elena grinned and walked over to the window to start looking for the tin plated ring. "Have you looked here yet?"

Zoe looked up from checking underneath the sofa. "Over there? No, not yet." She checked one more spot near the wall and got to her feet. "I'm going in the bedroom to look. You remember what it looks like, right?" she asked over her shoulder as she exited the lounge.

"How many rings do you lose around here?" Elena joked. "Is this the ring Eva gave you?"

A muffled agreement followed by a cry of anguish came from the bedroom.

"I'll take that as a yes." Elena chuckled, and continued her search.

"EUREKA!"

The triumphant cry came from the bedroom, causing Elena to burst out laughing. She walked over to the bedroom door and leaned against the doorframe, looking in at Zoe. The young dark-haired woman was sitting on the bed beaming and holding up the cheap tin-plated ring Eva had given her on the Patris. Her disheveled dark locks were falling over her eyes as she gave the ring a quick polish on her shorts and slid it back onto her finger.

Still standing at the doorway, Elena remembered the night she first met Zoe, and then Eva. She was feeling so alone, with no friends or family. She thanked God every day for that meeting.

****

The smell of the sea greeted Elena Mannheim as she walked out to the deck of the big refugee liner named Patris. She breathed in the sea air and exhaled loudly, so glad to be out of that cabin. Needing to share it with three other people, it didn't take long to discover that snoring by threes quickly became unbearable. It wasn't as if she wasn't used to sleeping in an overcrowded, dormitory-type environment. Having been forced to spend two years in Ber-

gen-Belsen concentration camp, she was pretty well cured of the need for quiet to fall asleep. There were exceptions, however. The fact that Mrs. Elimbos was snoring loudly enough to disturb the dead buried at sea was the reason she was out on the deck tonight.

"One more month," Elena chanted as she sat on a foldaway chair on the deck. She sighed. It was a chilly night, and she pulled the thin blanket she'd brought around her to protect against the wind.

"Excuse me, miss, but won't your parents be worried about you, out here alone at this hour?"

Elena turned to find a steward standing next to her and grinned. "I can't sleep, and I don't have any parents. I'm alone. Besides, I can take care of myself."

"Oh, I see. I'm sorry...um...take care you don't...uh...fall overboard," the steward said, then turned and walked off.

Elena raised her eyebrows to her hairline at the strange warning. She shook her head slightly and pulled the blanket the rest of the way up to her neck, then leaned back in the chair to gaze at the stars. She was indeed alone. Her mother had died in her arms back in Bergen-Belsen. Too weak and frail to fight off the infection that ravaged her body, she quietly slipped away one night. She had truly been alone after that, even though the barracks was filled to the rafters with women. She celebrated her fifteenth birthday alone, cleaning out the latrines. But, in the end, she didn't know how or why, she had survived.

Sensing something, she was startled to find that someone was standing just a few feet from her. "Hello," Elena tentatively said, hoping she was going to be able to speak to someone tonight and maybe have some company.

A dark-haired woman turned and grinned. "Hi."

"Have a seat. We seem to have the whole deck to ourselves tonight," Elena said as she motioned the young woman to the chair beside her.

"Thanks," the young woman said. "I'm Zoe." She stuck out her hand.

Elena smiled and shook the young woman's hand and watched as she sat in the next chair.

"It's kind of cool out here, want to share my blanket?"

Zoe grinned, scooting her chair right next to Elena's, and pulled some of the blanket over her legs. "Can't sleep?"

"Can sleep, Mrs. Elimbos won't let me," Elena corrected.

"How come?"

"Her snoring would wake even the dead that have been buried at sea," Elena said with a grin. "You have a snoring partner too?"

Zoe laughed. "Actually, I think I'm the one who snores. No, she's asleep. She was sick for most of the day with that flu bug, and she finally nodded off."

Elena liked the young woman; she had such an open and honest face. "I'm Elena. Where you from, Zoe?"

"Larissa, Greece, for most of my life, and more recently from Egypt," Zoe replied. "Have you got anyone in Australia?"

"No, I don't have any family. Just me, myself and I," Elena joked. "How about you?"

"My family was killed during the war."

"Kindred spirits, huh?" Elena whispered. "So you're by yourself then, as well?"

"No, not any more. I'm with my w...uh...friend." Zoe caught herself. She had spent all her time in Egypt not caring what people thought about her relationship with Eva; they hadn't covered it up. Eva had

warned her that on the ship, however, most people would be against their relationship, so they had to conceal it. That really annoyed Zoe, as she couldn't be herself around her lover.

"Your friend?"

"Yeah, Eva Haralambos. You may have seen her around: very tall, short dark hair, blue eyes. Can't miss her—she's like a lighthouse," Zoe joked.

Eva was taller than the majority of the passengers, which amused Zoe. Many of the young men tried to escort Eva to the dances they held every Friday night.

Elena nodded her head. She had seen the woman Zoe was describing. The tall woman always seemed rather aloof and cold to her. "Mmm, yes, I've seen her, but I thought she was a part of the ship's crew."

"What made you think that?" Zoe asked.

"She's not very friendly." Elena regretted the words as soon as she uttered them. "Look I'm sorry..."

"It's alright. You don't know her. She's quiet around people she doesn't know, and I'm sure that it looks like she's not friendly. But she is really the most loving and giving person I know."

"Look, Zoe, I didn't mean...well, it's...she's so quiet, and I don't think I've said two words to her. I've seen her around and I did hear her speak German once. Is she German?"

Zoe was quite surprised. Eva never spoke German if she could avoid it, and stuck with Greek or the English she and Zoe both studied hard to learn in Egypt. "She was born in Austria, but her parents were Greek," Zoe said quietly.

"Oh, she speaks quite fluent German. I heard her speak to a German couple when they were having some problems with their steward. That's why I

thought she was part of the crew." They sat in silence for a few moments. "Look, I'm sorry again for upsetting you."

Zoe was about to respond when she heard someone else come on deck, then frowned when she looked over and realised that it was Eva. "Hey you! Why are you out of bed and out here in the cold air?"

"I was wondering where you were," Eva said with a cough.

"You shouldn't be up here, love. It's too cold in this wind." Zoe lightly scolded the tall woman, frowning at her.

"It's too hot in the cabin, Zoe. I'll just stay out here for a few minutes," Eva insisted.

"Well, at least rug up." Zoe got out of her chair and fussed around the older woman, pulling the blanket that Eva brought with her up and around her head. "This is Elena." She motioned to the young woman still seated. "Elena, this is Eva Haralambos, my friend and the sick little puppy."

Elena laughed. She was enjoying her night even though she had put her foot in her mouth about Zoe's friend. She watched as the two spoke briefly to each other, then Zoe sat back down again.

"Thanks, mum," Eva said and gave Zoe a wink. "Hi Elena, I see you met my mother here."

"I have, yes. Are you from Larissa as well?"

"Not exactly. I met Zoe in Larissa," Eva replied quietly, sitting down in a chair next to Zoe.

"I was just saying to Zoe that I overheard you speak German, and I was wondering if you were German?" Elena never believed in beating around the bush and almost always spoke her mind, though it had gotten her into trouble more than once.

"She didn't take your head off, did she?" Eva asked as she looked at the love of her life, knowing

that Zoe was feeling edgy. "I speak German, Italian, Greek and English. I grew up in Germany."

"Oh," Elena replied.

"Come on, love, let's get you inside before you get worse," Zoe said, and pulled the older woman to her feet. "Elena, if you would like to join us, I know I would enjoy talking to you some more."

Elena looked at the two women. She liked them even though she had gotten off on the wrong foot with them. "Okay, are you sure you don't want to go back to sleep?" she asked Eva.

"Oh no, that's fine. Come on then."

She followed them back to the cabin as they walked in front of her. Zoe was still fussing over the older woman. Elena smiled when she saw Eva kiss Zoe on the cheek and slap her on the behind. They invited Elena into their cabin, which was quite small, and Elena tried to figure out how the tall woman coped in such a cramped room.

"Welcome to our broom closet," Zoe joked as she got Eva back in bed. She looked down at her wife in mock exasperation. "Can you please stay here?"

"You're not just friends, are you?" Elena asked, already knowing the answer. She had seen a few women who found love with other women in the concentration camp. It was forbidden, but that still didn't stop them. She asked her mother about it, and her mother said that love was love no matter who gave it. She thought it was unusual.

Zoe looked at Eva and shrugged, as if to say, "why not." "No. Zoe is my wife," Eva replied giving Zoe a lopsided grin. "I've wanted to say that all day."

"We just got married," Zoe said and grinned back.

"I know what you must be thinking," Eva said as

she looked at Elena.

"How do you know?" Elena asked

"Because if I were in your shoes, I would ask the same questions, and wonder why a German who wasn't a Jew is on a refugee ship," Eva said, then looked at Zoe and gave her a smile.

"That's true. I was thinking that. You're not a Jew, are you?" Elena replied.

"No. I'm a Greek that grew up in Germany. I'm not sure if that makes me a German. Not all Germans were Nazis."

"Most Germans were. My family fled Germany after Kristallnacht. You know what that is, don't you?"

"Yes," Eva replied quietly.

"Well, after they burnt down our shop, Mama and Papa decided that it was too dangerous and we fled. We went to Thessaloniki. Papa had a cousin there so we stayed with them. When Greece was invaded, we were trapped there."

"What happened?" Zoe asked as she poured Elena a cup of lemonade.

"Hitler's final solution. He was going to find and kill all the Jews. We were treated worse than animals. I remember the commandant of the camp had this cat...it went all over the place. It was treated much better than we were. I was at Bergen-Belsen camp until the last few months of the war, and then we were all going to be shipped to Auschwitz."

"I've heard stories about Auschwitz. Mrs. Hoffman, the lady I was translating for, was in that camp," Eva said.

"Well, they are all true. All the horror stories are true," Elena stated quietly. She didn't want to think about the camps because, if she did, she would lose any control she had over those memories.

"I'm sorry, Elena," Eva whispered.

"You know, Eva, I think those poor souls that died are the lucky ones; the survivors are the ones that have to live with the nightmares." Elena stopped. She didn't want to let those memories take over.

"How did you survive?" Zoe asked.

"I don't know. Fate, God, luck...I don't know. Everyone was being shipped off to Auschwitz. In the boxcar I was in, well, some of the men managed to get some of the rotten timbers pulled out and they jumped. I don't think the guards were aware of it. I remember seeing a patch of blue sky and thinking it might be the last thing I'd ever see. I just closed my eyes and jumped. I woke up a few days later. You know what I saw? This ugly shade of green of a tent. That's the first thing I saw. I've never been so happy to see that particular shade of green in all my life," Elena said and sipped her drink. "How did you two meet?"

"My stepfather was a German officer. I went with him to Larissa. Zoe wanted to kill me at first."

Elena looked at Eva and then at Zoe, who was giving the older woman a chagrined look. "She obviously didn't succeed," Elena said, lightening the mood slightly.

"No, it turned out that Eva was as much a prisoner as I was," Zoe replied. "I found out she was working with the Resistance."

"Doing what?"

"Forging identity papers through the local church," Zoe said proudly. "Very good ones too."

Eva had closed her eyes and sleep claimed her as Zoe and Elena talked into the night. Elena found her easy to talk to. They shared their dreams and their hopes. Zoe told her about Eva and their time together in Egypt, up to their finally boarding the Patris, bound for Australia.

****

"You're a goof, Zoe," Elena said as her friend looked up. Zoe had tears running down her face. "Hey, what's the matter?" She went to Zoe's side. "You found the ring. Why are you crying?"

"I thought I had lost it."

"It's only a cheap ring, Zoe."

Zoe brushed away the tears. "No, it's not. It's a part of Eva," she said quietly.

Elena smiled. For all the brashness and smart mouthed bravado that Zoe displayed, she had a sweet naiveté to her that endeared her to Elena.

"You are a part of Eva. Now stop being a goof, and let's clean up this place, or your Eva is going to have a major fit when she sees all this mess."

****

Eva was tired. It was hot, and the bus was crammed with people who wished they were elsewhere, just as she did. Eva stood and tried to hang on as the bus took a turn. Friedrich Jacobs would be coming over to their flat tonight. Her mind went over the previous night's events and she mentally shook her head. Her stepfather was alive. She didn't want to believe it, but she couldn't deny it when she saw the photographs. The burned and disfigured man was definitely her stepfather.

The bus stopped and Eva got off and exhaled. The weather was stifling hot, and she was sure that Zoe would be either in the bathtub or outside trying to cool off. It was exactly where she wanted to be.

She rounded the corner to her street and stopped. Zoe was indeed outside. She was barefoot and wearing the briefest little shorts and a T-shirt. Eva started toward the flats and saw that Zoe had a hose in hand watering the flowers, although she looked like she had watered herself more than the flowerbed. Her hair was soaked, and her lightly tanned and wet skin glistened in the sun. The drenched T-shirt clung to her petite frame, and a darker colored bra was visible underneath. The mere sight of her lover always managed to energise Eva, and she smiled at the smaller woman as she turned off the sidewalk and started up the front walk to the block of flats. It was good to be home.

Zoe turned and saw her wife, looking tired and hot, standing there with a grin. Zoe grinned back and turned the hose on her, making her squeal.

"Oh I needed that, thanks, love," Eva said as she tackled the young woman to the grass. Both women were now thoroughly wet as they fought over control of the water hose. They were interrupted by a throat being cleared—loudly.

"Miss Harlimbos!"

"Haralambos. God, will she ever get that right?" Zoe muttered as they both paused and faced a portly woman in her mid 60's. Mrs. Jenkins was standing there watching the two very wet, young women play with a scowl on her face. She shook her head.

"Mrs. Jenkins, how are you?" Eva asked as she got up and pulled Zoe with her.

"It's hot," Mrs. Jenkins said, stating the obvious.

Eva had just spent eight hours on a hot factory floor; of course she knew it was hot, but she bit back a retort. "Indeed," she said and gave the old woman a smile.

"Eva, can I call you Eva?"

Eva nodded her head. She was just too tired to start anything with this woman today.

"Eva, there is a dance coming up next week and my poor Harry...you remember I told you about Harry? Or did I tell Mrs. Deakin about Harry?"

Eva noticed the mischievous look in Zoe's eyes, the hose in her hand, and stopped her before she drenched the old woman. Suppressing a chuckle, Eva said, "Of course I remember Harry."

Zoe rolled her eyes at yet another attempt by Mrs. Jenkins to get Eva to go out on a date with a Jenkins nephew.

"Well, Harry will be in town. He's just back from the war and everything. A hero, you know. He fought in Greece, did you know that?"

"No, I didn't," Eva replied

"Yes, the poor dear got captured by the Germans, although he did say that a nice Greek family sheltered him for a few months before he got captured. You Greeks are so hospitable. Anyway, he's back and, well, the dance is next week, and he has no one to go with. Your sister told me last week that you only like Greek boys, so I was wondering...I know Harry isn't Greek, but he does speak Greek, and every time I hear him he sounds to me like he could even pass as a Greek."

Eva gave the old woman a half-hearted smile.

"I know you're tired, working in that factory all day. Have a think about it and let me know, all right? Harry will be ever so eager to meet you. I've told him all about you. Now, can you tell me who this belongs to?" Mrs. Jenkins handed an envelope to Eva, who took it and smiled.

"That's for us." She showed the letter to Zoe.

"It's foreign! Why don't they send mail in English so at least we know where it goes?" Mrs. Jenkins muttered. "You know, I should ask my Harry to teach me some Greek!" she laughed. "Now, think about what I said and let me know soon."

She turned to Zoe. "I'm sorry, Zoe, I don't think Harry will come with a friend, but I'm sure we'll find a nice young boy to go out with you to the dance." She gave Zoe a hopeful little smile, then waved at them and waddled off.

"That fat..." Zoe was stopped by Eva putting her hand over her mouth.

"Be nice, Zoe. Come on let's get inside."

Zoe put down the hose and shut the water off and followed Eva back into their flat. When she closed the door, she turned and hugged the older woman. "You smell like chocolate chip cookies! Well, like wet chocolate chip cookies." Zoe giggled and kissed her. "Mmm, you even taste like chocolate chip cookies!"

"Ah, thanks, I think," Eva replied. "I was in the cookie section today. Must have been over 120 degrees in there."

"I'll run a nice cold bath for you," Zoe offered as she headed for the bathroom to begin to fill the tub. Eva watched her walk off—the tiny shorts she was wearing were still damp, and clinging to every curve of Zoe's hips and rear. She stood there a moment, enjoying the sight, then followed Zoe to the bathroom.

Eva stood at the bathroom door watching her wife, and smiled. It was good to be home after the day she had, and to be greeted by the most important person in her life.

"So Harry is coming next week. Do you think I should wear the red dress, or the blue?" Eva teased, and Zoe stopped what she was doing for a moment.

"So you're going to dump me for the first pseudo-Greek you meet?" Zoe asked as she poured some perfume into the bath.

"Oh, absolutely!" Eva replied, grinning at Zoe.

Zoe closed the distance between them, looking up at the Eva's grinning face, and slid her hand under Eva's blouse. "Well, he can't have you," she stated, running her hand up Eva's back. "You're mine."

Eva shivered with delight as Zoe stood on tiptoe to meet her inviting lips. Passionately, she explored every inch of Eva's sweet mouth and when her teasing tongue met Eva's, both their bodies shuddered with electricity. Embraced in the euphoria of the kiss, Eva was oblivious to Zoe's wandering hand unlatching her bra, or of it falling to the floor. Not until Zoe pulled away did Eva become aware of the ache in her breasts or the tingling feeling running all over her body. Panting from excitement, she looked down at her bra and grinned at Zoe. "How did you do that?" she giggled.

"Practice," Zoe mumbled. She slowly unbuttoned each button until Eva's blouse joined her bra on the floor. Eva returned the favour and reached up under Zoe's T-shirt and unhooked her bra, then pulled her shirt and bra off with one motion. They continued helping each other quickly undress, until their beautiful naked bodies pressed together in an explosion of feeling.

"I love you, Zoe," Eva exclaimed with a passionate slur.

"Evy, you talk too much," Zoe said and took her lover's hand and led her out of the bathroom and toward their bed.

****

The grandfather clocked chimed six times as Eva came out of the bathroom with a towel around her body and another wrapped around her head. She entered the bedroom to find Zoe stretched out on the bed and smiling up at her. "I could get used to the smell of cookies," she said as she waggled her eyebrows.

Eva grinned and removed her towel to stand there naked, which got a whistle from her wife. "You like the view?"

"Oh yeah, very nice."

"You have way too much energy, young lady," Eva replied, putting on a light yellow shirt and beginning to button it. She was stopped by Zoe.

"Let me," Zoe whispered and slowly began to button the shirt. She stopped at the button below the collar and pulled it back slightly to reveal a small scar. "Does that still hurt?" she asked as she traced the scar left by the bullet that nearly killed her. She softly kissed it.

"Sometimes, when the weather changes," Eva replied, holding the smaller woman. They looked into each other's eyes, both of them all too aware of how close they had come to losing each other. Eva leaned down and kissed Zoe, putting all her love into the kiss.

The knock on the door interrupted any other romantic thoughts, and Zoe let out a frustrated groan, reluctantly letting go of Eva and flopping herself down on the bed. Eva grinned at her as she finished dressing, then walked out of the bedroom to get the door.

She opened the door to Elena, who was standing there with a large bowl in her hand. "Your timing is really lousy," Eva said and motioned for her friend to enter.

"Yeah, yeah. You should thank me. Zoe will wear you out before your time," Elena quipped as Eva closed the door.

"Did I hear my name?" Zoe asked as she closed the bedroom door.

"She said you'll wear me out before my time," Eva whispered to Zoe and stole a quick kiss.

"Have you been listening through the wall again?" Zoe wagged her finger at Elena.

"Didn't have to, I saw you two outside earlier, wrestling with the hose. I think Mrs. Jenkins is blind." Elena put the bowl down. "I bring gifts!" She uncovered the bowl of coconut balls.

"Beware Greeks bearing Gifts," Zoe mumbled as she ate a couple of the small balls.

"Yeah, but I'm not Greek, Zoe," Elena replied.

"Honorary Greek," Eva said as she picked up the letter that Mrs. Jenkins had given her. "Zo, who do we know in America?"

"That nice spunky doctor who saved your life," Zoe said and winked. "I forget his name."

"You saved my life, love, he just patched me up," Eva replied as she opened the letter. Before Eva could start reading, there was another knock on the door. Eva put down the letter and crossed to open it.

Standing at the door was a man with a cane in his hand. His hair was white, with a smattering of black. His clear blue eyes sparkled with a hint of mischief. He was clean shaven and wore a smart suit. Eva didn't recognise him and figured him for just another salesman. "Zoe, for you." She let the younger woman handle the salesmen, knowing they'd never return once Zoe finished with them. She turned to go back to her letter reading.

"Aren't you going to invite your father into your home?"

Eva turned around quickly at the voice. She knew that voice. Zoe quickly came from the living room followed by Elena.

"F...Father H?" Zoe was the first to speak as her wife was rooted to the spot, unable to move.

The man smiled broadly and winked. "What does a man have to do to get a kiss from his daughters?"

Zoe was the first to jump into Father Haralambos' arms, nearly bowling him over. Eva hung back, not fully believing that the man standing in front of her was indeed her father. A father she thought she had lost. Zoe was all over the big man, hugging and kissing him on the cheek.

"Zoe, you're going to kill me with kindness!" Panayiotis said and laughed as he was led, almost dragged, through the doorway and into the living room.

Eva watched her younger partner's exuberance. Zoe looked back at Eva and grinned, then caught Elena's attention. "Okay, Elena my dear, I think this is the perfect moment to go into the kitchen with me and tell me how you did those coconut thingies." She took Elena by the arm and steered her into the kitchen, closing the door and allowing Eva some privacy with her father.

Father and daughter stood for a moment, looking at each other. Tears ran down Eva's face as she closed the space between them and jumped into her father's embrace.

Panayiotis Haralambos was now content. He held his only daughter in his arms, and he knew if he died that moment, his life would be complete. "I love you, my child," Panayiotis said as he held the sobbing woman in his arms. His own tears tracked down his face. "Here, let me look at you." He held Eva at arms' length. "You're a bit skinny, is Zoe wearing you out or something?"

Eva laughed through her tears and brushed some of them away. "I missed you so much." She could still barely speak.

"Can we sit down?" he asked, as he gingerly made his way to the couch. He stretched out his bad leg, which was the lasting reminder of the train crash. Eva knelt beside him on the couch, still not believing her eyes. Her father was sitting in her lounge room. Alive.

"You don't believe it, eh?" he said, his eyes sparkling with happiness.

"D..Does Thanasi know? He didn't say anything about it in his last letter! You went back to Greece? How did you escape? Were you on the train when it blew?"

"Whoa, one question at a time!" He put up his hands in surrender at the volley of questions directed at him. "Before I answer those questions, tell me about yourself." He took Eva's still trembling hands into his, feeling her fingers wrap around his, and let her place them on her leg. "Are you happy, my child?"

She looked down at her hands entwined with her father's. "Well, I don't like the heat, and the language was hard to learn..." She looked back up into her father's eyes, and a broad smile lit up her face. "But, yes, Father, I'm very happy!" She lifted her arms to encircle his neck and placed a kiss on his cheek, then rested her head on his shoulder with a sigh. "Having you here makes me even happier."

"That's all that matters. I like your short hair, it suits you." Her former long hair was cut into a bob, and it framed her beautiful face. Father Haralambos lifted a hand to run his fingers through it. "Your mother had her hair like that." Panayiotis smiled. Eva looked so much like her mother he would have sworn that it was Daphne who had opened the door. "Now, do you think you can call Zoe back in from the kitchen so I can greet my other daughter again?"

Eva wiped away the remaining tears, then cupped her father's cheek and gave him a loving look. "Zoe, get out here!" she called. Zoe and Elena came out of the kitchen with a plate of cheese, olives and biscuits.

Father Haralambos roared with laughter at the sight. Zoe's sense of humour had survived he thought to himself. He remembered some years ago that he mentioned he hated the sight of feta cheese and olives. He hadn't thought Zoe would remember.

Elena looked at the three and wondered what was so funny about feta cheese and olives. She put the tray down on the table in front of the older man. "Hi, since these two are quite rude, I'll introduce myself. My name is Elena Mannheim," Elena said and extended her hand with a grin.

Father Haralambos chuckled. He liked the young woman. "Pleased to meet you, Elena. You may have guessed that I'm Eva's father."

"Wouldn't have guessed," Elena quipped back.

Elena sat down and watched as her two friends were all over him. She had never seen Eva smile like that before. It reached her eyes and made her look years younger. Zoe was her usual boisterous self, but Elena could tell that she also dearly loved the man sitting between them. She smiled at the two women as they caught up with the large, older man who called both of them his daughters.

Chapter 5

The corridor light bulb flickered on and off as Elena and Zoe closed the door, leaving Panayiotis and Eva in the living room. "Thanks for the coconut thingiess, El," Zoe said.

"Are we still going out tomorrow?" Elena asked, referring to their usual weekly excursion to Farmer's department store in the city. They had both discovered they loved to shop and had spent many hours window shopping. It had brought them closer together, in a strange kind of way. They also discovered that Eva passionately hated shopping, which amused them a great deal.

"Oh absolutely! I want to buy that blue shirt for Evy; it matches her eyes," Zoe said excitedly. Zoe had found the shirt after countless hours searching for a special gift for her partner. Her birthday was coming soon and since she didn't have money to give her a gift the previous year, she was going to make up for it.

"Okay, great. By the way, I love Eva's father."

"Oh yeah, I love him dearly. We have a lot to catch up on. I'll give you all the juicy bits tomorrow. Thanks for coming over," Zoe said as she watched Elena open her own door and disappear inside with a wave.

Zoe went back into her apartment where she found Eva nestled in Father Haralambos' embrace. She smiled. Eva had her eyes closed and a look of pure contentment on her face. "So, Father H, what happened with the train?" Zoe asked.

"Ah the train. Well, we left the station and I'm not sure how long we traveled for, and then I heard an explosion and that was it. I don't remember much of it. I woke up in a tent with people speaking bad Greek," Panayiotis laughed. "Very bad Greek. It wasn't until a few days later that I realised it was the Americans. I asked them to forward a note to you."

"We didn't get a note," Eva replied.

"Oh. You thought I was dead," Panayiotis said sadly. He had tried to send the note with a young medic who assured him he would pass it on. "I guess they had more pressing matters than playing postman."

"Eva was hurt too," Zoe said and took her partner's hand. "Muller tried to kill her."

Panayiotis was shocked. "What happened?"

"Reinhardt found out about us and Muller ordered my death. He would have succeeded if Zoe hadn't brought half the Resistance with her," Eva said and smiled at the young woman. "Reinhardt shot me."

"Oh my dear child! Are you okay now?"

"I am now. When the weather changes my shoulder aches, but I'm okay. I've got Zoe, and now I have you," Eva replied and hugged her father.

Zoe asked the obvious question. "So what happened after you woke up? Why didn't you come and find us?"

"I got moved to a hospital ship. I didn't know about it until I woke up again. That's when I met my angel."

"You died?" Eva asked.

Panayiotis laughed. "No, I met Alberta. She was my nurse—Alberta Fisherman." He looked at the expectant faces of his two daughters and grinned. "My wife."

Eva and Zoe looked at each other and then back at their father. "Your wife?" Zoe asked, as Eva was unable to even form a coherent thought at that point. "You left the priesthood?"

"Yes, I fell in love with her. She is my angel."

"Where is she?" Eva exclaimed as she found her voice. She was happy that her father had found happiness. She was just shocked, as she didn't think he would ever leave the priesthood. "Is she Greek?"

"No. She's an American, but she speaks fluent Greek, German, and Spanish. She's at the hostel. She wanted me to come alone tonight and break it to you gently," Panayiotis replied. He had been quite nervous about coming over.

****

He was nervous to the point that his tie was becoming one huge knot. "Pany, stop being such a scaredy cat, this is your daughter." Alberta scolded as she adjusted his tie. "She's going to fall over when she sees you."

"Come with me, angel," Panayiotis asked. He wasn't sure why he was so nervous. He loved Eva with all his heart and it was her face he imagined as

the train was leaving Larissa.

His wife had looked at him with a twinkle in her eye. "You need this reunion your daughter. I will meet her tomorrow."

"Alberta Haralambos, you're not making my life any easier."

"I love you, Pany, but you are such a chicken," Alberta laughed.

****

"Why didn't you come back?" Eva asked.

"The war in Greece was heating up and the Americans wanted the hospital ship out of harm's way, so we sailed away. I thought you would have gotten my note."

"The letter," Eva whispered and picked up the letter they received from Mrs. Jenkins.

"I mailed that when we left home. I married Alberta when we arrived in America, and we made our home there. I didn't know you were still alive. When you didn't reply to my letter, I thought you had gone back to Germany or..."

"I had died," Eva whispered.

"Yes," Panayiotis said. He remembered the pain in his heart when he realised that he wasn't going to get an answer to his letter. He cried that night; Alberta held him for what seemed like hours. "I lost hope that you were still alive."

"Oh, Father," Eva said and kissed her father. "I'm so sorry. I was in an American hospital unit in Larissa, and then we went to Egypt because you told Thanasi to take us away. We spent a year in Egypt and then we sailed for Australia."

"How did you know we were here?" Zoe asked.

Panayiotis grinned. "Thanasi told me."

"You saw Thanasi? When? He didn't say anything in his last letter," Zoe said excitedly.

"I asked him not to. Alberta and I ran into a friend of his. You remember Dimitri? Well I spotted him in town." Panayiotis stopped and took a sip of his tea. That had been a red letter day, as Alberta called them.

****

Panayiotis was limping towards the bakery to get his wife those little cakes she loved so much, when he turned the corner and froze in his tracks. Just a few feet away was a young man he knew instantly. "Dimitri?"

The man turned and asked, "Do I know you?"

Panayiotis mentally chastised himself. Of course he couldn't recognise him, for he had shaved off his long beard and wasn't wearing his black robes. "You are from Larissa in Greece?"

"Yes."

"My name is Panayiotis Haralambos..."

The boy's face lit up when he realised he was talking to the man that saved him from being a street urchin. "Father? Is that you? Mary, mother of God!" He picked Panayiotis up in a bear hug and began laughing. The people around grinned at his happy dance with the older man gripped in a tight embrace. "Father, I thought you were dead!"

"No, I'm alive. How are you my son?"

"Oh, I'm great! Wait until I tell Thanasi you're alive. He is going to flip."

"Is Thanasi well?"

"A little banged up, but that's war for you. Eva is going to want to swim here when she hears this news."

"Eva is alive?" he marveled. He had lost hope of

hearing from her, fearing she was dead. "And Zoe?"

"Oh, very much alive. They are in Australia, the land of milk and honey, or so I'm told. You know they have kangaroos that hop down the street there." The young man laughed. He couldn't believe his mentor was alive.

"In Australia?" Panayiotis said as an idea came to him.

****

"As you know, the civil war is still going on, but we managed to get Thanasi a message. He wrote back and he gave me your address."

"That little sneak." Zoe vowed to give him a piece of her mind in her next letter.

"So is my stepmother at the hostel now?" Eva asked. She liked the sound of that word. She wanted to meet the woman that had claimed her father's love. She must be pretty special to get him.

"Yes, and she isn't expecting me back tonight, so I'm all yours. Now, where can I rest my weary bones?"

"You can sleep in Zoe's room, and tomorrow I'll speak to Mrs. Jenkins, she's our landlady, about getting the spare flat, if you want."

"Hmm...living near you? That's perfect." her father exclaimed, causing both women to smile happily. He couldn't wait to tell Alberta about this. This was the Eva he knew and loved. But then he belatedly realised there were two bedrooms in the flat, and he frowned. "You have your own room?" he asked Zoe.

Zoe grinned. "Oh yeah."

Panayiotis looked between the two women. Eva had a serious expression on her face. "You're not together?"

"She's married, Father," Eva said and suppressed the grin that was threatening to explode.

"What?" His eyebrows rose and he half stood in surprise.

"Yep, see?" Zoe showed off the ring.

He took her hand. The simple band was on her ring finger, and the former priest frowned. He looked at both of them in shock.

Eva felt sorry for her father and she grinned. "Yeah, Zoe fell in love on the ship. She was asked and she said yes."

"Hey, I was in love long before then, I just got married on the ship. Seems it took 'somebody' a long time to get the courage to ask me." Zoe said with a teasing smile.

"Where is he?" Panayiotis asked, still trying to figure out the change.

"Who?" Zoe innocently asked.

"Your husband."

"Right here," Zoe replied and hugged Eva.

"I'm confused," Panayiotis complained.

Both of the girls lost their composure and burst out laughing. "Gotcha. That will teach you to surprise us." Eva said and hugged her father. "I asked Zoe to be my wife on the ship and she said yes; we've been married now for seven months."

Panayiotis grinned. "Does that mean I won't get any grandchildren?" Zoe lost her composure entirely and fell on the floor laughing. "I'll take that as bad news then," he said.

"Not unless Harry gets Eva pregnant, you won't."

"Who is Harry?"

"Eva's boyfriend," Zoe mumbled and then quickly looked away.

Panayiotis was confused again. "You have a boyfriend?"

Eva turned to her father. "Mrs. Jenkins has been trying to get me to go out with any number of her nephews since we arrived. She thinks I'm a good catch. She arranged for her nephew Harry, who was in Greece during the war and can speak Greek, to go out with me. Zoe told Mrs. Jenkins that I don't go out with men who aren't Greek so being resourceful, she set me up with a..."

"Pseudo-Greek," Zoe supplied.

"A pseudo-Greek. So I'm going to the dance with this Harry Jenkins."

"You are?" Zoe stopped and looked back at her wife.

"Have to, love, or else she will suspect something isn't right."

"I don't like it," Zoe said and went and sat in the opposite chair. "You could tell him you're not interested."

Eva looked at her father. He wisely decided to check out the kitchen, leaving the two of them alone. Eva went and knelt beside her sulking wife. She put her hand on Zoe's knee. "Zoe, come on, you know we have to go through with this ruse. You certainly know that I don't want to go out with Harry or any other man. What's the matter?"

"I don't like it that you're going to go out with him. He's going to have his hands all over you."

Eva suppressed a grin. Zoe was jealous. It was the first time she had seen the young woman acting this way, and in a funny kind of way, she found it endearing. Zoe had a pout that was so gorgeous, Eva wanted to kiss her senseless.

"Honey, he won't have his hands all over me. I promise he won't. I love you," Eva said and kissed her partner gently.

"He's going to think you are available, and then...you might..."

"Zoe Lambros, I don't believe you would even think that I would cheat on you," Eva tried to calm her wife. She wasn't sure where Zoe's insecurities had come from. "I love you and I always will. I'm here because of you, don't you know that?" she asked the young woman, brushing away Zoe's tears that started to fall.

"I'm scared," Zoe whispered.

"Of what? Harry? It's just a dance, love. Is that what you're scared about?"

Zoe nodded. "And Muller."

Eva held her wife in her arms. "He can't touch us now. We're not back in Greece."

Zoe looked up at her partner; her eyes held unshed tears that threatened to fall. "I don't want to ever lose you," Zoe said as her voice broke.

"I promise you, I won't ever leave you," Eva replied softly and bent down and passionately kissed her wife to reinforce her promise. "Ever."

Zoe sniffed. She looked into Eva's eyes and hugged the woman. She was terrified of what Muller would do if he knew that Eva was alive. It caused her many a sleepless night thanks to the nightmares. It was always the same dream, Muller standing over Eva's dead body, pointing at her and yelling that she had killed her lover. Zoe shuddered at the memory of her beloved Eva, dead on the floor. She couldn't bring herself to tell Eva.

Eva wiped away the remaining tears. "Are you feeling any better?" Zoe nodded. "Okay so do you think we can get Father out of the kitchen now?" Eva asked and grinned. Zoe nodded. "Father, you can come out now."

Panayiotis limped out of thc kitchen holding a plate with some coconut balls. He put them on the table. "These are nice." He sat back on the sofa.

"Zoe is feeling a little scared at the moment. We found out yesterday that Major Muller survived and he is here."

"Muller is in Sydney? How do you know?" Panayiotis asked his daughter. He watched as Zoe hugged the older woman.

The knock on the door forestalled Eva's response, and she got up and opened it. Friedrich Jacobs stood there with his hat in his hands. "Mr. Jacobs, please come in," Eva said, opening the door wider.

Friedrich entered to find an older man sitting rather stiffly on the sofa. Zoe had moved from her seat and sat next to him. She looked rather subdued, and he hoped he would not have a repeat of the previous night.

Eva made the introductions. "Mr. Jacobs, this my father, Panayiotis Haralambos. Father, this is Friedrich Jacobs."

"Pleased to meet you, sir. Uh, I thought..." Friedrich was confused. He thought Eva's father was dead.

"Are you Zoe's boyfriend?" Panayiotis asked. With all the mention of men being used as a ruse, the former priest thought he must be Zoe's friend.

"Oh no, sir, I mean...what?" Jacobs stammered and then shut his mouth. Zoe grinned.

"Mr. Jacobs is an investigator. He told us about Muller being in Sydney," Eva explained and sat next to her wife, putting an arm around her. "He came yesterday to tell us about it, but it kind of got out of control." She squeezed Zoe's hand.

"Oh, I see," Panayiotis said and nodded.

Friedrich sat down and opened his briefcase. He took out the folders. "We have located where Mr. Muller is living."

"Why don't you just arrest him then?" Zoe asked, hoping that was what he was going to tell them.

"We were going to, but they escaped this morning," Friedrich replied. "We traced them to a block of flats in Newtown."

"Who else is with him?" Eva asked.

Friedrich pulled out several photos and handed them to Eva. She looked closely at the men standing beside Muller, but didn't recognise any of them. That is, until she saw one particularly grim looking man. "Rhimes."

"Yes, we know. It seems Rhimes and your fa.."

"Stepfather. Her father is Panayiotis Haralambos," Zoe interrupted, raising her voice to make her point.

Friedrich couldn't believe he let that slip. He mentally slapped himself. And to do it when her father was sitting not two feet away from him. "I'm sorry, Miss Haralambos..."

Panayiotis was taken aback. He looked at Eva and they smiled at each other. She had taken his name, and he was extraordinarily pleased.

"Rhimes and Major Muller are connected with a group of ex-Nazis who have formed a network. The problem for Muller is that he needs medical treatments for his burns."

"What happened to Muller?" Panayiotis asked.

"The Resistance bombed his house while he was inside. He survived and escaped to Thessaloniki, but his burns weren't treated and they got infected," Jacobs replied.

"Couldn't have happened to a nicer boofhead," Zoe chimed in.

"Boofhead?" the former priest asked.

Eva chuckled. "Australian slang for idiot." She turned to Jacobs. "So what do you want us to do?"

"At the moment, nothing. We have to wait until he resurfaces."

"But why do you need us?" Zoe asked.

This was where Friedrich would have the major problems. He knew the feisty young woman would react angrily and he steeled himself for it. "We want Miss Haralambos to be the bait." He winced, waiting for the explosion to come.

"How?" Eva asked.

Friedrich was surprised. He glanced at Zoe who had her head down. "We can put it out on the Nazi grapevine that you will testify at Nuremburg against him."

"That isn't true, is it?" Zoe asked. She didn't want Eva to go back to Germany.

"No. We have enough witnesses in Greece and Germany. We don't need Miss Haralambos. He doesn't know that. It will also be leaked that you can testify against Rhimes and others, since you were close to them."

"I wasn't close to them, Mr. Jacobs. I was a witness to their brutality but I wasn't close to them," Eva responded. She held on to Zoe, who was ready to pounce on the hapless man. She needed to control her young wife's anger at Jacobs' comment as well as fight back her own fears. The possibility of Muller coming after her sent shivers down her spine, and she hoped that no one in the room noticed her trembling. She knew she had to do this, that monster could not be allowed to roam free, but the weight of impending doom loomed heavy on her heart. Somehow she had to catch the devil himself without getting her beloved Zoe caught in the middle.

"Miss Haralambos, I seem to be putting my foot in my mouth. My Greek isn't that good, so please excuse me for the poor choice of words. I meant you were close in the sense that you were with them...I mean you knew them." Jacobs tried to explain himself. "I didn't mean that you were close to them in that sense," Friedrich tried to get out of the mess he had made for himself. Maybe he should have gotten David to come with him.

He got up and retrieved his folders. "I'll be in contact in a day or so, after we get the latest field report." He put his folders in his back. "I'm pleased to have met you, sir." He shook Panayiotis' hand.

"Same here, young man."

Eva walked Jacobs to the door. "I will contact you in a few days."

"Looking forward to it," Eva mumbled as she saw the man out. She turned back towards the living room. "What a day," she said and sat down next to Zoe.

"Boring as usual," Zoe replied and gave her a peck on the cheek, causing the three of them to start chuckling.

****

"YOU! You killed her."

Muller stood over Eva's battered body, a gun in his hand. He was laughing at the sight of Eva's blood splattered on his clothes. In fact, blood was everywhere, on their clothes, the bed and the walls. Zoe looked down at her hands, at the blood on her hands, and she screamed.

Zoe bolted upright, freeing herself from the bonds of the nightmare. Her heart ached from the images of her lover, battered and bloody. Her breath came in shallow gasps as she wiped the sweat from her brow. She glanced at the nightstand and grimaced at the clock. It was 2:00 a.m. and, as had happened several times before, even in Greece, the same nightmare invaded her sleep.

Eva, my precious Eva, she thought and turned to look at her lover, contently sleeping on her stomach, the thin sheet pooled around her waist, exposing her scarred back. The moon's soft beams illuminated her broad shoulders, highlighting her silky hair in such a way that Zoe sighed at the sight. Lying back to watch her lover sleeping, Zoe propped herself up on one arm and gently traced the faint scars put there by the hand of her stepfather and uncle. She caught her breath as she touched the scar from the bullet that shattered her collarbone and almost took her life. Zoe softly kissed the scarred shoulder and reaffirmed that she never wanted to lose this woman.

Eva stirred and turned around. She opened sleepy blue eyes to gaze at Zoe. "What's the matter, love?"

"Couldn't sleep," Zoe replied brushing away Eva's bangs. "I had a nightmare."

Eva's eyes instantly misted and she scooped the younger woman into her arms and embraced her. She had woken a few times to Zoe's screams of "NO!" and she would sit and cradle her until she fell back asleep. But Zoe would never tell her what the dreams were about, and she felt frustrated as to how to help her.

"Eva, I'm sorry I got jealous about Harry," Zoe said softly as she laid her head against Eva's shoulder.

"It's alright. You don't have anything to worry about. You've already claimed me," Eva replied and kissed the fair-haired head. "You are the love of my life, why would I need to search for what I already have?"

Zoe looked at the love of her life and softly kissed

her. "I love you."

"I love you too, Zoe," Eva replied as she gave her wife another kiss. "Please, Zoe, please tell me what the dream was. I want to be here for you, but how can I when you won't confide in me?"

Zoe looked into those concerned blue eyes and knew she had to tell her. Taking a deep breath, Zoe held on to Eva as she shared her darkest nightmares. Eva closed her eyes as the tears came, for it was the same dream she had experienced many times herself, but it was Zoe who was killed.

"He can't hurt us any more," she whispered, "As long as we have each other, no one can hurt us ever again." Zoe laid her head on her partner's shoulder and the two held each other long into the night.

Chapter 6

Eva yawned. She was hot, tired, and she wanted to go to sleep. She glanced up at the large clock in the staff cafeteria and sighed. Another six hours to go before quitting time.

"Hey, Eva." A large man approached her. His white uniform was marred with black smudges, as was his face, making him look like a commando getting ready to drop behind enemy lines.

Earl Wiggins was a technician, fixing the huge machines that kept the assembly line working. He sat down next to Eva and leaned in. "What's the matter, did Zoe keep you up last night?" he asked and ruffled her dark hair.

Eva looked up at the big Aussie and gave him a smirk. Earl was the only friend Eva had on the factory floor. He was a jovial fellow and had introduced himself to Eva her first day at work. It wasn't long before he got through her tough exterior with his dry sense of humour. He made Eva laugh; and they soon became firm friends. It was the first time Eva ever had such a close friend, outside of Zoe. Eventually, she invited him and his partner Davey to dinner one night, which turned into a bonding session. Zoe ended up loving the big guy, too.

When they had first met, Earl tried to live up to his reputation on the factory floor as a ladies man, a reputation he had acquired on purpose and wasn't shy about. Even as they were becoming friends, he still kept asking Eva out within earshot of all the women. Eva eventually said "yes" one day, but only after Earl finally told her the truth about himself.

****

"Hey, Eva, can I speak to you?"

"Sure, Earl," Eva replied. "No, I won't go out with you," she quickly added as she stuck her hands in her pants pockets.

"Look, I know you're not interested, but can you still please go out with me?" Earl begged.

"Earl, I'm not the only woman on the floor. Go ask Alice."

The big man stood there fidgeting. He took off his protective hat and scrunched it up in his large hands. "Ah, Eva...look, I...I know you're gay. I saw you kissing your girlfriend a few weeks ago when she came to pick you up. I know no one saw you but me. I was in the cool room."

Eva was stunned. She looked down and tried to figure out how she was going to get out of this. The last thing she wanted was for that secret to get out. "So, what do you want, Earl?" Eva asked defensively.

"Nothing."

"Nothing?" Eva repeated.

"No."

"Earl, you must want something. I know if this got out I could be sacked for any number of reasons, so...?"

"Um, look, I'm in a...relationship...with a man. But I have a reputation here at work that I've worked years to get. I can't afford for the big guys upstairs to know I'm gay, or I won't make supervisor any time in my lifetime. So, please go out with me?" Earl pleaded. "I'm a really nice date," he added with a wink.

"Kiss me," Eva had said

"What?" Earl was confused.

"Kiss me!" Eva hissed, looking over his shoulder.

The big man bent down and kissed her tenderly, to which Eva responded by putting her arms around his neck and returning the kiss.

"Hey lookee...Earl bags another one!" Earl's supervisor cried out as he came near them. "Listen you two, try and control yourselves until you get to your room, okay?" He guffawed at his own joke and slapped Earl on the back. "Man, that was smooth. You took only two weeks to break the Ice Queen. You deserve a cold beer after work." He slapped the man again on the shoulder and left them with the sound of his laugh echoing down to the cool room.

"Thank you," Earl said and gave Eva a peck on the cheek.

"Don't you dare tell Zoe what I did, or else she'll have your hide." Eva chuckled and headed back to work.

****

"Hey, Earl," Eva said and yawned again. "Shut up and wipe your face. You been kissing your machines again?" She kidded him, reaching out to clean a smudge off his cheek and displaying the dirty fingertip.

Earl got up to grab a rag from his back pocket and scrubbed at his face with it, then leaned in close to Eva. "Well, did she keep you up all night? You know, my sweet woman, you should lend me that powerhouse woman of yours so I can teach Davey a few tricks," he said, then turned the chair around to straddle it as he sat back down.

"Now that's real macho, Earl." Eva grinned as Earl playfully slapped her on the head.

"Well, did she?" he whispered in her ear. To those around them it seemed like Earl was nuzzling her neck.

"No, she did not...and what Zoe knows would probably make Davey keel over," Eva mumbled back. She put her arms on the table and rested her head on them, stifling yet another yawn.

Earl laughed. "Pocket dynamite, that girl."

"Wasn't Zoe."

"Why are you so tired, then?"

"Let's go for a walk, maybe it will help wake me up." Eva got up from her chair, pulling Earl with her. He put his arm around her waist as they left the room.

"Hey, Earl, up for some nookie in the cool room, huh?" his supervisor called out, and half the room laughed.

"That man only has one thing on his mind," Eva said disgustingly.

"You have to forgive him, his mother dropped him on his head repeatedly," Earl replied, getting a chuckle from Eva.

They walked outside into yet more stifling heat, but with the breeze it was more bearable than inside. Earl pulled out a cigarette and lit it, and they crossed the street to sit on a brick fence overlooking the factory. "So...what's up?"

Eva turned to her best friend and gave him what he called her 1000 megawatt smile. "My father is alive."

Earl was confused. Eva had confided to him that her father was dead, and had also spoken of their adventures during and after the war. "Eva, sweetie, I think you're confusing Big Earl here."

Eva looked up with a grin. "I want you to meet him, Earl."

"Your father? But I thought he was dead?" he said, still confused.

"Well, remember when I told you about the train?" Earl nodded and Eva continued. "Somehow when the train exploded, he was thrown out or something. He woke up in an American medical tent, and the next thing he knew he was on a hospital ship heading for America. Do you believe that?" Eva beamed. "So then, they..."

"Wait, who is they?" Earl interrupted.

"His wife." Eva enjoyed the look of utter shock on the man's face.

"I thought you said your father was a priest!"

"He was. He fell in love," Eva replied.

"Eva, has anyone ever mentioned to you that your life would make a great wireless serial? Yours is better than *Dad and Dave*." Earl said as he shook his head and started to laugh.

"So, do you want to meet them?"

"Does Dad know about you and Zoe?"

Eva laughed and nodded. "Dad knows about Zoe, and we have his blessing."

"Well that's one bonzer bloke you got there, Evy my dear. Yeah, I would love to meet him," Earl said as he glanced down at his watch. "Come on, we'd better go back inside or else Timmy the Twit will go on the warpath." He took Eva's hand as they headed back to the factory across the street.

****

The department store was crowded, as shoppers began to browse and chatter. It had been a lean few years with the war on and money was scarce, but with the ending of the hostilities in Europe and then the Pacific, people began to spend some of their hard-earned money again.

A portly, middle aged saleslady was busy with the customers, a smile plastered on her face as she greeted every new customer that walked into her section. She watched as two young women entered and were browsing at the perfume section. She tried to see if either of them had a ring on their finger—her sales pitch about buying their husbands aftershave had worked like a charm all morning. The small dark-haired young woman had a few bags with her, and Nellie smiled when she saw the ring. "Not expensive, but these young kids don't have much. She probably got married before he sailed," she mused to herself.

"Good morning, madam," Nellie said as she smiled broadly. "Can I interest you in some after-shave for your husband?"

Zoe looked at Elena and grinned. Elena saw the twinkle in Zoe's eyes and she started feeling sorry for the poor saleslady.

"Sure," Zoe said and gave her bags to her friend

"Were you looking for a gift?"

"Yes, a birthday gift. I already got some clothes." Zoe sniffed at the aftershave, crinkling her nose.

"Oh, how wonderful! I'm sure your husband is a lucky man," Nellie gushed. She liked to get to know her customers better and then help them to select more than what they initially came in for. She looked at Zoe with a huge smile.

Elena turned away and rolled her eyes.

"I'm the lucky one," Zoe replied.

"Of course, of course. Now how old will your husband be?"

"Twenty six."

"Ah, a young man, with a beautiful wife. Any children?"

"No, none...we can't have any," Zoe said, giving the saleslady a sad look.

Elena coughed loudly to cover up her chuckles as Zoe played with the saleslady. She moved further away from her friend, trying very hard not to lose her composure.

"Oh, I am so sorry! You have your husband, though. That's the main thing," Nellie sympathized. She patted the young woman on the shoulder and wondered how serious his war wounds were. "We have an excellent range of aftershaves and colognes for men."

"Hmm..." Zoe sniffed at the various bottles. "Hey, El, come over here."

Elena returned to her side, a grin threatening to split her face, trying valiantly to control it. "Yep?"

"Do you think Eva would like aftershave for her legs? Hmm, no, I don't think so." She turned to the saleslady as Elena unsuccessfully hid a snort of amusement. "My wife doesn't shave...well, except for her legs of course."

Zoe started giggling as Elena finally burst out laughing with tears running down her face. The clerk had a look of total shock as Elena let the parcels drop and had to steady herself against the counter. Seeing the saleslady's face, Zoe was now laughing helplessly along with her.

Nellie's face turned a bright shade of red as Zoe and Elena continued to laugh at Zoe's joke. "You said you were married." Nellie said when she finally found her voice.

"I am," Zoe replied, still chuckling. "I'm married to the most wonderful, loving woman on the planet, and she loves me. Isn't that great?"

"Disgusting." Nellie huffed, turning away.

"Was it something I said?" Zoe asked Elena, who had finally regained her composure as well. "Come on, El, I hear food calling my name."

"You're a wicked woman."

"Oh, yeah!" Zoe replied and steered her friend out of the perfume section. She turned back to see the saleslady giving her a dirty look, so she stuck her tongue out. "Cow."

"You know, it doesn't matter," Elena said as she placed her arm around her friend's shoulder.

"Yes, it does," Zoe replied as she settled into the booth of the little tea house.

"If that woman was accepting of your love for Eva, would it make your love for her any stronger?"

"No."

"See? It doesn't make a difference. She's a narrow-minded old cow."

"Yeah, you're right. Did you like the blue dress I bought for Evy?"

"Gorgeous. It's going to match that white sweater you bought for her last week."

"I wanted to buy her that ring, but it's too expensive," Zoe sighed. She had spotted a gold band with sapphire gems a few weeks ago, and every time she passed the jeweler she saw the ring in the window.

"Oh, damn," Zoe muttered, as she spotted a familiar figure approaching and tried to hide behind a menu.

"What?" Elena whispered.

Friedrich and his friend David had finished their coffee break and were just leaving, until Friedrich spotted Zoe and changed direction, heading for her table. "Good morning, Miss Lambros," he said, extending his hand.

"Hi," Zoe replied with a weak smile. She didn't feel she could trust the man yet, but still politely reached out to give his hand a quick shake.

"And who are these gorgeous ladies?" David asked as he sat down next to Elena.

Friedrich rolled his eyes at David's comment. "This is my colleague, David Peterson."

"What's your name?" Elena asked, smiling at Friedrich. "I'm Elena Manheim."

"This is Friedrich Jacobs," Zoe supplied.

"I'm pleased to meet you, Mr. Jacobs."

Friedrich was stumped. "Ah, yes...uh..." He stuttered as a pink blush coloured his face and ears. Elena looked up at him and smiled. He didn't know how to speak to women, and even though David had coached him, he was still a lost cause.

"What my friend is trying to say is that it's a pleasure to meet you, too," David said and sighed. He was going to have to work on opening lines with Freddy again. The man was hopeless around women.

"Would you like to join us?" Elena invited Friedrich, since David was already seated. Zoe shot daggers at her friend at the suggestion but Elena ignored her.

"I'm sorry, Miss Manheim, but we really have to get back to the office."

"Oh, that's a shame," Elena replied.

"You know, I was just discussing with Friedrich how the dance is coming up next week, and we have no dates. Isn't that sad? Two eligible bachelors and no dates. Would you two like to join us?" David smiled.

Zoe was about to decline when she saw Elena's face. She was smiling at Friedrich. She turned to see an equally shy smile reflecting back from him. She sighed. Eva was going to go with Harry Jenkins, so this way at least they would be at the dance together.

"Sure." Elena turned around and stared at Zoe, who gave her a wink. "It's very nice of you to offer, Mr. Peterson," Zoe added.

"Excellent. Come on, Freddy, we have things to do, places to go, people to see. It's been a pleasure." He got up, putting his arm around his friend and steering Friedrich toward the door.

"That was a date." Elena said and turned to her friend.

"Really? Well, what do you know," Zoe replied and chuckled. "You like Mr. Jacobs?"

"He's cute."

"Not my type," Zoe replied with a smirk. "I like them taller."

Elena chuckled, then sobered. "Oh, no!"

"What?"

"I need a dress."

"Oh, no, what a dilemma." Zoe joked.

"Hey, what about Eva?"

"You can't go out with my wife," Zoe chuckled. "Eva already has a hot date with Harry Jenkins."

"So Mrs. J finally cornered her, huh?"

"Yeah. A war hero who served in Greece...she got around my 'Eva only goes with Greek boys' line. He even knows how to speak Greek. Go figure."

"Well, look on the bright side, you're going with David and I'm going with Friedrich, and Eva will be there."

"Who said David was my date?" Zoe teased and laughed at the crestfallen look her friend was giving her. "Oh, alright, don't make that face. You can have Friedrich."

"Come on, I want to go and buy a dress and some shoes and maybe some new perfume!" Elena said excitedly.

"Hey, let's go terrorise that saleslady again." Zoe said as she pulled her friend up.

"I don't know if she'll serve you now," Elena chuckled, then stopped. "Hey, how do you know Friedrich?"

"Long story. I'll tell you while you try and get some perfume from the nice lady."

They paid at the counter and walked away, talking excitedly.

Chapter 7

Alberta Haralambos looked into the mirror and sighed. She was a tall, beautiful woman with auburn hair. Bright blue eyes stared back at her as she appraised her appearance and watched a grimace appear. She so wanted to make a good impression on her husband's daughter.

"You look beautiful," her husband said as he wrapped his strong arms around her and kissed her tenderly on the neck.

"You're biased."

"Is there something wrong in that?"

"No, but..."

"No buts. You look beautiful. Eva will love you."

A sigh. "I'm not so sure."

"What do you mean?" Panayiotis asked, leaving her side to sit on the edge of the bed.

"I don't know if she'd like another mother in her life at the moment."

"My darling Ally...you are a nut. I love you, but you think too much. Eva is such a loving woman, even despite what she went through with that animal. She gives of herself wholly. Believe me, she won't hate you." Her husband gently tugged her over to sit next to him.

Alberta shook her head. "I can't believe that man is still alive." She was shocked when Pany had told her the news about Muller. "After all this time. It must be difficult for Eva."

"It is, but she has Zoe. Zoe is her anchor. And now she has us, too," he smiled.

"What's Zoe like?"

Panayiotis laughed. "Zoe is...a force of nature. She can be courageous and strong, and then turn right around and surprise you by her naiveté. She gives of herself completely, unconditionally. She reminds me of Saint Peter. So headstrong. She's not afraid to speak her mind and rushes in where angels fear to tread." He chuckled again. "Yes, that's Zoe. She lives life to the fullest. I'm surprised she survived the war."

Alberta smiled. It was obvious to her that her husband loved this young woman as much as he did his own daughter. "How old is she?"

"Eighteen, going on forty." the former priest chuckled.

"She's so young."

"She is indeed. The war didn't allow her to have a childhood. Her parents were killed by the Nazis, and she had no one after they died."

"She had you."

"Hmm, she had me, yes, but she suffered greatly the first few months after her mother died. We got through it, though."

"How did they decide to come here?"

"Zoe's idea. She got friendly with some Australian soldiers, and they sold her on the idea of wide open spaces and all of that. Eva wants Zoe to be happy, so off they went."

Alberta sat on the edge of the bed thinking. If she was going to impress Eva, that meant she would have to impress Zoe as well. She sighed.

Panayiotis chuckled. He knew his wife was nervous. It didn't take a genius to figure that out, but he also knew that Eva would like Alberta. They were so similar in temperament, and both were intelligent as well as beautiful.

"Don't worry. Eva and Zoe are going to love you."

"I hope so," Alberta whispered as she got up and went to her wardrobe to select another shirt.

****

Eva got out of the car and locked the door. The white Holden sparkled in the afternoon sun. Earl loved his car and buffed it to a shine every day. Though the new Holden cars were a beautiful design, Eva still couldn't see the attraction to what was just a car. However, she constantly heard enough about it from Earl to get an idea of just how much he adored it.

She grinned as Earl gave his car a pat on the bonnet. "Is Davey ever jealous?" she asked, leaning around her friend and patting the car herself.

"You know, you *are* a funny woman when you don't get any sleep." He took off his jacket and threw it through the open window. "Hey, is Zoe cooking tonight?"

"Yep. She cooks every night."

"Oh yeah, I forgot, you even burn water," Earl laughed. Eva's lack of cooking skills was a running joke between him and Zoe, and he enjoyed teasing his friend about it. His cooking skills weren't that great either, but he wasn't about to share that little tidbit with her.

Eva gave him a dirty look and bolted up the stairs to find the flat door open with music blaring out. She entered to find Zoe sprawled on the floor listening to a new record. She froze, staring at her wife, her eyes going wide.

Earl followed her in and also stared at Zoe in shock. "Holy Mother of God!"

Zoe grinned back at them. She had decided to cut her hair, which surprised both herself and Elena, since it was a decision taken on the spur of the moment. Zoe's formerly long hair was now cut short, similar to Eva's style.

"Well?"

Eva was stunned. She loved her partner's long hair, "Wow," was all she could manage.

Zoe laughed. "I think she likes it, Wiggy."

"I love it," Eva said and bent down to kiss her. Zoe raised a hand to tangle in the hair behind Eva's head as she kissed her back.

"Hey now...take that to the bedroom, you two." Earl said and chuckled.

The women ended the kiss and looked at each other with a smile. Zoe clasped Eva's hands as she straightened back up and let the taller woman help her to her feet, then turned to the big man beside her.

"Hey, Wiggy! How are ya?" She smiled up at Earl and giggled as she gave him a hug. The small woman's shoulders were barely above the large man's waistline, and her arms only reached halfway around his back.

"Hi there, Stretch. What's for dinner?" Earl replied, picking up the petite woman easily and engulfing her in a bear hug.

"Wiggy, I need to breathe!" Zoe laughed, trying to extricate herself from the bear hug.

Earl ruffled her new short cut as he gently set her back to the ground. "Love the new look," Earl whispered in her ear.

Eva had turned down the volume of the record player and put her bag down on the couch. She went into the kitchen and looked into the oven where a roast with potatoes and vegetables were nicely done. "Hey Earl, you wanna stay for dinner?"

"Nup, can't. I'm meeting my folks tonight," Earl said from the kitchen door. "It sure smells nice, though."

"Of course it does," Zoe said, and brushed past him giving him a slap on the behind.

"Hey, now! Eva, your wife slapped me on the bum."

"Lucky boy," Eva said as she passed him, heading to the bedroom to change, seeing Earl stick his tongue out at her in reply.

He smiled as he turned back to Zoe. "So, how are the preparations for the party coming?"

"Piece of cake. We can still use your place, right?" Earl nodded. Zoe had dreamt up the surprise party for Eva's twenty-sixth birthday and had made sure to invite all their friends to make it special for her partner. "Thanks, Earl," Zoe said, and gave him a dazzling smile.

"Anything for you, Stretch." He grinned back at Zoe, then turned toward the bedroom door. "Hey Eva," he called, "I gotta go and pick up the folks from Central. Spending the week with them is going to be lots of fun."

Eva returned to the kitchen as Earl was about to leave. "Hey, tell your mum I loved the chocolate cake she sent us."

"She sent you chocolate cake?" Earl turned and asked.

"Oh yeah, we overdosed on chocolate," Zoe replied and grinned.

"She never sends me chocolate cake," Earl groused.

Both women laughed at their friend. "Thanks for the ride home," Eva said as she walked Earl to the door and held it open.

"Hey, you rode in the Beast?" Zoe asked. She had nicknamed the car as soon as she saw it, the first time Earl brought it over to them to show it off. Zoe loved cars, and she couldn't wait until she was old enough to get her license.

They said their good-byes and Eva closed the door to find Zoe immediately wrapped around her. "Hi."

Eva smiled down at her partner. "Hi. The food smells nice."

"So do you," Zoe said and grinned. "I made some galaktoburiko for dessert."

Zoe loved to cook and experiment, but for this night they had decided to stick to Greek food to be safe. Zoe's food experiments mostly worked, but sometimes they didn't. Unfortunately for Eva, she was always the guinea pig. Zoe had gone on a Mexican food craze for a time, and one day tried her hand at Chili Con Carne. Eva found out what happens when you put too much chili powder in the Chili Con Carne, and she swore off Mexican food after that, despite Zoe's persistent attempts to get her to try it again.

They moved to the sofa and sat down together.

"So, you really like my hair?" Zoe asked, looking up at the older woman.

"Yeah, I do. You look gorgeous, Zoe," Eva replied. "It's going to take time to adjust to you as a brunette, but yeah, I like it."

"I was passing this hairdresser and they had a special on, so I did it."

Eva laughed. This was the impulsive and zany Zoe she loved so much. "Well, it suits you."

"Thank you," Zoe replied and stole a kiss. "Guess who we met up with at the shops?"

"Mrs. Jenkins?"

"No, our friend Friedrich Jacobs."

"Oh great. What did he want?"

"Nothing. He was having a coffee with a friend of his. El and I were shopping and we stopped off to get a cup of tea, and he saw us as they were leaving."

"That's nice," Eva said, relaxing back as Zoe settled against her.

"Hmm. You know that dance you're going to with Harry Jenkins?"

"Yep, how can I forget?" Eva grimaced.

"Well, I'm going, too."

"Oh? Who with?"

Zoe grinned. She knew her wife so well that the little lift of the eyebrow and the casual nonchalant look really hid avid interest. Zoe wasn't going to tell her she had figured that out. "His name is David Peterson, Jacob's friend."

"Huh?"

"Elena is going with Friedrich Jacobs. Her eyes nearly popped out of her head when they met."

"Elena and Friedrich?" Eva asked, not quite believing her ears.

"Yep. He stammered and ummed and ahhed. El went all shy and demure."

"Zoe, love, if I had to describe Elena, I wouldn't use demure in the same sentence."

"Well, she was. So in the spirit of friendship, I offered to double date with her."

Eva grinned. "It had nothing to do with me going to the same dance?"

Zoe frowned. "Hardly crossed my mind." She paused and then gave her partner an impish grin, "Well, not for a few moments, anyway."

They both laughed as the tea kettle began to whistle. Zoe got up to make some tea and Eva followed.

"So what do you think this Alberta is like?" Eva asked, leaning on the doorframe of the kitchen.

"Probably old and fat," Zoe joked as she poured out the tea. "I wouldn't worry."

"Who's worried?"

"You are," Zoe said as she poked her in the stomach on the way out of the kitchen. They settled at the kitchen table which was set out for the dinner.

"I'm a little nervous."

"Why?"

"What if she doesn't like me?" Eva asked taking a sip of her tea.

"What's not to like? You're gorgeous, you're intelligent, you're talented. Did I mention gorgeous?" Zoe replied and stole a quick kiss.

"You're biased."

"Hmm. Yeah, I am. Wouldn't you be in a pickle if I didn't think you were gorgeous, intelligent, talented, and let's not forget a fantastic lover?"

Eva laughed. "Have I told you today how much I love you?"

"Yeah, this morning." Zoe waggled her eyebrows.

"You're going to wear me out before my time," Eva mumbled. She looked at her wife with a wicked grin which earned a huge smile from her partner.

"My mission in life, Miss Haralambos. A difficult and dangerous job, but someone has to do it," Zoe replied, and they chuckled.

****

"Are you sure?" Erik Rhimes asked as he shoved his hands into his pockets.

"Yes, quite sure. Our contact inside the investigator's office tells me that she's here."

"Not possible. She's dead."

"Well, sir, our contact said she was here. I could get our colleague to copy the documents."

"Yes, do that," Rhimes replied.

The man nodded and walked away. Rhimes watched the street for a few moments and then went inside the block of flats. Entering his flat, he made sure the security bolt was fastened as he closed the door. He sat down heavily in the armchair and sighed. He didn't want to tell Hans that Eva was alive if he wasn't certain about it. He would wait until he had the documents in hand. If it were true, he wasn't sure how he would tell his best friend, or what they would need to do to eliminate her.

He would cross that bridge when he came to it.

Chapter 8

A light breeze whipped Eva's hair around as she leaned on the railing of the balcony and tried to relax, gazing off at the distant horizon. The sun had set just moments ago, still leaving the sky suffused with a slowly fading golden hue. She was distracted by a movement below and tore her eyes away from the sunset to see a neighbor wave at her as they left the block of flats. Giving the person a quick wave back, she tried to think if she even knew their name, only having met them once or twice in the hallway. Her thoughts were interrupted by the sound of soft footsteps behind her.

Zoe came out onto the balcony carrying a cup of tea and settled beside the older woman, leaning against her slightly as she raised the cup up to just in front of Eva's red lips. "Sip of tea?" she asked, and watched her wife move slightly to press her lips against the cup for a small sample.

"Mmm, that's good, love." Eva gave Zoe a smile and tried to ease into a small stretch of her back.

Zoe watched Eva's smile turn into a grimace with closed eyes. "Oh, my poor Eva," Zoe sighed, setting her cup down on the small corner table and holding her partner close, gently rubbing Eva's lower back as she laid her head on the taller woman's shoulder. It was more a show of sympathy and support, and while it didn't ease her pain, Zoe knew it still helped Eva deal with the discomfort. Eva's occasional back pains, another legacy of her stepfather's sometimes brutal abuse, required a more thorough massage for her to feel any relief.

"Has it been hurting all day?"

"Almost."

"It started at work, didn't it?" Zoe sighed, knowing Eva was stubborn enough to have stayed at work despite the pain. Between fears of Eva getting hurt and the frustration of working a lot of night shifts, she hated Eva working at that factory. Zoe had tried to convince her to quit many times, but Eva was always hesitant, saying they needed the money.

"Yeah...I was lifting some heavy boxes this morning."

"Eva! Why didn't you call Earl?" Zoe rebuked her gently, raising her head from Eva's shoulder to look up at her. They had had this debate before. Eva wanted to do things herself, and not have to rely on others around her, which Zoe thought was rather silly; and she did not hesitate to make her position known to her partner.

"I couldn't, Zo. He was busy doing something else, and I didn't want to call Jack. It wasn't until Earl and I went outside to talk during my break that it started to ache."

Zoe snorted at Eva's mention of her boss, Jack. She hated him. He was full of his own self-importance and made sure those under him knew he was in charge. Zoe took an instant dislike to him. He was rude, teasing and insulting Eva whenever he could, and he was also a racist. That alone made Zoe see red, but some of the jobs he also made Eva do, like the heavy lifting which aggravated her back, infuriated her.

"You want me to give you some vendouzes?" Zoe asked, still gently rubbing Eva's back.

"No! They hurt more than my back does," Eva replied with another grimace. She hated that treatment. Zoe had read about it in a book by a Greek doctor and thought it would help her back problems. Eva was dubious about it since it involved mentholated spirits and overturned cups. Zoe had tried it on her wife despite Eva's misgivings. It wasn't a success, not to mention that it was also very messy.

"What about I call Mr. Chang and he can try that needle thing."

"Acupuncture. No, I really don't feel like being a pin cushion tonight," Eva joked back to her concerned partner, trying to make her smile. "I'll be ok, Zoe."

Zoe looked back up at her partner and wished she could do something more for her. Eva hadn't told her about her back problems until they were on the ship heading for Australia. They had been in that cramped cabin with its tiny bed, and that had aggravated her back, forcing the confession. She had mildly scolded her partner for keeping that bit of information from her for so long.

****

Eva was quiet for most of the day as they sat in their cabin. The weather had turned cold, and it was raining up on deck. Zoe looked at her partner and sighed. Eva was generally quiet, but something was bothering the older woman as she lay on the bunk with her eyes shut.

"Eva, what's wrong?"

Eva opened her eyes and turned to Zoe. "My back hurts."

"When did you hurt your back?" Zoe asked as she knelt beside her.

Eva sighed. "I've had back problems for a few years now...since my mother died," she said quietly.

Zoe was going to admonish her for not telling her about it earlier, but thought better of it since she appeared to be in some pain. "Does it hurt all the time?"

"No, not all the time," Eva said softly.

"What do you normally do? Can I help?"

"I just need to lay here and rest. I think I aggravated it this morning by helping Mrs. Hoffman with that heavy case," Eva mumbled.

"Why didn't Mr. Hoffman do it? Damn, that has to be the laziest man I've ever met. Now you've hurt your back," Zoe said angrily. "Okay, I know something that might help."

Zoe went to their small food supply tucked away with the tea and a small urn. "What are you going to do with that?" Eva asked as she watched Zoe pour a little oil in a cup.

"My papa had back problems and Mama used to rub him down with some warm oil. I'm not sure if it helped, but Mama did this for years so I guess it must have had some benefit." She brought the cup over and set it on the chair, then helped Eva remove her shirt and turn over onto her stomach. Zoe warmed her hands with some of the oil and began a slow massage of Eva's lower back. "I'm not hurting you, am I?"

"No," Eva's muffled response came, as the older woman relaxed and let Zoe's hands ease the tension from her back. "It's nice."

****

"Hey, how about I give you a nice gentle backrub, hmmm? How does that sound?" Zoe asked as she rubbed her hand up across Eva's shoulders, then down again to her lower back. "I bought some nice rose scented oil today while I was out."

"A backrub? Just a backrub?" Eva teased with a tiny grin.

"Just a backrub. You're getting old and I don't want to wear you out too quickly," Zoe replied with a smirk. "I was reading the other day that they found an artesian well in a little country town called Moree. Remember I told you about how artesian water is supposed to be good for back problems?"

"Hmm, yeah I remember."

"Maybe we can take a trip to Moree when you get your holidays."

"Sure. I don't have my holidays for a few months. Where is Moree?"

"About fourteen hours by train. You need some time to relax from that factory, and we can do the artesian well thing."

"That sounds great," Eva replied as she spotted her father turning the corner and coming up the sidewalk. "They're here." She turned around in Zoe's arms and kissed her gently. "I'm so lucky to have found you," Eva whispered.

Zoe looked at her partner and wrapped both arms around her, hugging her gently and laying her head back down on Eva's chest. "I'm the lucky one," she whispered. They stood like that for a few moments.

"Come on, let's go back inside, they'll be here soon." Eva took Zoe's hand and they walked back into the apartment. She looked at the set table and smiled at the wattle, the red plant sitting squarely in the middle. Zoe loved the plant, which was native to Australia, and took every opportunity to cut two or three from the tree outside their building. Zoe loved the colour red. She had set the table with a white tablecloth and red and white napkins. The kitchen cupboards were painted red and white, which amused Eva, and they had tried to find dinner plates to match. They had finally found red and white plates when they had gone on a bargain search several weeks before, and a delighted Zoe had immediately bought them. These graced the table, as well.

"Okay everything looks great," Eva said, as she took a final look at the settings and the state of the lounge room.

"You look great," Zoe said and reached up to give Eva a quick kiss. Eva had changed into a stylish black pants suit with a baby blue coloured silk shirt, while Zoe wore a white shirt with her favourite jeans. Zoe took Eva's hand and they both walked to the door, opening it just as Eva's father and his new wife reached the top of the stairs.

Panayiotis grinned as he and Alberta entered. Eva took their coats and Zoe ushered them into the lounge room. "Alberta, these are my daughters, Eva and Zoe." Panayiotis introduced his wife to the other two most important people in his life.

Alberta shook Eva's hand and was about to shake Zoe's hand, but Zoe surprised her with a quick hug. Eva grinned at the bemused look on Alberta's face. They went into the lounge room, and Panayiotis sat down with a sigh. Zoe took his cane and leaned on it, giving the older man a smile as Alberta sat down beside him.

"I'm pleased to meet you finally after all the stories your father has told me about you," Alberta said as she tried to break some of the tension.

"I bet he left out a lot," Eva said and looked at Zoe with a grin. "He told us you're a nurse?"

"Yes, that's how I met your father. I was going to be shipped off to go back home, but things didn't pan out and I stayed on the hospital ship," Alberta explained as she turned and gazed lovingly towards her husband. It was fate that had brought them together that day. There wasn't any other way to describe it.

"I woke up and there was this angel. I thought I was dead," Panayiotis said, squeezing her hand.

Eva smiled. "Would you like some tea before we have some dinner?" She asked as she turned to go into the kitchen.

"I would love some, thank you," Alberta said. As she watched Eva walk to the kitchen, her trained eye could see the discomfort the young woman was in. Alberta turned to notice a concerned Zoe also was looking at Eva. "Does Eva have back problems?" she asked.

Zoe turned, a frown still on her face. "Yeah, sometimes," she mumbled. "Excuse me for a moment, please." Zoe got up and followed Eva into the kitchen. Eva was at the kitchen sink, having just swallowed two painkillers and washed them down with water.

"Hey," Zoe said and wrapped herself around the older woman.

"I'm okay. Just needed to take these," Eva explained as they stood together watching the kettle start to boil.

"You're not okay. You're going to see Dr. Stephanopoulos tomorrow, okay? Your back hasn't been this bad for ages...unless you weren't telling me."

Eva smiled. "It must have been the boxes today. A little rest will help. I'll take a sick day tomorrow."

"You mean I'm going to have you here all day tomorrow?"

"Yep. All day," Eva replied, taking the kettle and pouring the water for the tea. She smiled at her grinning partner, who took the kettle from her hand and poured out the rest of the water.

The sounds from the kitchen stopped, and Alberta and Panayiotis looked at each other. "I hope she's okay," Alberta said. "Pany, do you think if I offered to give her a massage, she would accept it?"

The former cleric smiled at his wife. He was pleased about her offer to help, but wasn't sure if Eva would let her. Before he could say anything, though, his wife got up and walked towards the kitchen, leaving him sitting alone on the sofa.

Alberta stopped at the door just as Zoe was giving her wife a kiss. She cleared her throat. "I'm sorry to intrude," she said with a smile as she saw Eva try to pull away from Zoe and Zoe keeping Eva right where she was. *The dynamics of this relationship are quite interesting*, Alberta thought to herself.

"We're bad hosts leaving you two out there alone. I'm sorry...um..." Eva stammered.

"Isn't she just so cute when she's shy?" Zoe smiled at her wife, turning back to Alberta. "So, Mrs. H, what do we call you, apart from Mrs. H?" she rambled.

Alberta chuckled. "Well, you can call me Ally if you like. That's what my friends call me."

"How about Mum?" Zoe suggested with a grin.

Alberta stood there feeling quite surprised. "Sure, if you want to."

"Hey, I never had a mother-in-law before." Zoe said with glee.

"Are you two married?" Alberta raised her eyebrows. She would have to speak to Pany when they went back to the hostel, and remind him of a small matter that he forgot to tell her.

Eva looked at Zoe with a half smile. It was obvious Alberta knew nothing about their relationship. "Eva and I got married on the ship coming out here. Does that bother you?" Zoe asked. She wondered why Father H hadn't told their new mother-in-law about them.

"No, it doesn't bother me at all." Alberta replied. "I think it's quite beautiful that you two have been through so much together, and that you would still find love. I don't understand it, but I never understand love anyway." Alberta smiled at the two women.

"Thank you," Eva said quietly.

"Eva, can I ask you a personal question?" Alberta asked, trying to get back to the reason she was in the kitchen in the first place.

Eva nodded and held Zoe's hand a little tighter.

"Does your back hurt? I'm a trained nurse, and I could tell by the way you walked. If you like, I could give you a massage. I know it's quite forward of me, but I think it would help you. I treated quite a few of the boys with back problems during the war."

Eva glanced down at Zoe, who was watching her with a questioning look. "It hurts occasionally. I lifted some boxes at work today and aggravated the problem. Thank you for your offer, but Zoe gives me a back massage every now and then."

Alberta wasn't that surprised her offer was refused. Pany had told her Eva was a private person. She wondered what that had to do with declining a backrub and she mentally shrugged. "Where do you work?" she asked.

"Westons Biscuit factory. It's not usually heavy lifting, but occasionally I do some," Eva replied.

Alberta was taken aback. Pany had told her Eva was well educated. She had attended university in Berlin and knew several languages. "I hope you don't mind my asking, but why are you working in a factory when you have such a high level of education?"

"We needed the work, and Zoe is going to school," Eva replied. She found she wasn't as uncomfortable as she thought she'd be with Alberta, and Zoe was beaming at her.

"Ah, I see. Maybe I can help you there. I've been told by the Immigration Department that they are looking for translators to help with the influx of refugees from Europe. You can speak several languages can't you?"

"She speaks fluent German, Greek, Italian, and of course English," Zoe said, smiling with pride at her wife.

"Excellent. Why don't you join me? I can speak Greek and rusty German. I've got an interview scheduled with them for tomorrow, would you like to come with me?" Alberta asked expectantly.

"That would be perfect, Evy. You could leave that factory and the night shifts," Zoe told her, trying to convince Eva of the benefits of quitting the factory.

Eva liked the idea of using her language skills for helping others. "I think I would like that." Before Alberta had a chance to reply, they heard a cough from the kitchen door and a frowning Panayiotis stood in the doorway.

"As much as I love watching the three of you bond, could you do it out here? And can we eat?" he asked, giving Zoe a wink.

They chuckled as Zoe bent down and started to remove the food from the oven.

****

Friedrich leaned back in his chair, and a smile played on his lips as he looked at the ceiling. He replayed the scene from the coffee shop in his mind. The young woman had caught his attention even though he was too seriously tongue-tied to give her any indication of his interest. At least David was there to help him out and get him a date. "Oh, damn!" he uttered when he realised something about the dance that hadn't occurred to him before.

The door opened and David walked through carrying some files. He set them down on Friedrich's desk. "What's the matter, Freddy old boy?"

"Um, I can't dance," Friedrich said rather dejectedly.

"Can you kiss?" David asked as he removed a file from the filing cabinet. When he didn't get a reply he turned around and looked at his frowning friend. "Oh, don't tell me you haven't kissed a girl yet?"

"Of course I have but, um..."

"But what?" David asked as he laid the file open and began scribbling notes and inserting them into the file.

"What are you doing?" Friedrich asked as he forgot David's question.

"I'm working on this file."

"I can see that. Why are you adding notes to my file?"

"For our friend." David replied knowing the little information he was doling out was getting Friedrich a bit annoyed.

Friedrich sighed. "Which friend?"

"Our janitor."

Friedrich gave him a confused look. "David, have you been drinking too many beers?"

David laughed. He brushed back his sandy blond hair and went back to writing. "I found out our janitor has ties with the Nazis. I thought it was a brilliant strategy for him to work for the government agency that dealt with Nazi criminals. He knew our every move, Freddy. That's why every time we would find out where these rodents were, they would leave before we got there. I didn't know who it was before, but I suspected that we had an informer inside the office."

"How did you find out?"

"Remember a couple of nights ago when Daniel told us where one of the houses was?" David asked as he looked up. Friedrich nodded. "Well, the next day when the Feds went to arrest them, nothing. The landlady told them that her tenants had left town. We have been working for months, with those rats knowing our every move. I suspected this weasel for some time, but I didn't have any evidence linking it to him conclusively."

"How can we use that to our advantage?"

"I'm not only a good looking bloke, but a smart one. Behold what I'm doing."

"You're writing in my files," Friedrich repeated, stating the obvious.

David handed him one of the papers he had written on. It detailed Eva's testimony against Rhimes and Muller.

"Do you think they'll buy it?"

"Of course. They already know Eva is alive."

"How?"

"Janitor Man told them. I let it 'slip' in the corridor with Daniel when Janitor Man..."

"Marko," Friedrich supplied. Janitor Man made him sound like a comic book hero.

"All right, then, Marko. When Marko finished work, I followed him. I couldn't see who he was talking to, but it must have been about Eva."

"So you're going to give him the file?"

"No, I'm going to give him what I want them to see." He pulled out a file that had been sitting in the pile he brought with him. "I've taken out information about Miss Lambros and certain other details." Friedrich watched as David continued altering the file. When he had finished, he slipped the new file into the filing drawer and buried the real file in the pile. "Come on, Freddy, I want to get something to eat," he urged his friend, picking up the rest of the files. "I'll teach you to dance as well."

They turned off the light and David waited as Friedrich locked the office. They walked down the corridor, the single light creating shadows down the narrow hallway. Stopping near the fire exit, they watched from the shadows for a few moments.

"Maybe he isn't," Friedrich started to say and then stopped as he saw the janitor stop in front of their office door with his mop and bucket. He looked down the darkened hallway for a moment before unlocking the door and entering their office.

"Okay, let's go, Freddy my boy. Are you sure you've kissed a girl before?" David teased as he ushered Friedrich down the stairs and shut the door behind him.

Chapter 9

Zoe was tired. She yawned again and tried to snuggle up in the downy comforter. Eva had gone with Alberta to the Immigration Department early in the morning, and Zoe was having a hard time getting back to sleep. After she had given Eva a gentle back-rub last night, they both had trouble sleeping. Eva kept tossing and turning to get comfortable, which woke Zoe every time she shifted. Almost as soon as Zoe drifted off again, Eva would start moving. It had been a very frustrating night.

She heard knocking at the door, and grumbled as she got out of bed and put on a robe. "This had better be good, or else," Zoe muttered. She opened the door to find Earl standing there in his white overalls. He didn't bother to be asked in, as he entered and started looking around the flat.

"Earl, what are you doing here?"

"Where's Eva? Jack is chucking the biggest dummy spit today."

"Jack can go and jump off the Harbour Bridge," Zoe mumbled and went into the kitchen to put the kettle on. Earl followed her.

"Zoe, this is important, Eva could lose her job."

"Good."

Earl stopped and scratched his head. "You guys didn't have an argument, did you?"

"No. We're fine."

"Hey, are you making me a cuppa?"

"No, I was making myself a cuppa...want one?" she asked the burly man, and for the first time since he arrived, she grinned at him.

"Thanks, mate, I need it. I really need a beer, but it's too early in the morning for that. So, what's up? Where's Eva?"

"Where were you yesterday?"

"Working."

"Working, huh? Did you know Eva lifted those heavy boxes yesterday?"

"Yeah, I know. I saw her," Earl replied. He wasn't sure where this conversation was going, but he could tell Zoe was getting a little annoyed with him.

"You saw her, and you still let her lift them?" Zoe asked angrily. "Where was Jack or the other guys?"

"Jack was watching her."

"Bastard. I swear, given half a chance, I would deck that stupid son of a bitch." Zoe was so furious she was fit to be tied. She hated Eva's supervisor; Earl had heard Zoe's rants about him many times.

"Where were you?"

"I was busy fixing a machine, Stretch. I couldn't help her. Why, did she hurt herself?"

Zoe put the tea in front of him, then opened the cool box and retrieved the milk bottle.

"Yes, she hurt herself. I've told her a million times not to lift that heavy stuff, but does she listen to me? Noooo," she rambled, angry with both Eva and Earl. "She tossed and turned all night! It hasn't been this bad in ages. Even the backrub I gave her didn't do any good," she fumed.

Earl shook his head. He had wondered why Eva was being so quiet during their break. He believed it was the reason she gave—that she was up very late and didn't get enough sleep. He was going to have a word with her when he saw her next.

"I'm sorry, Zoe, I didn't know. She didn't tell me about her back," Earl said, trying to placate his friend. He surely didn't want to be on the wrong side of an argument with Zoe at any time. He wondered how Eva handled this fiery young woman. "Is she at the doc's today?"

"Are you kidding? It would be easier for me to fly than to get Eva to go and see a doctor willingly," Zoe muttered as she sat down.

Earl smiled. Zoe's usual sunny personality was buried today due to lack of sleep and her worry about Eva. Zoe looked up and caught him grinning at her. "What?"

"You're cute when you're pissed off."

Zoe broke into a half-hearted grin. "Oh, shut up and drink your tea." They each sipped their tea as the mid-morning sun lit up the small kitchen. "Are you sure she didn't tell you anything about her back?"

"Nope, nothing. We went to morning tea, and she kept yawning. She told she was tired because you both were up late, but she didn't tell me her back hurt."

"If she wasn't hurting so much I would smack her," Zoe muttered into her tea.

"Ooh, sounds kinky," Earl replied and got a smack on the head for it. He winked at Zoe, and they both chuckled.

"So, why are you here again?" Zoe asked after a few minutes.

"I need to find Eva."

"Why? She's off sick. They do allow her to take sick days, don't they?" Earl nodded. "So what's the problem?

"No one knew she was taking a sick day."

"Huh? Didn't Eva call in?"

Earl shook his head. "I don't know. Jack came up to me and asked me where she was, and I said I didn't know," Earl replied, not telling Zoe about the rude remarks Jack made in addition to asking him where Eva was. "I had a half day today, so here I am, in search of my missing best mate."

"Tell Jack to shove his job up his arse."

"Zoe, I love it when you talk dirty," Earl said and ruffled Zoe's already disheveled hair. "Come on, so where is Eva?"

Zoe sighed at Earl's persistence. "She's gone to the Immigration Department with her stepmother to apply for a translator job."

"Hey, that's great, Zoe," Earl exclaimed. He had been urging Eva to find another job ever since they had become good friends. "So, what's the old lady like?"

"She's nice. We had a great time last night. She's a nurse, and she sure tells funny stories about some of her patients." Zoe tried to stifle another yawn. "I like her."

"What does Eva think of her?"

"Eva likes her, too. You know Eva, she takes a bit of time to warm up to strangers, but Mum..."

"Who? Mum?" Earl gently teased.

Zoe slapped his arm as Earl chuckled. "Mum put her at ease and got her talking, which I must say was quite a challenge last night. Father H was his usual funny self. Eva called Mrs. J over, and Father H talked to her about the flat downstairs." A knock sounded at the door just as she finished speaking. "What is it around here today? Central?" Zoe grumbled and walked over to open the door, finding Elena standing with her dresses in her hand.

"Morning, sunshine! I need your advice," Elena said as she came in. She caught sight of Earl and waved. "Hey, big guy, how's Davey?"

"Morning, El. Davey has gone bush for a few days."

"How come? Can't stand you any more?" Elena joked with the big man. She loved Earl like a brother and had spent quite some time with him and Davey. "Hey, you look a bit rough," she said to Zoe. "Saw Eva this morning, told me not to wake you until eleven a.m."

"It's not eleven a.m. yet," Zoe grumbled as she looked at the clock on the wall.

"You are such a grouch in the morning. Earl's here, so I thought it was safe to knock." Elena held up the two dresses to display them. "I can't decide...do I wear the blue or the red?"

"Didn't we have this conversation at the shops?" Zoe asked her friend.

"We did, but you didn't give me an answer."

"I dunno, ask Wiggy," Zoe mumbled and walked back into the bedroom to change. When she had dressed and combed her hair, she came back outside to find Earl trying to teach Elena how to dance. She stood and grinned at her two friends, a huge man and a tiny young woman, attempting to waltz.

****

The Immigration Office was full of people waiting their turn. The various chairs were all occupied as the queues were going at a snail's pace. Eva sat with her stepmother on two very uncomfortable wooden chairs, awaiting their interview.

"How's the back?" Alberta asked, already knowing the answer since Eva kept shifting to find a comfortable position.

"Aches a bit, but not as bad as last night," Eva replied.

"How did you hurt it initially?"

Eva sat silent for a moment, not sure what to reveal about herself. Out of respect for her stepmother, though, she decided to let a little of her past surface. "I was beaten by my stepfather."

"Oh," Alberta said quietly. "I'm very sorry to hear that."

"Dad didn't tell you?" Eva asked shyly. She wasn't sure what her father had told his wife about them.

"No, he told me you and Zoe had gone through some very rough times with your stepfather, but he didn't tell me any specifics. It's okay, Eva, that's a private thing between you and your father."

Eva wasn't surprised to find out her father told Alberta about their time in Greece, but was grateful that he didn't reveal too much. Eva liked Alberta a great deal, but she also liked her privacy. "It's a long story," Eva said quietly

"Well, after we finish here, we can go and have some lunch and talk if you'd like," Alberta offered.

"I would like that," Eva said and smiled shyly at the older woman.

"Miss Eva Harlambis?" a middle aged man asked aloud as he called Eva to her interview. Eva shook her head as her surname was once again butchered.

As the stepdaughter walked after the short balding man, she turned and gave her stepmother a grin.

****

Erik Rhimes was not in a good mood. He had spent the morning trying to get in touch with his contact in the Investigations Bureau. He had been told not to contact the man unless it was extremely urgent, but he thought that this was urgent. Having had no luck in locating the man, he had decided to go back home. He watched dourly as several trains sped past him. He had just missed his train and there would be a long wait until he could get another. He sat down on the hard bench and lit a cigarette.

"Looking for me, Herr Rhimes?"

Rhimes jumped as he turned to the voice. Marko stood with his hands in his pockets and grinned. He was a middle-aged man with thin graying hair, of middling height, and sporting a thin mustache. It was the ridiculous mustache that made him look quite comical, Rhimes thought. Rhimes disliked the man, but he would deal with the devil himself if it meant his safety and that of his friends.

"Where have you been? I've been trying to contact you."

"My day off today. Thought I would take a leisurely walk. It's quite fortuitous I ran into you, isn't it?" Marko asked as he sat next to Rhimes on the bench.

Rhimes looked at him and frowned. "What do you have for me?"

"Well, from reading her file, I would say you are in a heap of trouble," Marko answered, taking out a cigarette of his own and lighting it. He took a drag and exhaled the smoke, watching it as it drifted up.

Rhimes tried to control his temper with the man. "Do you have a copy of the file?"

"You know that's against the law, Herr Rhimes," Marko replied with a smirk.

Rhimes closed his eyes and counted until his temper was under control. He couldn't afford to kill this idiot, not until he had what he wanted. "How much is this going to cost me?"

"I have a figure in my head. Maybe we can get some coffee and discuss it."

"Fine, whatever. Lead the way."

Rhimes followed the man from the subway and across the street into a coffee house. Marko led him to the end table and sat down. He waited until the waitress took their order before reaching into to his pocket and retrieving a piece of paper. "Before we discuss our little business transaction, why is this woman so important?"

"None of your business, Mr. Berckett. I paid you well for the information you have supplied to us, but I don't think it's in your best interests to ask so many questions."

Marko still retained the little smirk on his face as the waitress came back with their order. "Herr Rhimes, I have something you want desperately, and I can't figure out why. Was she your mistress or something?" Marko chuckled at the thought of Rhimes being together with the young woman that he saw a photo of in the file.

Rhimes refused to rise to the bait and his patience was wearing thin. "No."

"Okay, so you don't want to discuss it. How about we discuss how you will make me a happy man, and then I can make you a happy man. How does that sound?"

"Fine," Rhimes spat out.

"I'm assuming you don't have this much on you?" Berckett asked as he handed Rhimes a note.

Rhimes' eyes bulged at the number written on the piece of paper. "No, I don't carry that kind of change on me," he verified and handed the note back.

"A Nazi with a sense of humour." Berckett chuckled, and watched Rhimes over the top of his coffee cup as he took a sip. "How about I meet you someplace, and then we can exchange gifts."

Rhimes sighed. He would indeed give Mr. Berckett a gift, but he doubted the man would enjoy it. He needed that file, so he would deal with the devil and hope he wasn't going to burn in hell for it. "Fine." Rhimes took out his pen from his jacket pocket, scribbled an address on the napkin, then folded it and gave it to Berckett. "Meet me there at 7 p.m. tonight. I will have your gift."

"Excellent. It's been good doing business with you, Herr Rhimes," Berckett said as he got up and left the coffee shop, leaving Rhimes alone with his coffee.

"Indeed," Rhimes said and shook his head.

Chapter 10

The interviews had gone on for a hour or so, then they had undergone the physical examination which was compulsory for all Australian public servants. She had waited patiently in the busy public waiting area for Eva to finish, and finally caught sight of the familiar tall young woman. She watched as Eva shook hands with her interviewer and walked towards her with a grin. Alberta was quite pleased with herself. She had been accepted into the service, and now she would have her stepdaughter with her also. She couldn't wait to tell her husband. Alberta shielded her eyes from the sun's glare as they left the Immigration Department building. "How did it go?" she asked as they crossed the road.

"It went well. He brought in a couple of translators to test me on the languages I know, which was quite a surprise. The physical was a bit on the achy side."

"Why?" Alberta asked. Her physical went quickly and smoothly.

"The doctor prodded my back a bit. He said my duties didn't involve lifting or anything that would aggravate my back problem, so he didn't see it as a cause for rejecting my application."

"That's good...isn't it?" she asked her stepdaughter.

"Oh, that's very good! I don't mind not lifting heavy boxes or working night shifts," Eva replied with a chuckle. "Zoe is going to be so happy that I'm quitting the factory."

Alberta held the door open as they entered the tea house. She had discovered it on one of her explorations of the city. A waiter showed them to a little corner of the room where they were seated at a table with quite comfortable seats and offered the menu. The tea house was nearly empty since their lunch hour rush had finished.

"Can we please have some water?" Alberta asked the young man, who nodded and went to fill her request. She pulled out a packet of aspirin and took out two of the pills. "Now I want you to take these with the water," she said, as the waiter brought them two glasses. "Those hard chairs gave me a backache, so I can't imagine what you're feeling like."

Eva smiled at her stepmother. Her back was aching a little, and she had forgotten to take her painkillers when she left home. She accepted the aspirin and swallowed them down with the water. "Thank you, Ally. That's sweet of you."

Alberta grinned. "Nothing sweet about it. If I returned you to Zoe with another backache, she might be a little miffed that I didn't take care of you."

Eva chuckled. "I like you."

Alberta's grin widened. Pany had told her that Eva would need some time to get to know a new person, and that it took a great deal of trust for her to open up and accept anyone into her life. "Thank you, I like you as well. Your father told me so much about you before we came, it's almost as if I've known you all my life. I hope we can become very good friends, Eva."

"I would like that," Eva agreed shyly.

Alberta's brown eyes twinkled as she watched Eva look at her menu, the tip of her tongue sticking out as she tried to decide what to eat. "Did they tell you where you'll be working?"

"George Street Immigration Centre. They had enough Greek translators, but they didn't have many for Italian and German."

"Excellent! That's where I'll be as well. I thought I would be going to the Circular Quay office, but I'm so glad we'll be working together." She took a sip of her water and gave Eva a more serious look. "Your father was going to speak to Mrs. Jenkins today about the flat downstairs from you. Does it bother you that we might live so close?"

Eva looked surprised at the question. She wanted them close. She had missed having family nearby. She loved Zoe a great deal, but also wanted to have her father and stepmother around. They would feel like a real family again. "No. I would love it. I know Zoe would like that as well. I haven't had much family around since my mother died. I've missed it."

Alberta wasn't surprised, but she was pleased that Eva's response had been so enthusiastic. She knew her husband wanted to be near his daughters, so that arrangement had worked out really well. She wasn't sure what she would have done if there had been a problem. The waiter came back to take their orders and as he walked away, Alberta looked at Eva. "How old were you when your mother passed away?"

Eva looked down at her menu. "She died before my eighteenth birthday, the ninth of November, 1938."

Alberta was shocked. A tragic event on what should have been a joyous occasion for the young girl. "I'm so sorry. If you don't want to talk about it..."

"No, that's okay. She was killed by someone who thought she was a Jewess on the Night of Broken Glass. I think that night was a turning point in my life."

Alberta nodded. She knew about that infamous night. She had huddled beside the radio listening to news reports which made her sick to her stomach. She also heard a firsthand account from a Jewish family that had fled Germany with only the clothes on their backs. Their shop was destroyed and all the hard work they had put in to build up the thriving grocery had gone up in flames.

"I heard stories about that night. Tragic," Alberta replied.

Eva grimaced and kept her head down, staring at the menu. "I participated in it," she mumbled. She was quite sure with that revelation, her stepmother would be disgusted and not be so quick to like her. She was still disgusted with herself for participating in Germany's night of shame and the start of a nightmare for many Jews.

Alberta sat watching Eva with a sad smile on her face. The obvious self-loathing Eva was showing made the older woman want to hold her. She knew that all the young people were forced to belong to the Hitler Youth, and as the daughter of an army captain, she didn't have a choice. "How did you participate?"

Eva continued to hang her head. "I went with my friends, and we burnt down a synagogue," she whispered.

Alberta nodded at the waiter who had returned with their order and waited until he had left. She sat looking at the young woman. "You didn't...?" She left the question hanging.

Eva looked up, unshed tears glistened in her eyes. "I was a coward, Ally. I did nothing to save the rabbi or the synagogue. I'm as much a killer as if I had dealt the blows or lit the fire."

Alberta took Eva's hands and held them tight. "Oh, sweet child, you aren't a coward. We all do things that in hindsight would seem to be extremely wrong. But you have to think of what you were like when you were eighteen, and not look at the past through the eyes of a twenty-six year old. The woman I see before me is gentle, kind, and loving. I don't think that eighteen year old Eva would have been any different. But the eighteen year old young woman was doing what her peers wanted her to do."

Eva sniffed. "If I had not gone with my friends, my mother would still be alive," she said quietly.

"Eva, look at me for a moment." She lifted Eva's chin and brushed away the tears. "If you had been in the house, you would have been killed. I don't think you being at home would have stopped whoever killed your mother."

"I'm sorry," Eva said as she took out a handkerchief, wiping at her eyes and blowing her nose. "I haven't talked about my mother for a long time." Eva took a deep breath and took a sip of her tea.

"You have nothing to be sorry about," Alberta said as she scooted her chair over and gave the younger woman a hug. "You're not responsible for your mother's death."

"My stepfather thought so," Eva whispered.

Alberta's heart broke as she watched Eva try to deal with memories that were obviously still painful. She wished she had an aspirin to fix those as well. "Is that when you hurt your back?"

Eva nodded. "He beat me," she sighed. "He didn't care that I was out on Kristallnacht, but he found out that I was a lesbian that night as well. It didn't sit well with him that a German officer would have a deviant for a daughter," she said bitterly.

"Eva, you are not a deviant. Anyone who loves as much as you do isn't wrong."

Eva smiled grimly and wiped away an errant tear. "Not many people think like you do, Ally."

Alberta sighed. It was true that many people saw homosexuals as sick individuals, but she couldn't find it in her heart to hate someone because they chose to love another person of the same gender. It was abhorrent to her to think that a God of love would be so cruel as to hate and condemn a soul that loved another. "Eva, my Bible tells me that God is love, therefore I choose to believe that all love between consenting adults is right in His eyes. You love Zoe, and you were willing to travel to the other side of the world to make her happy. You provide for her. You were willing to work in a factory to support her. There is absolutely nothing wrong in that. I know Zoe loves you, too. Her eyes light up like Christmas lights when you're around."

Eva smiled. "Zoe was my saving grace. She saved my life."

"I'm sure Zoe would say the same thing about you," Alberta replied and gently brushed away Eva's bangs. "That young woman worships you. I've only just met you both, but I could easily see the love she has for you."

"I never thought I could love anyone so much," Eva whispered.

"I know. When I met your father, I thought I knew love, but getting to know him and being with him gave me a new understanding. How did you meet that little minx, anyway?" Alberta asked, wanting to steer the conversation back to a happier topic.

Eva chuckled. "Never get Zoe mad." They both laughed as Eva went on to relate how Father Haralambos suggested Zoe be hired as her maid and general assistant. Alberta laughed with the young woman as she was regaled with Zoe's antics.

****

Zoe was slumped on the sofa, her feet up on the armrest as she found a comfortable position to listen to Benny Goodman. She enjoyed listening to his music and closed her eyes to let it wash over her. As the song ended, she glanced up at the clock and wondered when Eva was going to be home. As if on cue, the door opened and her partner walked through with some shopping bags in hand, followed by Alberta. Zoe jumped up and ran the few steps to greet her wife. "Hey, you're back! How did it go?" Zoe asked expectantly as she wrapped herself around her partner.

Eva grinned as she tried to hold both Zoe and the grocery bags. "We both made it."

Zoe squealed with delight and kissed Eva in celebration. "Thanks, Mum!"

Alberta beamed at the young woman. "My pleasure, Zoe."

"So, did you behave yourself?" Zoe asked as Eva attempted to put the shopping bags down. "How's your back?"

"Fine. And I always behave myself," Eva replied with a grin.

Zoe snorted. "Oh yeah, like the time..." Her story was cut short by the arrival of Mrs. Jenkins and Panayiotis at the still open door. Eva let go of Zoe as soon as she noticed Mrs. Jenkins, and went over to the sofa.

Alberta watched the little interplay and wondered what was going on, when moments before the two were attached to each other like Siamese twins.

"Elise, I would like you to meet my wife, Alberta," Panayiotis introduced her to Mrs. Jenkins, who had taken an instant liking to the older man. Zoe's eyes went wide at the mention of their landlady's first name by her father-in-law. She rolled her eyes when Mrs. Jenkins began to sing the praises of Greeks and their way of life.

"So, Eva, you're going to get new neighbours!" Mrs. Jenkins exclaimed. She positively adored the older man who had been so charming and flattering. She could easily see where the taller young woman got her dark looks from. They talked for a short while until Mrs. Jenkins had to leave. They watched her waddle down the hallway before she suddenly stopped and headed back. "Oh, Eva, I nearly forgot. Harry told me to tell you that he will be by at 7:00 p.m. tomorrow for the dance." She waved again and waddled off.

"Who's Harry?" Alberta asked.

"Eva's boyfriend," Panayiotis replied and watched as his wife's eyes went round.

"I'm confused," Alberta admitted and watched as Zoe began to put the shopping away. The young woman had gone very quiet as she walked into the kitchen.

"Dad, I think Zoe is a bit sensitive about Harry," Eva admonished as she walked past her father and into the kitchen to unruffle some feathers. She stood in the doorway, watching, as Zoe put the shopping away. "Hi, safe to come in?" Eva asked.

Zoe looked up and smiled. "Why wouldn't it be?"

"You had your pouty face on," Eva replied, stopping Zoe from putting away any more of the groceries and gathering her in a hug.

"I don't have a pouty face," Zoe argued, then grinned.

"Yes, you do. It's usually followed by your look at my woman the wrong way again and I'll deck you face," Eva joked which got Zoe giggling. "Want to come with me to the factory to hand in my resignation?"

"You bet. Can I tell Jack where to shove his job?"

Eva shook her head. "No. Jack could make life difficult for Earl if you do that."

"Boofhead. I had this all planned out. We were going to go down there and tell him to shove the job right up his arse," Zoe muttered.

Eva chuckled. "Nope. Sorry, Zoe, can't do that. Come on, let's go back out before Ally and Dad think we don't like them."

She held the younger woman's hand as she led her back to the living room.

****

The traffic noise hit them as they jumped off the tram. Eva took Zoe's hand and led her through the afternoon crowds towards the factory. Eva held the resignation letter in her hand. As they entered the building, they were overwhelmed by the oppressive heat and noise.

Zoe frowned. “I hate this place,” she muttered as they walked through to the main office. A moment later, she saw Jack round a corner, heading straight for them. “Oh, shit.”

“Well, well, well. If it isn’t Miss I-Hurt-My-Back. What happened, Eva? Did Earl get a bit too energetic for you?” He laughed at his own joke.

Zoe was fuming as she stood next to Eva, who kept a calm expression on her face. She handed the resignation letter to Zoe to hold and took a step forward. Eva was an inch taller than her former supervisor, and she stepped right up into his face.

Eva grinned. “Tell you a secret, Jack.”

“Yeah?”

“Sex with Earl is mind blowing. You know, the first time we did it, I couldn’t walk for hours. Maybe if you ask him nicely, he might show you how to love a real woman instead of the plastic models you’re used to.” She smirked as she patted his cheek and walked off, leaving him slack jawed.

Zoe grinned as she watched her wife walk into the office. “She’s right, Jack. You could use a good lay,” she whispered to him as she walked past, following Eva into the office and chuckling at his expression.

****

Hans Muller sat on the sofa and watched as Rhimes looked at the clock and paced. He had been watching his friend for over an hour as he wore a path in the carpet.

“You can’t do it here.”

“Why not?”

“You’re going to get blood on the carpet and Mrs. Neiler will be upset,” Muller replied with a grin.

Rhimes grinned back at him, despite the seriousness of the situation.

"Hans is right, Erik. Mrs. Neiler is none too happy if we just get beer on the carpet," Klaus piped up from the corner, waving the gun he was cleaning.

The knock on the door prevented Rhimes from replying as he pulled out his gun and looked through the spyhole on the door. He unlocked the door when he saw Marko Berckett outside and quickly ushered the janitor inside.

"Gentlemen, I'm pleased to meet you."

Klaus grunted and continued to clean his weapon. Muller nodded as Berckett sat down. "So, do you have what I asked for?"

"It all depends. Do you have the file?" Rhimes asked.

Berckett smiled as he produced a file from his briefcase and handed it to Rhimes, who flipped through it. He handed the file to Hans. "Well?" Berckett asked. He was getting a nervous twitch as he looked at Muller's scarred face, watching him read.

"The bitch is alive. That's her," Muller muttered as he stared at the photograph of his stepdaughter.

"Does that mean I get my money?"

"You're going to get something better," Rhimes said as he sat down next to the janitor.

"W..what?" Berckett stammered.

"Actually, I'm going to give you a choice," Rhimes replied as he pulled out his weapon and held it to Berckett's head. As the man looked at Rhimes, his face went a pasty white. "Okay, choice number one is that I kill you here."

"Mrs. Neiler doesn't like blood on the carpet," Klaus muttered from the corner.

"Bb..blood..on the ca..carpet?" Berckett stammered as he soiled himself.

Muller looked down at the puddle with disgust. "She doesn't like that, either." They were toying with the man, who had by now realised he had walked into a trap and probably wasn't going to come out alive. "Choice number two would be for Klaus to take you on a nice scenic trip to the Blue Mountains. Would you like that?" Rhimes asked, still holding the gun to the man's temple. "Since Mrs. Neiler isn't going to be happy with us getting blood on the carpet, I think option number two is best, don't you?" He looked over at the man cleaning his gun in the corner of the room. "Klaus, please escort Mr. Berckett out."

Klaus was a mountain of a man, and as he stood up to his full height of 6'5", Berckett's eyebrows shot up. He towered over the short janitor and grabbed him roughly by the arm.

"Oh, before I forget. Thank you so much for the file," Rhimes said pleasantly as he watched Klaus and Berckett exit.

Chapter 11

The sun filtered into the bedroom, causing Zoe to open her eyes and then shut them again at the bright light. She had left the curtains open, much to her disgust. She wanted to sleep in and cuddle with Eva. She was going to spoil her wife today. That was the plan.

She cuddled closer to the sleeping woman beside her, and rested her head on her arm to watch Eva sleep. A smile played on Eva's slightly parted lips which caused Zoe to grin. They had spent a tender and loving time together last night. After Zoe had finished with a light back massage, she surprised Eva when she began a very slow exploration down her back with feather light kisses and caresses. Eva normally took charge during their lovemaking, but Zoe had decided it was time to reverse that a little and pamper her lover. Zoe's grin widened at the memory of the happy little grin her wife usually wore right after what Zoe called "all the bells and whistles going off."

She loved to watch Eva's face as she slept, and lightly traced her wife's high cheekbones, smiling as Eva stirred at her touch and slowly opened sleepy blue eyes. Zoe smiled as those eyes gazed at her.

"Hi." Eva said in a rough, sleepy voice.

Zoe replied with a soft, but passionate kiss, which woke her partner right up. "Hi, how's your back?"

"Back? Oh...no back pain," Eva replied, scooping up Zoe to pull her close. "I think you found a cure to my back problems."

Zoe chuckled. "Dr. Zoe to the rescue. You're staying in bed today."

"Can't. I have to..."

Zoe leaned back to face Eva with a scowl. "You most certainly are. Well, at least for the morning. It's Saturday, and that means you have a day off. So I'm going to pamper you," she said and nuzzled her partner's neck. "And, you're going to enjoy it," she finished, then kissed Eva passionately, as if to emphasize her words.

Eva smirked when they finished the kiss. She didn't have the luxury of sleeping in on most days, and the last couple of months had been tiring, especially with the increased hours she spent at work. She hated the night shifts which took her away from Zoe, and she knew Zoe felt very alone not having her there during the nighttime hours. She doubted that the translating section of the Immigration Department worked night shifts. "Okay," Eva said to the serious face still hovering above her.

Zoe was taken aback. She had expected Eva to offer at least some resistance. "Who are you, and what have you done with my wife?" she asked playfully, then raised up on an elbow and brushed a stray, sleep-tousled lock of hair off Eva's forehead. Zoe leaned down to give Eva a soft kiss, then raised back up to look at her with gentled eyes. "You need to rest, love. All this work is really stressing you out. I hate it when you come home and you're just so tired. I hated it when Jack treated you like a pack mule. I hate it when your back hurts, because when you hurt, I hurt," she said as she caressed Eva's cheek. "I love you so much."

A tear escaped and slowly tracked down Eva's face. "I love you, too, Zoe."

Zoe gently wiped away the tear. "Hey, I didn't mean for you to cry. I just want you to relax today. I'll make you the nicest, juiciest, biggest breakfast, and then I'll give you another massage..."

"But, my back doesn't hurt," Eva interjected.

"Who said anything about your back hurting?" Zoe replied in a sultry voice with a smirk. "I read about some new relaxation techniques that involve a lot of kissing," she said leaning down and again kissing Eva's sweet lips, "lots of exploration of skin," and nuzzling Eva's neck while sneaking her free hand down to gently rub circles over the flat stomach below her, eliciting a little moan from her partner, "and lots and lots of loving," she finished, and moved up for a long sensuous moment of exploring her wife's lips while her fingers continued to stroke fire over Eva's belly.

"Oh, I like that," Eva said a little breathlessly.

Zoe grinned as she watched Eva close her eyes and sigh contently. "Then that's settled, you stay here all nice and relaxed," Zoe told her, and gave her a quick kiss before scooting out of bed.

Eva watched as Zoe picked up her robe, put her slippers on, and padded out to the kitchen. She smiled. "Whatever I did to deserve her, thank you," she said as she gazed up at the ceiling.

****

They spent the morning eating breakfast in bed while Zoe read the paper to Eva, then spent a long time exploring Zoe's new relaxation techniques. By the time the afternoon rolled around, they were both quite relaxed and enjoying their day together. It was mid afternoon when they heard a knock, and Zoe padded to the door as she put on her robe. She opened the door to Elena standing there all dressed up, ready for the dance.

"El, why are you dressed already?"

"I was nervous," Elena said as she came in. She frowned when she saw both Zoe and Eva in bathrobes. She shook her head at them.

"What's the matter, El?" Zoe asked and she gave her friend a smirk.

"Nothing," Elena replied, moving to the sofa. She was too nervous to joke with her friends. Earlier, she had tried on six different dresses, and nothing was right.

Eva gave Zoe a grin and sat next to Elena. "You're nervous."

"Does it show?"

"Not too much," Eva replied with a grin. She got up from the sofa and padded into the bedroom, reappearing a few moments later dressed in tan shorts and a T-shirt.

Zoe came out of the kitchen and whistled at the sight of her wife's long legs. "Nice view. Where are you off to?" she asked as she gave Elena an orange juice.

"I thought I would take a walk, get some exercise," Eva replied, tying the laces of her gym shoes.

"Didn't get enough exercise this morning, huh?" Zoe teased as she followed Eva to the door and kissed her. Elena spluttered, spilling her orange juice, and began coughing.

"You okay, El?" Zoe asked, turning to pat her on the back.

Eva shook her head and reached over to give Zoe a quick kiss before leaving.

Zoe watched the door close and sat down next to her friend.

"Hey Zo, can I ask you a question?"

"Sure."

"It's a bit personal."

"Okay."

"What is it like with Eva? I mean were you...um..." Elena stammered. She had never discussed sex with Zoe and had never even broached the subject before. "I mean...were you a virgin when you...um..."

Zoe watched with fascination, seeing her usually cool and very confident friend being uncharacteristically shy. "Was I a virgin? Back in Greece?"

"Yeah," Elena said as she took a gulp of her remaining orange juice.

"Yes, I was. Eva was my first lover, and my last," Zoe replied and smiled.

"Um...were you nervous about...you know...doing it?"

"You mean having sex?" Zoe teased her friend and got a chagrined look back. "Sorry, El, I don't usually talk about sex with you, and it's a little unsettling. Okay, I'll get serious. Was I nervous?" Zoe thought back to the night that they first expressed their love for each other. She had been angry with

Father Haralambos and that stupid train, and had run off in the rain, gotten soaked to the skin, and was thoroughly miserable until Eva showed up and took her up to her room and began to remove the wet clothes.

****

Zoe started to unbutton her blouse, but Eva pushed her hand away. "We can't have you catching a cold after..." Zoe looked up for the first time and saw the sheepish grin on Eva's face, "...all, uh, can we?" Not sure how to interpret Zoe's expression, Eva stepped to the side and retrieved a blanket.

"This is very romantic, isn't it? Somehow I didn't think it would be quite like this...me being wet, cold, and covered in mud, Despina yelling at me..." Zoe teased as she tossed her blouse to the floor, her shyness about revealing her own body forgotten. She looked up into blue eyes, losing herself in their depths.

Eva smiled. "You were thinking about it...about me?" she asked, and placed the blanket around her friend's shoulders.

Zoe blushed. "Well...um...not all the time I mean...oh, hell, I don't know what I mean," she groaned, and let herself fall into Eva's embrace, listening to her chuckle. Zoe looked back up into Eva's eyes, which made her forget what she was going to say.

Eva herself was just beginning to admit to her feelings for this teenaged girl, really a young woman, who was wrapped in her arms. She had resisted her feelings for so long. Didn't want to get involved with anyone. She had cut herself off and maintained that icy exterior. She had built the walls around her heart to prevent anyone from hurting her again, and to stay safe from her father. She had managed to stay remote and aloof, until the day she had met this young woman. Zoe had gone in and begun to break down the walls she had worked so hard at building.

They held on to each other for a few more moments. Zoe was quite content to stay where she was, and realised she wasn't cold anymore. I wouldn't mind staying in her arms forever, *Zoe thought to herself, as Eva wrapped the blanket around her tightly. "Eva... I..I've never fallen in love with a woman before...I've never even been in love before," Zoe said softly, finally admitting her feelings out loud. She hoped Eva felt the same way.*

"Well, that's...What did you say?" Eva suddenly realised what Zoe had just said. Eva never thought she would hear those words again. Nor dared to think of saying them herself.

"I've fallen in love with you," Zoe repeated softly, looking into eyes that reminded her of the Aegean. "This is all new to me. I've never felt for anyone the way I feel for you."

"Maybe we..." Eva said hesitantly. She wanted to believe what Zoe was telling her, wanted so much to feel that finally she could love again.

"When I said you weren't going to be alone, I meant it, Eva Muller. I just said I was new at this, and, well, you're just going to have to show me."

"You surprised me, Zoe," Eva said quietly as she gazed at the blanket-covered woman. Her chestnut coloured hair was matted with mud, but eyes that shone brightly looked up at Eva with emotions that Eva thought she would never again see directed at her.

"Oh? How so?" Zoe asked as she looked at her friend. She cocked her head sideways and watched

the now fidgeting woman that held her.

"When I told you about Greta," Eva said, looking down at Zoe.

"I didn't freak out, is that it?"

Eva nodded. She wasn't sure what would happen when she revealed her love for another woman to Zoe. She couldn't believe it had only been a little over a week since she had confided in the younger woman. She remembered how Zoe held her as she told of her pain, and the regular beatings her father inflicted to get her "perversion" out of her. The beatings she endured at the hands of her uncle on orders from her father. The shame of being berated by her aunt. The rapes by her uncle's friends as he tried to find her the "right man for the job."

They spent the night talking. It felt good to be able to tell someone the whole truth. She had revealed a little of what she went through to Father Haralambos, but not the full story. She didn't think she could voice her deep pain, and she never could, until Zoe came into her life. She had to make certain that Zoe knew where they were headed. She owed her that much.

"Why should I freak out? You were hurting, and you needed a friend so badly," Zoe said quietly, looking into Eva's eyes.

"You are special, very special, to me," Eva quietly said, and, cupping Zoe's face in her hands, she slowly leaned over, pressing her lips to Zoe's. Gently at first, so as to explore the sweetness of this young woman, Eva slowly became more aggressive until she could feel the excited response from Zoe and sought to quench her desire.

"Oh, boy!" Zoe exclaimed as they parted.

"Good or bad?" Eva asked.

"Oh, good! Better than good!" Zoe exclaimed as

they shared another kiss. "Much better than when Tasos kissed me."

Eva looked down at her and her brows furrowed together which caused Zoe to start laughing. "Are you jealous, Fraulein Muller?" Zoe asked with a grin.

"No...I mean...yes...how...when did you kiss Tasos?"

"Let's see, now." Zoe pretended as if she was trying to remember, then smiled up at her friend. "I was twelve years old, and it happened at the back of the chicken shed. Very sloppy kissing." She laughed. "My brother, Mihali, came out and stopped us. He told me that if I kissed a boy, I would have a baby." They both laughed as Zoe continued, "Which I believed, and I never kissed anyone again!"

Eva looked down her own tall frame. "Well, I'm not a boy, so I can't get you pregnant."

Zoe looked Eva up and down. "You certainly are not *a boy."*

They looked at each other. Eva frowned. "You know, this can be very dangerous for you." The thought of her father laying a hand on Zoe made her angry and fearful. She could withstand his beatings again if she had to, but not Zoe.

"For me? What about you?" the young woman asked, wrapping the blanket around the older woman as well.

"He'll hurt you if he finds out. I don't want to see you going through what I've been through. You are a very gentle soul, Zoe, and if it means we can't take this further..."

"And you are a hard bitten Nazi, right? How do you feel about me, Eva?" Zoe's eyes narrowed.

"I love you, Zoe, but I don't want to put you in danger. I don't want to see you hurting."

Zoe sighed with frustration. She reached up and

tenderly caressed Eva's cheek. "Eva, you may not have noticed this, but we are in a war. I'm in danger merely walking down the street. I can get shot just for looking at a solder the wrong way."

"My father..."

"Your father is an abusive man, who hurt you physically and mentally just for loving someone. Father Haralambos told me that when we find love, we should accept it. We don't question it, we don't deny it."

"Father Haralambos said that?" Eva asked.

"Yes, he did. I don't think he was speaking about us, but I do know how I feel about you. My brother described it once as Heavy Like." Zoe chuckled as she remembered her older brother describing his feelings for his latest girlfriend. Zoe stopped and mimicked her older brother. "He said, 'Zoe, there are three stages to a relationship—Like, Heavy Like, and Deep Love. I'm in the second stage, Heavy Like. When I get to stage three you can shoot me, because I'll be useless'," she chuckled quietly. "So, I'm in stage two, and I think there isn't any cure to stop it from going to level three." She grinned up at Eva. "I wouldn't want to be cured."

At that, Eva leaned down and softly kissed her again.

****

"Hello...Zoe...come back to me, please!" Elena said as she waved her hand in front of her friend's face.

Zoe blushed. "Sorry. I was just thinking."

"I'm sure. You had that goofy grin on your face."

Zoe smiled. "What's the question again?"

Elena sighed. "Were you nervous about having sex with Eva?"

"Oh, right. Doing it," Zoe teased her friend. They chuckled and Elena gave an exaggerated sigh. "Yeah, I was nervous. I hadn't really even kissed anyone before, that doesn't count Tasos.."

"Who's Tasos?"

"A boy I kissed at the back of a chicken shed."

Elena chuckled and waited for Zoe to continue, watching as her gaze focused on the past once more.

"She had the softest lips," Zoe said, smiling at the memory of Eva's gentle kiss when they finally told each other how they felt.

"Too much information there," Elena said with a grin.

"Oh, okay. But, she does," Zoe teased, then got serious. "I was very nervous. After I had my bath we talked for a long time, just cuddling and kissing until I felt ready."

"What's it like?"

"I...don't know what it's like with a man, El. With Eva, she's gentle and loving," Zoe replied. "You haven't gone to bed with Friedrich yet, have you?"

"Not yet," Elena replied, giving Zoe a grin. "We've talked on the phone a few times. It's easier for him to talk when he doesn't have to face me, I think."

"That could be a problem when you two want to kiss," Zoe said with a mock frown. "You could invent phone sex. You know, he gets all hot and sweaty talking to you."

Elena laughed. "I don't think Friedrich would like phone sex."

"I'm amazed he can even talk to you on the phone," Zoe chuckled, remembering the stammering young man they had encountered at the coffee shop.

"He really is the sweetest man," Elena said with a dreamy look in her eye.

"You have got it bad, El," Zoe said as she pulled her friend up from the sofa. "Come on and let's find you a different dress, since you can't even drink orange juice without spilling it." The two friends laughed as they walked out to go and get Elena a change of clothes. Zoe smiled to herself. She thanked God that Eva was her first lover. She knew she was spoiled.

Chapter 12

Zoe leaned on the doorframe and watched Eva as she dressed. A small smile played across her lips. Eva wore Zoe's favourite dress, an apricot rayon outfit with sequins and beaded trim. Eva hated shopping, but when Zoe caught sight of the dress she knew it was perfect for her wife, and Zoe was determined, almost dragging Eva into the store to try it on.

Eva looked up at the mirror and saw her watching. "How do I look?"

"Gorgeous," Zoe replied, moving over to give her a hug. Zoe had finished dressing herself moments before. She normally didn't wear dresses, but she finally—after hours of searching, and testing Eva's patience—agreed on a black silk, faille and white organdy dress with a dropped waist. Zoe would have preferred wearing pants with a suit, or even her favourite jeans.

"You look great, too," Eva said to the smaller woman holding her and kissing the top of Zoe's head. She smiled and pulled Zoe's body closer, smelling a subtle hint of perfume she assumed Elena convinced Zoe to wear.

Eva sighed, savoring the moment, and rested her head atop her partner's. "Thank you for today."

"I didn't do anything special, just got you to relax a bit," mumbled the smaller woman into her shoulder. "We can do my special relaxation techniques again tomorrow, if you like."

"Hmm...let me think on that," Eva replied and closed her eyes, then grinned. "Do you still have some more cherries?"

"Oh, yeah!" Zoe grinned as well, patting Eva's side. "Lots of them." She had found some new season cherries and fed them to Eva in bed in increasingly creative ways, until soon it had turned into a rather interesting, delightful game.

"You have yourself a deal," Eva said quietly and leaned back a little, cupping Zoe's face in her hands and tilting it up to gaze into her eyes. She slowly closed the distance, pressing her lips to Zoe's, gently at first, as she explored the sweetness of her wife. Eva's kisses slowly became more aggressive, until she could feel her partner's body start to melt into hers, and felt Zoe's arms slide around her neck, tangling fingers in her hair.

They both groaned when they heard the knock at the door. "I'm going to kill whoever is outside that door," a flushed Zoe muttered, as she followed Eva out of the bedroom.

Eva opened the door and a grinning Earl leaned casually against the frame, with his jacket draped over his shoulder. "Don't you look squish," Eva said as she looked at Earl, who wore a black tuxedo with a red bow tie.

"Of course," Earl said as he leaned down and gave his friend a kiss on the cheek and then spared one for a still red-faced and scowling Zoe, as well. "What's the matter with you?"

"Nothing a cold shower wouldn't fix," Zoe mumbled.

Earl chuckled as he took a seat to wait for his friends to finish dressing. Eva went back into the bedroom, followed by Zoe, who pinched Earl's cheek as she passed by. Earl half-whined an "ow!" and gave the retreating Zoe a mock glare. Zoe responded by sticking her tongue out at him just before disappearing into the bedroom. Earl chuckled and got up from the sofa, going over to check out a few of Zoe's new records.

"Where's your date?" Eva asked from the bedroom.

"I'm all alone tonight," he replied, and watched the two women exit the bedroom together. "You are looking at Mr. Security Man." He struck a Superman-like pose, which got Zoe giggling. He waggled his eyebrows back at her. "You clean up nice!" he teased Zoe, getting a hard poke in reply. "So, Miss Zoe, when do I meet this David Peterson?"

"Oh, um...David, yeah...well, he should be around soon. He's coming with Friedrich. That's Elena's date."

"And, Eva, of course, your date is...?"

Eva was about to answer when they heard another knock on the door. She opened it to find a young man in an Army uniform. His brown hair was slicked back, and his brown eyes crinkled when he smiled. He held a cane in his hand.

"Harry, you old dog!" Earl shouted and engulfed the surprised man in a bear hug.

Eva and Zoe stood together with a confused look on their faces.

"Earl Wiggins, dear God, man, it's been a long time!" Harry replied and returned the hug. They both turned to the two women with large grins.

"Eva, this is one of my oldest and dearest friends, Harold Jenkins," Earl said, and slapped himself on the head, realising that Harry was Mrs. Jenkins nephew. "I didn't know your aunt was Mrs. J! Harry, this is Eva Haralambos and this is Zoe Lambros—two of my best friends."

"You poor things, I'm sorry to hear that you have to put up with this man." Harry said and slapped his friend on the shoulder.

"Pleased to meet you, Mr. Jenkins," Eva said, ushering the men inside.

"Please, call me Harry. I don't think I can go through a dance with you calling me 'Mr. Jenkins.' I'm going to be looking around for my father."

Zoe liked the man who sat on the sofa, and she was quite taken with his charm. "You were in Greece during the war?"

"For a short time. I was captured by the krauts, but I did spend a month with a Greek family, who hid me from the patrols until I got unlucky and they caught me. When did you come back?" he turned and asked Earl. "You weren't in Europe?"

"No, mate, I was up the Kokoda track fighting the Japs," Earl replied.

Eva was aware that Earl had spent time in the Australian army, but they never really discussed it. Davey had told her he was in New Guinea during the war, and that it had been a tough time in the jungle, repelling a Japanese invasion force. They were the only defense standing in the way of a Japanese invasion of Australia. A small battalion of Australian soldiers withstood and beat back 2000 well-trained and battle-hardened Japanese soldiers. Davey was proud of his partner, but Earl didn't want to think, or talk, about his experiences.

"Oh, that was rough," Harry said quietly, knowing the sacrifices made and the men they had lost during that campaign.

"Yeah," Earl replied quietly, and they sat in silence for a few moments. "Okay, enough war stories! You're taking my best mate here out on a date. What are your intentions towards this lovely young woman?"

"Earl!" Eva said in mock outrage. Secretly, she loved the way he was looking out for her, like the big brother she never had.

"No, wait, I want to hear Harry's answer to this," Zoe interjected.

"Yeah, Harry, tell us."

Harry was bemused. "Well, let's see...some dancing, a little romancing, and..." he stopped when he saw Earl shake his head. "No dancing?"

"That's allowed."

"Okay...no romancing?" Harry muttered good-naturedly, "What am I going to do all night if I can't romance this gorgeous woman?"

"No romancing the shiela."

"Hey! I'm here, you know." Eva said as she cuffed him.

"Ow," Earl quietly moaned, "You're a dangerous woman."

"Believe it," Zoe said.

"Okay, I'm allowed to dance, but not to romance?" Harry asked as he looked between Earl and Zoe. Eva had sat back, and was watching the two people she loved the most try and act protective.

"Yep," Earl replied, nodding his head.

"Why?"

Earl smiled broadly. "Harry Jenkins, meet Eva's wife, Zoe." Eva and Zoe were both shocked at Earl, blurting out about their marriage to his friend. "You two look like your eyes are going to bulge out! Relax, possums. Harry was best man at my wedding."

"And what a wedding that turned out to be!" Harry slapped his friend on the back and laughed. "I don't think I could ever eat prawns again and not think of..." he stopped when he caught Earl's glare. "Okay, that's a story best left in the annals of history," he finished and gave his friend a smirk. He turned to the two women. "So I can't romance you, because your wife will kill me, right?"

"Yep!" Zoe piped up.

"Okay, how about dancing?"

"That's not a problem, but don't handle the merchandise," Zoe supplied as Eva lost her composure and laughed, hearing yet another person at the door.

She shook her head as she went to the door to answer it. She opened it to find a man with neatly combed blond hair and green eyes that held a touch of mischief, his attractiveness making Eva take an instant dislike to him. She had seen David Peterson's type before—men who thought they were irresistible to women.

David Peterson stood awkwardly, feeling Eva's blue eyes gaze at him as he played with the bouquet of flowers in his hands. "Um, is Zoe here? I'm David Peterson."

"Zoe, your date is here," Eva turned and called out.

Zoe arrived at the door and gave Eva a slap on the rear. "Behave yourself," she muttered. "Hi, David, come in," Zoe welcomed the blond man. She took him by the arm and brought him into the living room as she introduced everyone.

"Would you like to put those in some water?" Eva asked sweetly. Zoe turned and gave her a quizzical look, which Eva ignored on purpose as she gestured David to follow her. As soon as David entered the kitchen, Eva closed the door quietly and turned to the surprised man.

He wasn't expecting her to be attracted to him, but he imagined she did already see that he had some charm and wit. He cleared his throat and grinned, showing white, even teeth. Eva smiled sweetly at him. "Touch my wife tonight, and you die," Eva told him pleasantly as she stood inches away from him. "Understand what I'm saying?" The man simply nodded as he stood aside, and let Eva open the door and walk back out into the living room with the vase. He sighed. He was going to have a very boring night.

****

Muller was furious. He stared down at the photograph in his hand. Eva's smiling face looked back at him. The photo also showed a blond-haired man laughing and holding Eva closely.

"She doesn't look like a lesbian to me," Rhimes said, looking over Muller's shoulder.

"This is a fake," Muller muttered.

"Hans, why are you so quick to believe she is a lesbian? Who told you?"

"Reinhardt told me."

"Both times?" Rhimes asked his friend. Muller nodded.

"Could it be he simply didn't like being spurned?"

"No. When I confronted Eva with the accusations Reinhardt made, she didn't deny them."

"Was she conscious at the time?" Rhimes asked. He knew about the beating Muller had given his daughter, and it had shocked him. He hadn't known at the time why Muller had lost control, and he hadn't asked. Muller just called him and told him he needed a doctor to come to the house, and to get someone who would be quiet about what he saw.

Muller glared at him. "This is a fake. I know my own daughter, Erik."

"Not well enough, if she is a lesbian, my friend," he replied, softening his jibe. "What does the rest of the file say?" he asked as he picked up the folder. He looked through the statements and shook his head. "We need to get out of here." Muller sat with the picture in his hands, and his head down. "Hans, did you hear me?"

"Ja, I heard you."

"Well?"

"I want her dead," Muller replied, scrunching up the photograph.

"Hans, listen to me. They have enough evidence here to have us shot. They won't catch us if they can't find us...I'll get Klaus to..."

"No! I want to do it this time. I sent Reinhardt the last time, and the fool probably got himself killed. I need to do it myself," Muller insisted. His one arm was badly burned, but he was determined to manage to kill his deviant daughter.

Rhimes sighed with resignation. They would have to do what Muller wanted or else he wouldn't leave. "Alright, my friend. Let's wait for Klaus to come back, and then we will go."

"Good," an irritated Muller replied.

****

The group had finally decided to leave for the dance. Earl, Harry, and Eva went in Earl's car, followed by David, with Zoe, in his car, and then Elena and Friedrich. They parked under the jacaranda trees, and could already hear the music coming from the building.

"It's a beautiful night, isn't it?" Zoe said to David as they walked along.

"Yes, very beautiful," David muttered. He kept his hands in his pockets as he walked next to the young woman. Zoe smirked at him, and realised Eva must have had a little chat with him in the kitchen.

"Hey, Zoe, this looks great!" Elena said as she came up behind them, holding hands with Friedrich.

The two friends bumped into each other and chuckled. They entered the big auditorium filled with people. The band was apparently still playing some soft music before getting into the swing of things.

Eva and Harry sat in their seats, which were a few tables from where Zoe and Elena were. Eva winked at Zoe and then turned to her date.

"So, how long have you been married?" Harry asked.

"Seven months," Eva replied.

Harry poured some wine and offered it to her. They sat in silence for a few minutes as the conversation ground to a halt. Eva enjoyed the music and sipped at her wine. She turned to see what Zoe was up to and frowned when she saw Zoe also had a glass of wine in her hand. She knew Zoe normally didn't drink, and never in public since she had just turned eighteen. Eva decided to keep an eye on her wife.

The night was still going slowly for Eva, as Harry tried to get her to talk. He wasn't such a bad bloke after all, she'd decided, but none of the subjects he'd brought up so far warranted much conversation from her. It wasn't until he mentioned his love for photography that Eva's ears perked up. She was an avid photographer when she was in Germany, but hadn't had an opportunity to indulge in her passion for quite a few years. Once they found a common interest, they talked for quite a while, the conversation becoming animated and quite lively at times.

David was also having a very dull evening. He danced with Zoe a few times, but also kept an eye focused on what Eva was doing. He was relieved when he was called outside, but his relief quickly turned to real concern on finding out the police had discovered Berckett's body. It had been pure luck that a hiker had stumbled on the body as he was making his way up a lonely trail. David excused himself and pulled Friedrich from the dance floor as the band ended their song.

"What is so important that you have to drag me away?" Friedrich hissed. He was enjoying himself, and he found Elena to be a lovely young woman. He noticed he quickly got over his stammering after Elena had joked with him a bit, and he realised she was truly interested in getting to know him.

"Daniel just told me the police found Berckett."

"And?"

"He's dead, Freddy."

"Oh," was Friedrich's terse reply.

"We have to go stake out the flat."

"NOW?" Friedrich hissed.

"Well, I don't think they're going to wait until the dance finishes, do you?" David said with irritation. They were close to arresting the Nazis, and there was no way he was going to miss this opportunity. "Look, since the girls are here, they won't be targets."

"Okay, okay." Friedrich muttered.

****

The car slowed down and pulled over, right after it rounded the corner. Klaus stopped the car and shut off the lights.

"Wait here," Muller ordered the driver as he opened the back seat door and got out. Rhimes got out the other side and followed him down the path, pulling out a paper and checking for the flat number. They wore jackets, and kept the collars up and their hats pulled down low to reduce their chance of being identified.

"It's number five."

They casually walked down the corridor and stopped at the door to #5. "Won't she be surprised," Muller muttered. He quietly knocked and they waited. Not hearing a sound after a minute, Rhimes looked down the darkened hallway and was just about to kneel to start picking the lock, when Mrs. Jenkins popped her head out of her door. "Can I help you, gentlemen?"

"Good evening, um...we're looking for Eva Muller."

"Eva Muller? There isn't any Eva...oh, wait, you mean Eva Haralambos, don't you?"

Rhimes looked at Muller. "Ah yes, since her husband died she must have changed her name..."

"I didn't know Eva was married. The poor child...she lives with her sister up in number twelve, but I don't think they are in now. They've gone to a dance."

"Oh. Thank you for telling us. I'm Erik and this is my brother Hans. We're Eva's uncles."

"Oh, how nice!" Mrs. Jenkins enthusiastically replied. "*Kali nikhta*," she said in Greek, feeling rather proud of herself.

Rhimes gave her a huge smile. "*Kali nikhta*," he repeated. "You said you didn't know when they would be back?"

"No, you know young people these days...staying out 'til all hours."

"Yes. Hans and I have traveled a long way to see our favourite niece," he hinted, hoping she would rise to the occasion.

"Oh, you poor things. I'm sure Eva wouldn't mind if I let you into their flat. Just let me get the master key. It's a shame you missed your other brother, he was here just half an hour ago..." Mrs. Jenkins was still talking as she re-entered her own flat. Rhimes looked at Muller and just shrugged. She re-emerged a moment later, and began to slowly trudge up the stairs, followed by Rhimes and Muller. She stopped at #12 and opened the door for them. "I'll tell Eva when she comes back..."

"No! I mean...no, please don't do that. We wanted to surprise her," Rhimes explained as he placed a kiss on the back of Mrs. Jenkins' hand. "Thank you kindly, madam, for your help tonight."

The plump old woman blushed. "Oh, you Greek men are so gallant. Think nothing of it. Have a good night." She waved before closing the door behind her and making her way back downstairs.

Rhimes watched the door close, and could only shake his head at their good fortune.

****

Elena was miserable. Her big date with Friedrich was a total fizzer. He had to leave with David, which left her alone with only Zoe to keep her company. But, by now, Zoe was getting quite a bit of attention from some of the young men, dancing and having a very nice time. Elena just sat glumly, nibbling at a biscuit and sipping her punch.

Eva frowned, watching as Zoe danced. She would have to step in soon and take her home, but she did look like she was having a good time. She watched Zoe head outside, and her eyes narrowed as the young man Zoe had just danced with followed.

Zoe was feeling warm. She had had a few drinks, which she thought were rather mild and didn't seem to affect her at all. Her dancing partner seemed a nice fellow, and he followed her outside when she decided to clear her head up a bit with some fresh air. It was getting quite stuffy in there.

"Hey, Zoe, how's about a kiss?" the young man asked with a grin.

Zoe looked at him blankly. "No."

"No?"

"No."

"C'mon, just a little kiss." He caught her and held her against the brick wall. He was moving to kiss her when he felt himself being grabbed and thrown backwards.

"She said no," Eva growled, and shoved the man aside. She watched him get up, and he looked about to charge her, when Earl took hold of his collar with one large hand and bodily dragged him away. Eva turned to her partner and embraced her.

"I don't feel so good," Zoe mumbled.

"You're drunk, love," Eva said and kissed her brow.

"Eeeva... I can't feel my legs anymore." Zoe looked down, and wondered why she could see her legs, but couldn't feel them.

Eva sighed. Zoe was going to have a massive hangover the next morning. "Zoe..."

Zoe looked up and grinned. "I love you."

"I love you, too, my love, but you're drunk, and we need to go home."

"Oh...kay," she mumbled into Eva's chest. "I like it here, it's so nice and soft..."

"Is everything alright?" Earl asked, as he came back outside after throwing the troublesome young man back in through the door.

"Zoe is drunk, and I want to take her home. Can you drive us back?"

"No worries. I'll just tell Phil that I'm leaving." Earl turned to go inside.

"Earl, thanks."

"Anything for you, you know that," Earl replied, and went to arrange for his absence.

Earl told Elena and Harry they were leaving. Harry decided to stay on and have a bit of fun. That's exactly what Elena knew she wasn't going to have that evening, so she followed Earl. Once in the car, Eva sat in the back with Zoe, who was starting to get very amorous, while Elena sat up front with Earl.

"How's she going back there?" Earl said, and quickly looked behind him.

"Hanging on," Eva mumbled, as she once again tried to get Zoe's hands off her breasts. "Zoe!" she whispered, "Please, not now."

"But I like your breasts...they're so very nice...and soft... and..." Eva cut off Zoe's ramblings, putting her hand across her mouth as Earl and Elena snickered.

"I feel sleepy," Zoe mumbled a few minutes later, and snuggled against Eva's chest, promptly falling asleep.

Earl parked the car in the closest open space, but they'd still have a little walk to the girls' flats. Eva got out, rearranging her dress, and was about to gather Zoe up to carry her inside when she was tapped on the shoulder.

"Let me," Earl said.

"I can do it," Eva replied.

"No, you can't. You're going to hurt your back again, and I won't hear the end of it from the drunken sleeping beauty, so hand her over. Besides," he smirked, "it wouldn't look ladylike."

Eva scowled. To hell with ladylike. However, she knew he was right about her back. It was still healing, and although Zoe wasn't very heavy, the weight probably would aggravate it again. She reluctantly stepped aside and let Earl pick Zoe up. Looking almost tiny in his big arms, Zoe just snuggled up against his broad chest and softly snored.

"Oh...she's going to be one sick puppy tomorrow," Elena said, trying to sound sympathetic, but unable to stifle a grin. She saw Eva's head turn, but the tall woman's glare was spoiled by the twitch at the corner of her mouth. "I know, sorry. It's just that I've never seen her like this before."

"Actually," Eva gave up and let her grin show, "neither have I. I hope she doesn't get too sick."

"Bite yer tongue," Earl replied quietly. "Don't listen to them," he whispered to the young woman still blissfully asleep in his arms.

Eva shook her head as she walked with Elena, who had a hand clamped over her mouth to quiet her giggles. They climbed the stairs and bade goodnight to Elena at her door. Finally at their flat, Eva put the key into the lock, opened the door, and entered.

"Well well, well...Eva, how nice of you to drop in." Rhimes greeted them with a gun in his hand. "Please, do come in."

Chapter 13

Friedrich sighed, with a disgusted look on his face. Here he was, sitting on a wooden crate in a dark, empty flat. He didn't want to be here. He wanted to be back at the dance with Elena. Exhaling loudly, he glanced over at David, who was also perched on an empty milk crate. They had managed to get into the vacant #5 flat without the landlord's notice, and decided to wait there for Rhimes and Muller to show up. They left all the lights off and were keeping their vigil in the bedroom, in case the Nazis decided to kick the front door in and surprise the occupants they thought were there.

Friedrich wondered how Elena was getting along back at the dance. He had been enjoying the company of the young woman very much, and then to be dragged away during one of the few times he had enjoyed himself at a dance. He grimaced, thinking about Elena giving up on him and allowing another man to take her home. Turning to the party responsible for his current state of mind, he gave David an angry glare.

"Alright. I know you're angry with me," David said quietly.

"I'm not just angry with you, I'm so pissed off I could shoot you," Friedrich hissed back. They had brought their guns, and David was relieved that at least Freddy wasn't the type to wave his around in anger. Still, David wasn't sure whether Friedrich was serious or not. He had never seen his friend so angry. *Maybe he really did want to stay at the dance,* he thought to himself. He and his date did seem to be having a good time, and he had to admit that, for Freddy, having a good time going out, not to mention having a date, was rather unusual. He promised himself that when they finished with this problem, he would make it up to his friend by sending them to dinner at the most expensive place he could find. He hoped Friedrich would hold off shooting him for that long. "Look, mate I'm sorry, but..."

"Just shut up, David," Friedrich retorted angrily.

David looked at him and sighed. He wanted desperately to try and apologise to his friend, but in the mood Friedrich was in, he knew he wasn't going to get anywhere. He took his flashlight out and shielded most of its glare as he pointed it at his watch. If Rhimes and Muller were coming there tonight, they had better do it soon, or else his only accomplishment for the evening would be having one extremely angry Friedrich on his hands. He wasn't sure which circumstance would be more dangerous.

They spent the next half an hour in silence, sitting and listening, while David also kept watch on the front door. They grew tense several times, hearing footsteps pass by in the corridor, but none of them stopped at their door. They were both growing impatient, and still nothing was happening. Friedrich finally broke the silence. "Tell me something, did you have to give Berckett the file yesterday? Couldn't it wait?"

David frowned. "Friedrich, as much as I want to improve your love life, I don't think waiting until the dance ended would have been a good move."

"It would definitely have helped my love life since I didn't have one before," Friedrich muttered. "I don't think they're going to turn up any time soon, David. It's already getting late."

"Let's wait a little longer."

****

Eva closed the door quietly, smothering the light from the hallway and leaving the darkened room bathed only in the moonlight that leaked through the windows and the balcony door.

"Please leave the lights off," Rhimes ordered, motioning for them to remain where they stood.

Earl stayed quiet, still holding Zoe, who was soundly sleeping and oblivious to the danger around her.

"So, Eva, we meet again," Rhimes said and cocked the gun he pointed at her. "You are looking as gorgeous as ever."

"I wish I could say it is a pleasure, but it's not," Eva muttered. She turned to the noise coming from the shadows near the balcony, and knew her stepfather was there as well. Hans Muller stepped into the moonlight coming from the sliding balcony door. His face was half shrouded in shadows, but there was just enough light that she could see the scarring from the fire on his face and neck. She grimaced.

Rhimes sat down on the sofa with his gun aimed at Earl. Earl planted both feet and held Zoe in his arms, keeping Rhimes in sight but not wanting to outright stare at either man, not knowing how they would react. Zoe had curled up against his chest and he could hear her slightly snoring.

"Why aren't you dead?" Muller rasped as he stood in front of Eva and shoved the gun barrel under her chin.

"Lucky, I guess," Eva answered quietly. She watched his eyes squint and she tensed, expecting to be hit, but it didn't happen, which surprised her.

"Aren't you going to introduce your friend to your father?" Muller asked, looking at Earl and the girl he held in his arms.

Eva scowled, "You're not my father and never have been."

"Ah, how soon they forget," Muller said over his shoulder to Rhimes, who was shaking his head.

"Who do you think gave you all the nice things you had as little girl? I did." He grasped her chin and turned her face towards him. "Who do you think gave you the money to go to university? I did. Who do you think loved you and gave you everything you wanted? EVERYTHING!" he hissed into her face.

"You were a bastard child, and you still are a bastard child. If I hadn't married your mother, you would be a good-for-nothing, uneducated peasant, starving in some village," he spat out as he yanked her hair back and pushed the gun hard into her throat. "How did you repay me? You brought a *whore* into my house." he growled into her ear. "You're nothing but an ungrateful slut!" He yanked hard on her hair again. "I'm going to kill you, and I want you to know that I'm going to enjoy it. It's just a shame that whore of yours isn't around. I would have enjoyed killing her in front of you."

Eva tried not to look at Earl's precious bundle, and prayed that the shadows would hide Zoe's features from her stepfather.

Muller released Eva with a jerk and stepped over to Earl, who stood rock still with the sleeping Zoe in his arms. "Who are you?" He pointed the gun at Earl's face.

"I'm Eva's fiancé, Earl Wiggins. Who are you?" Earl asked, knowing exactly who the madman in front of him was.

"Fiancé, eh? Well, then, I'm your father-in-law," Muller's voice rasped and he began to laugh. He leaned towards Earl. "You're a big, strapping young man. How much is she paying you to fuck her?"

"She doesn't pay me to...fuck her, sir," Earl replied, looking down at the man standing with a gun aimed at him. "I do it willingly."

Rhimes chuckled from where he sat.

"Is that so?" Muller asked.

"Yes," Earl replied.

Muller scratched his scarred chin. "So, tell me, son-in-law, since you fuck her willingly, does your fiancée have a distinctive birthmark anywhere on her body?"

Earl dislike of the man in front of him had quickly turned to hate. What he really wanted to do was throw Zoe on top of him, then beat the shit out of the man. However, he didn't think throwing Zoe at Muller would make either Eva or Zoe very happy. He forced himself to remain calm and took a better hold of his precious cargo.

"She has scars on her back from your hand, if that is what you are talking about...sir." Earl said through gritted teeth. He wanted to turn and offer comfort to his friend, but he stayed rooted to the spot holding Zoe a little tighter in his arms.

He remembered clearly the day when he accidentally noticed Eva's scars. It had been a hot muggy day and the factory floor was unbearably hot. Eva normally wore a T-shirt underneath her uniform, but for some reason that day she didn't. They were the only two working on the machine, and they both sweated profusely. Eva's shirt was plastered to her back and when Earl noticed the faint scars outlined from inside the cotton shirt, he made a joke about Eva and Zoe being on the kinky side. The look Eva had given him would have killed him on the spot. He still cringed every time he remembered his crass comments. Not until later did Eva tell him about their origin, which only made him even more ashamed of his comment to her.

Earl's response surprised Muller. Maybe Reinhardt was wrong. The Eva he knew would never wear a bathing suit, or any dress which exposed her back. Yes, it was possible that snivelling, incompetent fool had been wrong all along. "Who is that?" He pointed the gun at Zoe and Eva shifted slightly, her fears boiling to the surface. She was prepared to rush Muller and hope to God that she wasn't going to get Earl or Zoe killed.

She was very relieved that Zoe was asleep. She didn't want Zoe involved in this and hopefully they would find a way to get out of this mess without her waking up. If Zoe woke up, their deception would dissolve as soon as she opened her mouth.

"My sister," Earl said smoothly.

Muller used the barrel of his gun to brush away Zoe's bangs from her eyes as he took a good look at her. "Hmm, she doesn't look like you."

"She says that's a good thing," Earl replied as Rhimes again let out a chuckle from where he sat.

"Can I put her in the bedroom? She's getting a little on the heavy side."

"Hmm...okay," Muller replied taking both Eva and Earl by surprise. "Put her down and come back here and be with your 'fiancée'."

Earl slowly made his way into the bedroom and laid Zoe gently on the bed. He put the covers over her and smiled when she curled around the other pillow with a grin on her face. He turned to leave when his eye caught sight of a cricket bat in the shadows near the door. He looked back at Zoe and smiled. He had given her the cricket bat a few weeks ago when she took an interest in the game. He picked up the bat surreptitiously just before he got out of the bedroom. He noticed Rhimes sat on the sofa his back to him and Muller was taunting Eva.

"EVA, DOWN!" Earl yelled as he heaved the bat with all his might and smacked Rhimes in the head causing the man to fall unconscious from the sofa to the floor, his gun going off before it dropped from his hand.

****

David sighed and yawned. He was bored. Friedrich was right, they weren't going to make it tonight. "Freddy, let's go. I don't..."

David broke off as a gunshot was heard and he ran to the door, followed by Friedrich. "Oh hell!" he yelled and stopped when he ran into Mrs. Jenkins. She had been awake and unable to sleep; she heard the gunshot and then the door of the vacant flat opening.

"Who are you?" she demanded. "What are you?" she followed up when she saw their drawn guns.

"We work for the government, ma'am," David answered, wanting desperately to run up the stairs.

"What are you doing in the flat?" Mrs Jenkins demanded. "I had two other men here tonight..."

"What?" Friedrich asked.

"Yes, Eva's uncles came looking for her," she began, but David and Friedrich bolted for the stairs taking the steps two at a time. "Humph! How rude." She stood there for a second listening to the men run up the stairs, then decided she had better go sort out the problem herself.

****

Muller turned at the shout and Eva took advantage of the distraction and hit Muller on his scarred neck. He let out a scream and turned, then met with Eva's knee to his groin which dropped him to the ground groaning. Eva kicked him and picked up the gun and held it against his head. "Move and so help me, I'll kill you," Eva growled into his ear. Muller groaned and stayed face down on the carpet.

Eva and Earl looked at each other and then the door burst open. Earl stood in front of Eva with his bat raised and swung the bat as soon as he saw the gun. The bat slammed into Friedrich's head, and he went down in a heap next to Muller. David followed his friend into the room and stopped dead in his tracks.

"Wait!" he yelled as Earl swung the bat again, and David ducked.

Mrs. Jenkins followed David and switched on the lights. Elena came racing into the flat and gaped in amazement at the occupants. Eva was sitting on her stepfather holding the gun to his head; Rhimes was sprawled on the carpet and Friedrich was out cold.

"I think I missed something," Elena muttered. "Friedrich?" she asked in alarm, spotting the man she was enjoying the evening with not an hour before now lying on the floor at her feet. "Friedrich!" She dropped to the floor, cradling the unconscious man's head.

Panayiotis and Alberta rushed from their flat when they heard the shots, as did their neighbours. Alberta made her way to Eva. "Are you okay?" she asked and gently touched her arm. Eva nodded. "Where's Zoe?" she asked in a panic when she didn't see the young woman.

"Asleep, in bed." Eva grinned. "I think Friedrich needs some help, though." She indicated the young man lying a few feet away. Elena looked up as Alberta knelt beside them.

Panayiotis surveyed the assorted bodies on the floor and looked down at his daughter. "Are you alright?" he asked, going to one knee and cupping her face with his hand. Eva nodded and Panayiotis gave her a kiss on the brow. "Who is that?" Panayiotis indicated the prone Muller.

"Father, that's Hans Muller."

"Well I'll be," Panayiotis said he went down on all fours and lowered his head to Muller's eye level, recognising him belatedly. "Well, if it isn't Major Muller.

"Who are you?" Muller asked and grunted.

"Father Haralambos, at your service. Why is my daughter sitting on you?"

Muller's shocked expression caused Panayiotis to chuckle. "You're supposed to be dead!"

"I'm very much alive, thank you," Panayiotis replied.

"You're her father?" Muller looked at him in disbelief.

"Indeed. That *is* my beautiful daughter that's sitting on you. You are a stupid man, Muller," Panayiotis said as Eva assisted him up.

Eva looked around the room. Alberta and Elena were helping a grimacing Friedrich slowly sit up, as he still looked a bit unsteady. Earl also was kneeling beside him and talking to him. David had just handcuffed Rhimes and sat him up. She shook her head in disbelief at how the events turned out. She spotted Mrs. Jenkins standing at the door with a shocked expression on her face.

"Eva, what is going on here?" Mrs. Jenkins asked, looking around the room.

"Um..." Eva looked up and tried to find a good excuse for two Nazis and a government investigator to be sitting on her floor with a dazed expression on his face and couldn't find one good reason to offer the older woman except the truth.

"Come with me, Elise, we need to have a little chat," Panayiotis said as he came up behind Mrs. Jenkins and steered her out of the flat. He looked back at Eva, who had a very relieved look on her face, and gave her a wink.

The door to the bedroom opened, and a very groggy and still drunk Zoe staggered out, stumbling over Rhimes who was still on the floor in front of the sofa. Eva looked up and saw Zoe kneel beside Rhimes, looking at him in confusion. "Do I know you?" Zoe asked, leaning into the semiconscious man. When she didn't get an answer she pushed Rhimes, who promptly fell over. "Humph," Zoe muttered, stumbling again as she tried to get back up. She decided that since her legs wouldn't work she'd just sit. So she did, cross-legged, on the floor.

Eva had watched Zoe's antics with concern, but also with a small bit of amusement. She sighed, seeing her partner's head start to droop as she sat there on the floor, and decided it was time to get Zoe back to bed. David had just finished handcuffing Muller, and she handed him the gun as she got up and went over to kneel beside her wife. "Zoe..."

"Hmm?" Zoe looked up at her with a lopsided grin.

Eva grinned back at her wife's cute expression. She had never seen Zoe drunk, and despite the seriousness of the situation, she couldn't stop herself from giving the young woman a kiss. "We need to go to bed."

"Ooh!" Zoe exclaimed and jumped on Eva, who lost her balance and fell backwards with Zoe landing on top of her.

"What do you have...um..." Zoe stopped and frowned.

"What's the matter?"

"I feel sick," she muttered.

"Hmm. You're going to feel even sicker tomorrow," Eva said as she sat up with her partner and kissed the top of Zoe's head.

"Why are there so many people in our home?"

"I'll tell you tomorrow."

"Okay," Zoe mumbled, and wrapped herself around Eva as she was hauled to her feet. Eva carefully led her back into the bedroom and closed the door on the chaos outside.

****

Eva sat on the edge of the bed and watched Zoe sleep, smiling down her. She had managed to get her into her Bugs Bunny T-shirt after Zoe finished retching a few times. She leaned down and gave her partner a kiss before tucking the blanket back around her.

She left the bedroom, padding quietly over and opening the door to the balcony. A gentle breeze was blowing as she stood outside watching the stars twinkle above. It had been quite an evening, one she would never forget. One chapter of her life was now closed, she thought.

Earl looked out from the kitchen when he heard the balcony door open. He had been busy when the police and the ambulance finally arrived. He had taken over and made sure Eva was with Zoe and that they weren't disturbed. He and David gave their statements, and promised to take Eva down to the station the following day for hers, which appeared to appease the police. He got a call later from Elena that, apart from a mild concussion, Friedrich was going to be okay. Earl winced at the memory of the bat hitting Friedrich's head. He would have to make it up to Friedrich with an expensive dinner for the couple when he got out of hospital.

He stood quietly in the kitchen, watching Eva on the balcony for a few moments, hoping his friend was coping okay with all the stress of the past few days. He was relieved that his batting practice on Muller and Rhimes had gone so well. If only he could do as well when it came time to bat for his cricket team. At least he could tell Zoe her bat passed his test with flying colours. He chuckled at the thought. Earl dried his hands on the towel over his shoulder and walked over to stand behind his friend, putting his arms around her shoulders.

Eva looked up and leaned back into his chest.

"Happy birthday, Eva," he whispered and kissed her on the cheek.

Eva was surprised. She had forgotten all about her birthday. She looked up at the tall blond man and smiled. "Thank you."

"How's Zoe?"

"She's sleeping. She was sick a couple of times, but I managed to get her to go to sleep finally."

"She makes a happy drunk, doesn't she?" Earl chuckled softly. He was sure his young friend would be mortified when told about her antics of the evening. He was looking forward to seeing her reaction. Earl cleared his throat. "Um, I have an apology to make to you."

"Oh?"

"Mm hmm. I'm sorry I was so crude earlier."

Eva frowned, and then realised he was talking about Muller. "You have nothing to apologise for, Earl. You saved our lives."

"I want you to know that I would be a very happy man if you were my wife."

Eva was touched by his comments. She looked up at him and reached around to cup his face with her hand. "Thank you, my friend."

"So if Zoe ever decides to toss you away, you know who to come to," Earl joked, trying to lighten the mood.

Eva chuckled. "I think Dave may have something to say about it."

"Dave likes threesomes," Earl chuckled, with Eva joining in.

"I don't think Zoe would let me come and play at your house any more if you said something like that to her," Eva replied and gave him a gentle slap on the arm.

"Ah, yes, well, it will just be our little secret," Earl suggested and hugged her.

Chapter 14

Eva woke to the sounds of someone moving about outside. She could hear voices. She quietly got out of bed, put on a robe and padded to the living room, closing the bedroom door quietly so as not to wake her partner.

Earl was standing at the front door talking with a neighbour. He looked back when he heard a noise and waited until Eva got to them. "Eva this is my mate Reggie. He lives at number 20."

Eva recognised the man she had seen a few times in the hallway. They had a nodding acquaintance. "Pleased to meet you, Reggie."

"Finally I get to speak with the most beautiful woman in the building," Reggie said as he gave Eva a huge grin.

"Oh, knock it off." Earl chided his friend. "Reggie will fix the door, if that's okay with you."

Eva looked at the door which had seen better days. The lock was totally destroyed and a massive hole had taken its place. "Yeah, that's fine," Eva said and yawned. "Sorry, it was quite a night."

"Yeah I heard. Were those really Nazis?" Eva nodded. "Wow!" Reggie exclaimed. He had heard the stories going around the building about what happened at number 12 during the night. The whole place was buzzing with the news. "Is everyone alright?"

"Everyone's fine," Eva mumbled.

"Okay enough gossiping. When can you do it?" Earl interrupted, knowing Eva was tired.

Reggie looked at the door. "Well I can patch it up so you can close it, but it will be tomorrow before I can put in a new door since today's Sunday and nothing is open."

Earl looked at Eva who nodded. "That's fine. I think we'll be in for most of the day today," Eva replied.

"Good. Talk to you later, mate," Reggie said and took another look at the door, jotted down some figures. "Have a quieter morning, Eva."

Earl closed the door and Eva looked up at him and sighed. "I think the whole building knows we're here now."

Earl chuckled. "I think they knew you were here before. It makes *Dad and Dave* sound boring with you around." Earl said referring to one of Eva's favourite comedy shows on the radio. Earl had introduced her to the hilarious show and Eva loved it's down to earth humour about a father and son team that never had a dull moment in their lives. "Hey, you want some breakfast?"

"Hmm...I would love a cup of tea."

"Coming right up. Is the drunk still asleep?"

"She was when I got up."

"Go back to bed and I'll bring you a cuppa. Now shoo." Earl gently pushed his friend towards the door and watched her as she entered the bedroom.

Eva took off her robe and got back into bed just as Zoe was beginning to stir. "Argh," Zoe groaned as her head pounded and her stomach was doing flip flops. She opened her eyes and then shut them against the bright glare. "Kill me now," she moaned.

Eva scooped her up and cuddled her as Zoe continued to moan from her self induced drunken bout. "You don't want to die."

"Yes, I do. Quickly."

Eva tried to hide the smirk but wasn't fast enough as Zoe glared at her. "Don't look at me like that. How many did you have?"

"It wasn't the drinks. I was run over by the Beast," Zoe muttered.

"No, love, you were drunk as a skunk, last night."

"My head hurts!" Zoe continued to moan, "I only had a couple of drinks!"

"My little two pot screamer." Eva chuckled and kissed her tenderly.

"Ow. That hurts," Zoe said and burrowed her head under the covers. "Last thing I remember is someone asking me for a kiss. That wasn't you was it?"

Eva smirked. "Nup. Wasn't me. It was a blond-haired boy."

"Oh, no. Did I kiss him?"

"Nope. I asked him not to."

Zoe opened her eyes and looked at Eva's smug look and laughed, which she regretted soon after. "Ow. Then what happened? You didn't hurt him did you?"

"No, I just convinced him not to try and kiss you. Earl threw him out," Eva replied and brought up the blanket and settled it around them.

"There's something you're not telling me."

"You know, you are very cute when you're drunk."

Zoe cringed. "Oh, no. What did I do?"

"You get very...amorous."

"I'm amorous all the time," Zoe said and waggled her brows which caused her to grimace. "My whole face hurts. Let me hear all the gory details."

Eva chuckled. "Well I thought you had enough and were quite drunk; I decided to take you home."

"How?"

"Earl." Eva knew this would cause Zoe to moan and she wasn't disappointed. "And Elena."

Zoe's face took on a pasty white colour as the blood drained from her face. Her two friends who she loved dearly were going to torment her about this forever. She just knew it.

Eva stroked her hair as she held her partner, knowing that what she was going to tell her would probably mortify her. "You were groping me in the car."

"I WHAT?" Zoe raised her voice and again regretted the move as she held her head in her hands and moaned, "Please tell me I didn't do that."

"Yeah, you did. You were undoing the laces on my dress and sticking your hand down my cleavage..." Eva couldn't stop the chuckle as Zoe's eyes went wide. "Elena and Earl were up front."

"Oh God, this can't get worse." Zoe looked at Eva when she didn't agree with her. "Please tell me it doesn't get worse."

"It gets worse."

Zoe burrowed underneath the blankets. "I'm not leaving this room ever again." She uncovered her head, her disheveled bangs askew, and Eva grinned and kissed her. "What did I do?"

"You told Earl that I had soft breasts." Eva laughed out loud at the look on Zoe's face. "And they were very soft to sleep on and other things." She held Zoe as the younger woman's face went a bright shade of red. "Then you did the best thing you could have done."

"I made love to you in the back seat of Earl's car and I don't remember it?" Zoe supplied.

"No, although that would have been memorable."

"You're enjoying this aren't you?"

Eva nodded, which got her a slap on the belly from her wife. "You fell asleep," Eva said and watched Zoe's relieved face. "That's when things got hairy."

"Huh?"

"We had a visit from Muller and Rhimes last night."

Zoe forgot about her hangover and turned towards Eva. "Are you okay?" she asked and checked for obvious damage to her partner. She then noticed the small bruise on Eva's throat. "You're hurt!"

"No, love, I'm alright."

"You have a bruise on your neck and I know a hickey when I see it and that's not a hickey."

Eva fingered her neck for a few moments and smiled. "Muller stuck his gun there."

"Tell me what happened."

Eva began to recount the story from just after they entered the flat and what Earl had done with the cricket bat, which got a snort from Zoe. She filled her in on how Friedrich and David came rushing through the door only to be met by Earl's flying bat, which got a chuckle out of Zoe. "Is Friedrich alright?"

"Well, he didn't look too good last night. David rang from the hospital to tell us that he had a concussion. Elena was most upset and spent some time holding him. I think they like each other."

"I think El is quite taken with him," Zoe agreed and wrapped her arm around Eva's waist. She looked up at Eva and grinned. "Did you really kick Muller in the balls?"

"Yep."

"Way to go, wife!" Zoe celebrated with a quick kiss. "Should have blasted him there while you had the gun." she muttered.

"Things got a little interesting after that."

"Interesting?"

Eva nodded. "You woke up and stumbled over Rhimes who was lying on the floor and then you sat on the floor grinning. When I tried to get you to go to bed you pushed me over and fell on top of me, and you were telling me what you would do to me when you got me in bed."

Zoe let out a belly laugh despite the pain in her head. "Oh my God. Tell me no one saw that."

"Um...let's see: there was Earl, David, Elena, Ally and dad, Mrs. Howitz from across the hall..."

"ARGH!"

A light tap was heard and Eva called to Earl to come in. Earl opened the door and brought in a tray with toast and tea. He put the tray down and looked down at Zoe who had burrowed herself under the blankets. "You told her?" Eva nodded and Earl patted the lump under the blankets. "Hey, Stretch, I want to ask you about something."

"What?" the muffled reply came.

"How do you get Eva to scream out your name, I didn't quite hear it when you told everyone last night."

Both Eva and Earl began to laugh as Zoe moaned loudly, "Go away, I hate you."

"I love you too, Stretch. By the way I have the perfect hangover solution."

"What?"

Earl took the mug from the tray. "It's two raw eggs..." He didn't finish as Zoe threw back the blanket, her hand over her mouth, and jumped off the bed and raced to the bathroom. Eva hit Earl on the arm as she chuckled and followed Zoe.

"Must be something I said," Earl muttered as he took the tray back to the kitchen

****

Eva sat on the sofa; Zoe was stretched out, her head in Eva's lap, as soft music played. Eva had spent the morning tidying up the flat while Zoe was trying to get over her hangover. Earl had stayed around while Reggie fixed the door and then cooked them a light lunch.

"Everything's done." Earl said quietly as he leaned over Eva's shoulder to gaze at the sleeping Zoe. "How is she?"

"She's okay. I think the headache is gone," Eva replied and stroked Zoe's hair. They both looked up when they heard a knock on the door. Earl opened it and then closed it again.

"Earl, what's the matter?"

"I think you need to wake sleeping beauty."

"Why?"

Earl came over and cupped her face in his hands. "Humour me."

Eva shook her head. “Zoe,” she whispered in her lover’s ear. “Come on, love, time to wake up.”

“Don’t want to,” Zoe mumbled.

“Yes, you do, sport,” Earl said and picked her up and set her on her feet. He leaned down and whispered in her ear.

“Oh,” she replied and rubbed her eyes. Eva got up and was about to open the door when Earl barred her way. Eva was confused. Zoe gave her a smile and wrapped herself around Eva’s waist. “Okay, Wiggy.”

Earl opened the door.

“SURPRISE!” Panayiotis Haralambos led the greeting as he entered the flat, followed by Alberta, Elena and Earl’s partner Dave. Eva was surprised, as she hadn’t been expecting a birthday party.

“You did this?” she asked Zoe, who was beaming at her.

“Yep, but I didn’t plan on getting drunk. It was supposed to be at Earl’s place, but he kinda moved everything here.”

Eva looked at Earl who was handing out party hats to everyone and streamers. “Happy birthday, you old thing,” Earl said and kissed her. She was speechless. She was usually aware when Zoe was planning something.

“Are you surprised? I wanted to make this special for you,” Zoe said and looked into Eva’s eyes which had started to glisten with tears. “I love you.”

“Thank you, love,” Eva replied and bent down and gave her wife a tender kiss as the party got underway around them.

Other Books from

RAP

Darkness Before the Dawn
By Belle Reilly

Chasing Shadows
By C. Paradee

Forces of Evil
By Trish Kocialski

Out of Darkness
By Mary A. Draganis

Glass Houses
By Ciarán Llachlan Leavitt

Storm Front
By Belle Reilly

Retribution
By Susanne Beck

Coming Home
By Lois Cloarec Hart

And Those Who Trespass Against Us
By H. M. Macpherson

Restibution
By Susanne Beck

Printed in the United States
2084

9 781930 928152